Wreath of Deception

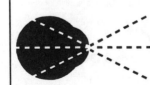

This Large Print Book carries the
Seal of Approval of N.A.V.H.

WREATH OF DECEPTION

MARY ELLEN HUGHES

WHEELER PUBLISHING

An imprint of Thomson Gale, a part of The Thomson Corporation

THOMSON

GALE™

Detroit • New York • San Francisco • New Haven, Conn. • Waterville, Maine • London

THOMSON

GALE

™

LIBRARY OF CONGRESS CATALOGING-IN-PUBLICATION DATA

Hughes, Mary Ellen.
    Wreath of deception / by Mary Ellen Hughes. — Large print ed.
    p. cm. — (Wheeler Publishing large print cozy mystery)
    ISBN-13: 978-1-59722-395-9 (softcover : alk. paper)
    ISBN-10: 1-59722-395-6 (softcover : alk. paper) 1. Widows — Fiction.
2. Large type books. I. Title.
PS3558.U3745W74 2007
813'.6—dc22   2006031483

Published in 2007 by arrangement with The Berkley Publishing Group, a member of Penguin Group (USA) Inc.

Printed in the United States of America on permanent paper
10 9 8 7 6 5 4 3 2 1

For Dad, Edmond V. Lemanski,
who fixed all those sore throats,
stomachaches,
and amazing hot fudge sundaes.

ACKNOWLEDGMENTS

Many thanks to the talented crafting people who generously shared their time and expertise: Julie Black, of Black-eyed Susan Florist; Rebecca Myers, of Rebecca Myers Jewelry Design; Heidi Hess and her lively group of stampers; scrapbooker Angie Palmer; knowledgeable knitter Kay Wisniewski; theatrical advisor Jim Hughes; awesome website designer John Baker; and ever-patient pharmacist (and sister) Barbara Gawronski.

I am specially grateful to my agent, Jacky Sach, for generously pointing me in the right direction; my editor, Sandy Harding, for her terrific manuscript polishing skills (and who is a joy to work with); and the many other hard-working people at Berkley who helped turn my loose pages into a book.

Many thanks to fellow writers and critiquers: Janet Benrey, Ray Flynt, Sherriel Mattingly, Trish Marshall, Marcia Talley, and Lyn Taylor, for always catching what I didn't see, and who served the greatest cakes.

Last and best, to Terry: my support in so many ways, who always encouraged me, kept me on track, and never minded fixing his own breakfast.

CHAPTER 1

The first shaft of sunlight pierced through the hole in her bedroom shade, and Jo, who had been awake and watching for it, jumped out of bed. Wrapping herself against the mid-September chill in her raggedy but cozy terry robe, she padded into her small kitchen, wondering if she'd actually slept at all. She had memories of a jumble of thoughts as she tossed during the night, but couldn't clearly separate persistent worries from those same fears morphed into dreams. What she was sure of, sleep or not, was that she didn't truly need the coffee that she automatically began to fix. Adrenaline pumped through her veins, and she was already running, internally, on all cylinders.

This was it — the day she had been planning and working toward for weeks. The make-or-break day. If it went well, Jo would be able to stay on in Abbotsville, Maryland, pay her rent, eat. If it didn't, well, she might be losing those last five pounds quicker than she'd expected.

She watched the coffee drip into the carafe, breathing in its fragrance. When the machine finished its routine of gasps and sputters, she slipped out the carafe and poured herself a mugful. Wrapping her hands around the mug for warmth, Jo carried it to her back door and gazed through the glass at the tiny yard. The scrubby grass sparkled with dew, and the leaves of the spindly dogwood already showed tinges of red. The sun, higher now, filtered through her neighbors' towering trees and made the scene nearly pretty. It was far different, though, from the steel and brick view through the loft's windows in New York.

Jo winced at the thought. In some ways, it seemed a lifetime ago, although it was only months. She crafting her jewelry, and Mike making his wonderful metal sculptures from pieces he molded and shaped with his acetylene torch until one day that very torch malfunctioned and exploded, annihilating the loft, Mike, and her entire life as she knew it.

Mike was her life, her love, and losing him, as well as all they had built together, was devastating. But she had somehow managed to pull herself together — the

need to survive truly works wonders —
gather Mike's small life insurance money
and invest in a shaky future for herself.
Every penny she had, along with loans that
would likely keep her in servitude to the
First Maryland Bank until dementia set in,
had been sunk into Jo's Craft Corner,
whose grand opening was less than three
hours away.

Jo shivered at the thought — from excite-
ment or fear? she wondered. Likely both.
The countless steps leading to this day ran
through her mind: first and foremost, tracking down the store in an affordable district
of Abbotsville, with the help of her amazing
friend, Carrie. Then the necessary wares,
including boxes and boxes of supplies for
every craft imaginable. There were beads,
flowers, yarn, paper, stamps, paint — all
painstakingly arranged in what she hoped
was a customer-friendly manner. Plans for
workshops she and Carrie would conduct,
ads taken out for the grand opening, the
clown hired to pass out freebies and bal-
loons and hopefully attract families with
craft-loving moms and dads, refreshments,
music. Had she thought of everything? If
not, it was too late now. Another shiver-
producing thought, but she banished it.

At least the weather, the one thing over

which she had no control, was promising. A cloudless sky would let the sun shine brightly, and the temperature, if the last couple days were a predictor, should warm up nicely, bringing people out of their homes. It might even be hot by afternoon, which would be just fine with Jo, because it would draw more thirsty people to her free punch and cookies, which were situated deep inside the store and required customers to stroll past her beautiful, extremely purchasable wares.

Her wares. Jo suddenly pictured the store as she had last seen it at eleven o'clock the previous night, before stumbling home for a couple bites of cold pizza and collapsing into bed. Should she have put more Halloween items near the front? Yesterday she'd worried over making Jo's Craft Corner look too much like a Halloween-only store. But that holiday, she began to think, was a big seller. She should probably capitalize on it while she had the crowd there, and move the pumpkins and ghosts to the front. Quickly.

Jo plopped her coffee mug in the sink and whisked off her sleep shirt on her way to the shower. She still had to pick up ice and set up the huge punch bowl she'd rented. She should double-check the stamping section — had Carrie unpacked the box that arrived late yesterday afternoon? How about the racks of scrapbooking papers? Had they been filled enough? How, where, what . . . ?

Jo's mind ran as fast as her legs, which propelled her from shower, to closet, and out to the car in double time. Out on the road she had to brake suddenly to keep from running a red light, and she glanced around with relief noticing that traffic was light this early on a Saturday morning — not that it was ever truly heavy in Abbotsville.

Once inside the store, she took a few deep, calming breaths. "Don't let yourself turn into a crazy," she commanded, smoothing down her short dark hair, and carefully realigning the fringed paisley scarf she had added to brighten her white silky blouse and black slacks. Then she promptly turned into a crazy, zigzagging up and down the aisles, filling her arms with pumpkins and branches of autumn leaves and ghouls. Only the rattle of keys in the door brought her to a stop.

"My gosh, have you been here all night?" A plump woman in a navy jumper, holding several white paper bakery bags, stood in the doorway, backlit by the morning sun.

"Carrie!" Jo hurried over with her load, shedding leaves as she did. "We have to move the Halloween things before anyone comes!"

Carrie smiled, letting the door swing closed behind her. "Jo, take it easy. It's at least an hour before we open for business. Plus no one in their right mind's going to show up until an hour after that. Trust me, Abbotsvillians are not early risers on week-ends. Sit down and have a bagel. I bet you haven't had a bit of solid food."

"You mean today, or this week?"

Carrie tsked disapprovingly, then moved behind the checkout counter and began spreading out the goodies she'd brought. "You won't impress customers, you know, if you pass out face-first into the punch. Take a breather. Everything's going to be fine."

Jo set down the autumn leaves and pump-kins and sank onto a tall stool beside the cash register.

"Guaranteed?"

"There's no guarantees in life, sweetie. You should know that by now."

Jo sighed. "Yes, I do." She grabbed one of Carrie's breakfast treats and breathed in its delicious freshness. "But at least there's blueberry bagels. Thanks, Carrie."

Carrie shrugged, her way of accepting gratitude for as long as Jo had known her, which was years — since her first day at

Thomas Jefferson High, to be exact, when they encountered each other in the girls' bathroom. The meeting was not one she would have expected to produce a lasting friendship — Carrie had walked in to the sound of Jo retching prodigiously in one of the stalls. But instead of a hasty retreat, Carrie had called over the door, "Scared out of your gourd, huh?"

Jo, startled enough to pause in mid-heave, had managed a shaky, "Uh-huh."

What followed, once she splashed enough cold water on her face to risk frostbite, was Jo spilling out her fears to a sympathetic Carrie about not knowing a soul in this terrifyingly huge school, which Jo's parents had enrolled her in after transplanting them all to Maryland not one week before. Carrie had proceeded to take her in hand, earning Jo's undying gratitude and friendship.

Interestingly, in the years following, it was Jo who was the more adventurous one, going out for cheerleading and drama, activities largely dominated by "cool" cliques to which she never belonged, then signing up for challenging art courses, followed by art school, and eventually heading off to New York to begin life as a starving artist.

Carrie made quieter choices, playing second piccolo in the band, signing up for

Home Ec courses, and later marrying her high school sweetheart and moving with him to Abbotsville, not far from, nor much different from the town they grew up in, to begin her chosen career as wife and mother.

But, whereas Jo's life was full of drama, spiked with highs and lows, Carrie's seemed a calm sea of contentment, managed with a quiet strength that showed itself only when needed. It was never needed more by Jo than after Mike's horrible accident. When Jo, dragging herself out of the ashes of her life, had searched for a way to go on, knowing she couldn't manage on what her jewelry making alone had been bringing in, Carrie suggested a craft store in Abbotsville.

The idea slowly took root, its attractiveness, Jo realized, owing much to the distance it would put between her and the painful memories of her loss. Jo's mom, now living out her widowhood in a retirement community in Florida, had urged her to come there. But setting up anew near her old friend, who also volunteered to give up time from her comfortable life and add her considerable skills at needlework to the store's offerings, carried the most weight.

"Eat!" Carrie ordered, breaking into Jo's reverie, and Jo realized she had been staring into space.

She hastily bit into the chewy treat. When she could again speak, she asked, "Why did you come in so early? I thought we agreed you'd get here at ten."

Carrie grinned and fiddled with the end of her long blond braid. "I woke up early and started thinking you should have a bigger Halloween display near the door."

Jo grinned back. "Great minds, huh?"

"For sure."

Carrie got to work setting up a rack for the display, and Jo, nibbling at her bagel, joined in, bringing straw to nestle around the plastic pumpkins and gourds, and draping orange and black material behind a grinning scarecrow. As Carrie sprayed canned cobwebs around the edges, Jo went back to the storeroom to look for more acrylic paints that could be used for decorating costumes and masks.

The storeroom was jammed with boxes, some stacked on shelves six feet high. All this stock, she thought, gazing at it with amazement. Would she ever sell it? Who would have guessed that she would ever be running a business? She, who had always scorned the more practical things in life to flourish in what she did best — art. Now she would be keeping books on inventory and toting up sales, and grateful to have sales to tote up. She ran her finger down the rows of boxes, checking labels for acrylic paint, and worried: would this town have enough interest in arts and crafts to keep her in business? Carrie seemed convinced of it, and Carrie certainly knew the local market better than she did.

"But you'll have to have something for everyone, Jo," she'd said, when Jo first wanted the store to concentrate on what she knew best — jewelry making.

Good advice, but it required such a huge stretch for Jo. She had been involved in her specialty so long, she had to relearn, or in some cases discover anew, many of the other aspects of arts and crafts. Soon she would be expected to be the knowledgeable source of information for her customers on all corners. Could she handle it?

"Jo, while you're back there, can you grab the broom?" Carrie called out.

Now that, at least, she could handle. "What'd you spill?" Jo called back.

"Oh, nothing much. Uh, do we really need to have all the beads separated by color?"

"What!" Jo shot out the door.

"Just kidding." Carrie stood near a revolving rack of craft magazines. "But you might want to pick up a mousetrap or two later on."

"Uh-oh." Jo trotted over and looked down at a corner niche Carrie pointed to. Several black, disgusting mouse droppings lay there.

"Ugh! Think I can get the landlord to take care of it?"

"Well, probably not as quickly as you'll need. You don't want little mousies setting up nests in your lovely yarns, there. I can get Dan to do it."

"No, Dan's done enough." Carrie's husband had pitched in to set up Jo's fixtures and racks, running his tools for hours, saving Jo a bundle. "I'll take care of it." Jo said it bravely, adding emptying a mousetrap to her list of things that as a single woman she now needed to do, but would really, really rather not.

Carrie lifted an eyebrow, but said, "Okay," and proceeded to sweep up the little mess.

"Oh! I just remembered," Jo cried. "My wreath! I haven't hung my autumn wreath on the front door yet!" She went to the back of the store to her office cubicle, where she had left the carefully wrought creation.

"It's beautiful," Carrie commented as Jo carried it forward. "And the perfect thing to welcome your arts and crafts customers. It's like having a sign that says, 'You too can make this — come in and learn how.' "

Jo smiled. "I thought it turned out rather

well. I plan to have new ones for each season." She took the wreath outside and hung it on the brass hook that Dan had already installed for her, then stepped back to look, pleased with the arrangement of dried flowers and berries, all in lovely autumn colors on a circle of graceful leaves. Her eyes roamed contentedly over the entire storefront. *Her* storefront, with her name on it: Jo's Craft Corner. She let out a satisfied sigh. Until her brain registered the clock just inside the window.

"Oh, Lord, look at the time!" Jo hurried back inside, dashing to the storeroom for the forgotten paints. "When did we tell the clown to show up?" she called out to Carrie.

"Not until eleven."

"Good. Hopefully the Abbotsvillian slug-a-beds will start straggling in by then. At what I'm paying him per hour, I'd hate to waste too many of his minutes."

"Charlie would have been glad to do it."

Jo remembered the look on Carrie's fifteen-year-old when his mother first suggested it: the flash of horror and panic quickly masked by his usual gloomy disdain. What an interesting clown he would have made.

"Being a clown is hard, Carrie. It takes a lot of training," Jo said, restating much of what she had said that first time to save Charlie from what he clearly considered a fate worse than death. "The guy the agency's sending is a pro. He'll be great."

"These shoes are killing me," Cuddles the Clown moaned through his painted smile. "And the heat out there! Nobody told me you wouldn't have an awning! These costumes don't come air-conditioned, you know."

"Here, have some more cold punch." Jo handed him what must have been his fifth cup, and he'd only been working an hour. At this rate she might have to run out in the middle of the day for more. Cuddles should have called himself SpongeBob. But at least he had the sense to limit his complaining to the lulls between customers.

Shrill screeches sounded from the sidewalk as a family with twin toddlers made its way to the door. Jo handed Cuddles his basket of freebie handouts and flyers, and took back the empty punch cup.

Cuddles's shoulders drooped. "Great. Two of them. Wonder which one will kick me first."

"It's happy time, Cuddles," Carrie called

out. "Just keep thinking of that paycheck at the end of the day."

Cuddles muttered, and tramped over to the front door. "Hey, kids!" he cried, flinging it open and inducing frightened screams.

Carrie rolled her eyes at Jo.

"He's better with the older ones," Jo said, smiling weakly.

"At least he hasn't actually chased anyone down the street. Yet."

"It's probably too hard to run in those floppy shoes."

"And he'd get sooo hot in that costume, too. Good morning!" Carrie greeted the latest arrivals. "Welcome to Jo's Craft Corner."

The young mother, who showed a remarkable ability to tune out the screams of her children, looked around with delight and declared, "I've been just *dying* for you to finally open. There's nothing like this around for *miles*. Do you have stuff for scrapbooking? I have piles of pictures of the twins, and I saw what my cousin Ali did with her photos and I want to try it too."

"We have a whole section over here," Jo said, struggling not to flinch at the continuing shrieks.

"And we'll be starting classes on scrapbooking next week. Tuesdays, at seven,"

Carrie added, as Jo led her customer to the scrapbooking area.

"Oooh, that'd be terrific!" the woman chirped. "Honey," she called to her husband, who had been left holding on to the wailing toddlers, "put my name on the list, will you?"

As she browsed through the scrapbooking area, more people walked in, heads bobbing to the circus music that played outside, thanks to Dan's sound-system setup. They glanced around the store with pleased oohs and ahs, and before long Jo was busier than she could have dreamed, showing customers around, explaining about various decorative items, ringing up sales.

The *ca-ching* sound was music to her ears, but just as important was the steadily growing list of women interested in taking her various workshops. This wasn't going to be a one-day wonder. She was actually drawing what might become regular customers. She caught Carrie's eye at one point, as they crossed paths in mid-bustle, and Carrie gave her a thumbs-up sign.

Things were going great — except, that is, for the miserable clown. He was in and out continuously with complaints: the music drove him nuts; the kids, the heat, the shoes drove him nuts; if his regular job paid him a decent wage he wouldn't have to take these kinds of gigs. Carrie's sullen teenager, Jo thought, would have been a regular David Letterman next to him.

Amazingly, though, Cuddles didn't seem to be having a negative effect — except on Jo's patience. His presence alone in his colorful costume, combined with the cheery music, appeared to be enough for the brief time her customers came in contact with him. One woman, astonishingly, even asked her for his name, explaining she'd like to have him for her child's next birthday party. Jo stared at the woman openmouthed, suspicions of child abuse leaping to mind. But wide eyes returned her gaze innocently, so Jo suggested she ask Cuddles himself for his card, and hoped the prospect of another job might lighten him up some.

She continued to be busy enough to forget about this regrettable accessory to her grand opening, until, at two minutes to four, Cuddles came dragging in.

"My time's up," he announced, leaning one weary elbow on the counter.

"So it is," Jo agreed in surprise after glancing up at the clock, whose hands, as far as she was concerned anyway, seemed to have spun around madly. She handed her latest customer her bagged purchase with thanks, and pulled open a drawer for her checkbook. "Who shall I make it out to?" The entertainment agency in Baltimore had never actually told her this man's real name, and she presumed he wouldn't want "Cuddles" written on the check.

"Kyle Sandborn."

Jo looked up. Somehow she'd never have picked him for a Kyle.

He misread her expression, saying, "You might have heard the name. I've acted at the Abbotsville Playhouse a lot."

"Really? No, I'm new here, and haven't been to the theater yet. But I'll certainly look for you in future productions."

Kyle/Cuddles gave her his first genuine smile of the day, though it seemed to require his last reserve of energy, and reached for the check. "Mind if I change in your back room?" he asked, barely waiting for her answer before turning in that direction.

"No, go right ahead."

He left the basket of handouts with her and flopped toward the stockroom in his big shoes. Jo's attention was quickly moved to another customer — a woman who, joyfully, had filled the store's hand-carry shopping basket to the brim with items, many of them foam balls and cones, and packets of sequins and ribbons in Christmas colors.

"I know it's only September," the woman bubbled, "but I can't wait to get started on Christmas projects. It's always been my favorite holiday of the year."

"Mine too," Jo said, smiling. "In fact, I'll be giving a class on making Christmas wreaths if you're interested."

No sooner had she packed the Christmas lady off than a crashing noise pulled her attention to the opposite side of the store.

"Missy, I *told* you not to touch that!" A child's wail rose up from the floor, and Jo hurried over to inspect the damage. A display Carrie had set up of handmade teddy bears dressed in the costumes of various movie characters had been pulled down and lay in shambles on the floor.

"I'm *so* sorry," the mother cried. She struggled to calm her sobbing three-year-old with one hand while reaching for fallen bears with the other.

"Don't worry about it," Jo assured her. "They're not breakable." She picked up Rhett Butler and brushed him off, then found Scarlett, uncharacteristically shy and hiding in her green velvet gown behind the needlecraft kits.

"Jo, there's someone here with a question

about making beaded necklaces," Carrie called out.

"Be right there," Jo responded, and plopped the bears as best she could back on their stands, starting to feel like she had not stopped moving since she'd arrived early that morning. Had she had lunch? She wasn't quite sure. She vaguely remembered Carrie's eleven-year-old, Amanda, showing up with a platter of edibles, but what they consisted of Jo couldn't recall.

"Bead necklaces, you say?" she said to the interesting-looking woman at the front of the store, who had long, unnaturally black hair, and '70s, hippy-styled clothing despite a youthful, twentysomething face. An Ab-botsvillian? Jo wondered. If so, she had much still to learn about her adopted town.

That customer was replaced with another, and then another, and Jo could hear her voice beginning to crack in her dry throat from all the explaining, directing, respond-ing, and thanking she had done over the hours. Finally, the dinner hour approached, and the crowd thinned.

"Thank you, ma'am, and do come again," Carrie said to their final customer, then fol-lowed her to the door, clicked off the circus music, and turned the lock. She spun around to face Jo and threw up her arms.

"It's over! You're grand opening was a success. You did it!"

"*We* did it," Jo corrected. "My gosh, what a day! I can hardly believe it." Jo ran her hands through her hair and plopped down on the stool. She picked up the stack of sign-up sheets from the counter and grinned. "Customers! Real, live customers who want to come back again and buy my wares."

"Well, of course! How could they not, with all the beautiful things they can make from what you have here?"

"And the sales today! I could barely keep up with it."

"We were both running our legs off, and we deserve a reward. I've already talked to Dan. He's taking us out to dinner to celebrate."

The idea sounded great to Jo, but as she watched Carrie turn off lights, and saw Dan's black Chevy Blazer coming down the street, it occurred to her she had a lot of cash sitting in the drawer.

"Just a minute." Jo pulled bills from the drawer and began stuffing them into a canvas bank bag.

"You're not taking that along, are you?"

"Uh-uh. I'm going to stash it where a

burglar wouldn't think to look. Right behind the needlepoint kits. What do you think? If you were a burglar, would you find it there?"

"You really need a safe."

"You're right. I guess I just never truly believed I'd have money to worry about. Until now." Jo grinned, and grabbed her pocketbook.

"Dinner at Alexander's," she said, "and it'll be my treat."

The last light she saw Carrie flick off, before hustling up to the front door, was that of the storeroom.

CHAPTER 2

Alexander's was a welcome change from the noise and bustle of the last several hours. Jo had chosen this out-of-the-way restaurant for that very reason, and glanced around blissfully at its muted decor of dark browns and greens. Soft music caressed her ears, which still buzzed from the endless calliope tunes.

"This place is weird," Amanda declared.

"Amanda," Carrie admonished her preteen, but Jo laughed.

"Try to bear with it, honey. Your mom and I need to decompress."

"They have weird food, though," Amanda persisted. "Stuff like Vitello allo, uh, Scalogno. I don't even know how to say it."

Charlie slouched in his chair sullenly. "Can I send out for a cheeseburger and fries?"

"No, you can't." Dan scowled at his son. "And sit up straight. Miss Jo is celebrating tonight, and the least you can do —"

"How about we all stop at Baskin-Robbins for ice cream on the way home?" Carrie jumped in, calming the waters as Jo had seen her do more than once, lately. Charlie, at fifteen, seemed bent on alienating all around him. Jo remembered her godson as a bright and engaging child, but it seemed hormones had sent most of his charm packing and put him at odds with both parents — particularly his father.

Dan had enthusiastically coached Charlie's early soccer games and elementary basketball efforts. At thirteen, though, Charlie dug in and flatly refused to participate anymore. Carrie confided that Dan was not happy, especially since he saw Charlie putting energy into very little else, least of all his schoolwork. Carrie was growing very worried about him, Jo could tell, though she tried her best to be upbeat.

Jo regretted choosing this teen-unfriendly restaurant, but it was too late now. "They do have spaghetti and meatballs," she suggested. "They call it Pasta Alexander here."

Amanda brightened up, and Jo thought she saw in Charlie's eyes a flicker of interest, which he quickly covered with gloomy resignation.

"Well," Jo said, closing her menu, "it looks

like Jo's Craft Corner just might be around for a few more weeks."

"Not just around, Jo, you have a hit!" Carrie cried. "It was like Abbotsville has been just *drooling* for you to show up and open that store."

Dan nodded. "Looked like a pretty good opening."

"My friend Lindsey and I are going to make matching friendship bracelets," Amanda announced. "Mom's going to show us how. I think they're neat, and maybe everyone else — the girls, I mean — at middle school will come in to buy your beads and stuff, Aunt Jo."

"Amanda, that would be so great." Jo beamed at this girl who seemed to be following in her mother's footsteps, taking pleasure in cooking and home crafts. But, she had yet to enter the scary teens. With that thought, Jo glanced once more at Charlie, who now stared at the ceiling, possibly hoping for an out-of-body experience to survive his current ordeal. The arrival of the food, however, livened him up enough to joke around with his sister over slurping up the spaghetti, which Carrie wisely ignored as long as no one at the table — or nearby tables — was getting splashed with red sauce.

Jo, Carrie, and Dan launched into ideas for the future of the craft store, and Jo allowed herself to start feeling optimistic, something she had resisted for weeks. Too much confidence, she was convinced, almost guaranteed failure. Look, after all, what had happened in New York. She and Mike were doing great. Mike was getting gallery shows for his sculptures, and orders were increasing for her jewelry. Jo was convinced their future was set. Then boom, it all went up — literally — in smoke. Jo swallowed the lump that rose in her throat. It was much safer, she reminded herself, not to tempt the gods, so to speak, with high expectations. But from today's results, things did look promising.

By the time she sipped her coffee, Jo's mood was mellow. The glass of excellent merlot earlier hadn't hurt. The check came and Jo snatched it before Dan could, saying, "This is my treat. A very small way of saying thank you to you guys, for all the help you've been giving me."

A chorus of "We were glad to, it was nothing, don't be silly" rained down, and Jo ignored it all with a grin, scribbling her signature on the dotted line.

They squeezed back into Dan's car and headed to the store where Jo's Toyota waited, all thoughts of Baskin-Robbins forgotten after Alexander's excellent dessert cart had appeared. She hugged everyone — even a stiffly resisting Charlie — before waving good night from beside her car, whose door remained shut. Jo planned to take a final look inside her store, and had avoided mentioning that to Carrie, instead implying she was driving straight home. If Carrie suspected Jo wanted to go back in the store, she and Dan would have insisted on coming in as well, for safety's sake, dragging the kids along too. And it would have been totally unnecessary. Besides, Jo wanted — perhaps selfishly — this quiet moment to herself. She wanted to bask in the golden memory of her store flooded with customers, of people thrilled with her beautiful craft supplies, and many enthusiastically buying.

She unlocked the front door, then relocked it behind her, switching on one low light that allowed her to see most of the store, although dimly. She then strolled the aisles, thinking over the highs and lows of the day, but mostly the highs: the woman who claimed she belonged to a knitting club and would bring her entire group to see Jo's beautiful yarns. Jo credited Carrie with doing a wonderful job overseeing that department.

Then there was the man who asked Jo to come see him about setting up a craft show at the country club in October. Its purpose would be to draw new members to the club, but it would be great exposure for Jo's Craft Corner as well.

When she came to the needlework kits, Jo checked on her cash bag. She wondered if she should take it home with her, but then noticed that supplies had thinned in the nearby stamping section, many of the papers apparently having sold well. She might as well double-check that they had plenty in stock, she decided, and she continued on to the back room, bending down on the way to pick up and replace a fallen wreath form. She flicked on the storeroom light and paused, considering where the stamping papers would be. Her gaze wandered the shelves until something caught her eye near the end of one of the rows, something colorful on the floor. Gradually, it registered that what was on the floor was not store stock, and she focused more carefully. It was something, no, it was *two* somethings. Eighteen inches high, fuzzy, and with swirling reds, golds, and greens. Cuddles's big floppy shoes? Had he left his costume behind?

Jo had no memory of Cuddles/Kyle actually leaving the store once he had been paid. She did remember his request to change here in the back. An ominous feeling took root in the pit of her stomach, and Jo moved closer to the odd shoes apparently standing there on their own. Why would he just drop his costume and leave it? Would he be that careless of something that could be quite costly to replace? Jo came to the end of the shelf and the answer to all her questions. Her hands flew up to her mouth, stifling a cry.

Cuddles had not left his costume on the floor. In fact, Cuddles had not left his costume at all, but still wore it as he lay there, huge shoes pointing to the ceiling, baggy pants spread wide on the floor, and a new, dark red stain added to the colors in his shirt.

Cuddles, despite the wide grin still painted on his face, would smile no more. Cuddles was dead.

CHAPTER 3

Red lights flashed and radios crackled as strangers trampled in and out of her store, most brushing past Jo as if she were invisible. Hovering just outside the front door, Jo clutched her arms tightly to keep from shivering, the cool night air not as much a factor as the shock over what she had recently discovered.

Cuddles the clown really *was* dead. Denial had leapt up protectively at first, trying to convince Jo that the clown was simply sleeping, passed out, or, least likely, joking. But the relentless sight of the blood on his chest, plus one awful touch of Cuddles's lifeless, cold hand convinced her otherwise. Jo had stumbled backward and staggered to the front of the store where she'd left her pocketbook, fumbled for her cell phone, and called 9-1-1. Afterward she had waited there, numbly, until finally hearing sirens.

Then mass confusion had taken over. Now she watched helplessly through the window, while others took command of her store.

As a parade of people tramped in and out of the back room, doing God knows what to the poor dead clown back there, a tall man of about forty arrived whom she overheard identified as Lieutenant Morgan. He quickly disappeared into that room himself.

Someone put a paper cup of coffee in her hand and she thanked him, holding the cup but ignoring its contents. More coming and going, and Jo's coffee cooled. Finally, she set the cup down on the sidewalk and grasped her arms tightly once more.

"Jo! Jo, are you all right?"

Jo turned to see Carrie running down the sidewalk with Dan close behind her. Both soon engulfed her in a hug, making her aware of just how badly she needed one.

"Bonnie Smithers called," Carrie explained. "She said police cars were all over the place here. We were scared to death something had happened to you."

"It's Cuddles. The clown. He's back there, dead."

Carrie looked toward the storeroom wide-eyed. "My God! And you found him?"

Jo nodded.

Dan's mouth pressed grimly into a straight

38

line. "What happened?"

Jo shook her head. "I don't know. There was blood. I don't know if he fell on something or what."

"Oh, Lord." A strange look passed over Carrie's face.

"What? What are you thinking?" Jo asked.

"Nothing. I mean, oh, I don't know. It's probably terrible to think of at this time. But I just wondered if your insurance covers something like that? Things like accidental death on your property?"

Jo stared at Carrie, not getting it at first. Then she got it. "Oh, Lord," she echoed. "You mean, maybe I could be sued?"

Carrie nodded.

"I have no idea if that's covered. But what could have happened there that would be my fault? I keep paper and paints back there, not spears jutting upward, for heaven's sake, waiting for the unsuspecting to fall onto."

"You said there was blood. Did you see what might have caused it?"

"No. But I didn't hang around too long looking."

A uniformed officer came up to them. "Mrs. McAllister? Lieutenant Morgan wants to talk to you."

Carrie and Dan started forward with her

but were stopped by the officer. "Just Mrs. McAllister for now."

"We'll be right here," they said to her, and Jo nodded gratefully. She still felt shaky, and now began to worry about exactly what had happened to the hapless clown in her storage room. The officer led her to an alcove of the store, near the yarns. The lieutenant stood there, appearing, oddly, to be in search of the perfect set of knitting needles for his next project. He turned at her approach and held out his hand.

"Mrs. McAllister? Russ Morgan." He shook her hand briskly, then looked down at his notebook. "This is your store?"

"Yes. Today was my grand opening."

"And you hired this man, Kyle Sandborn, to work for you?"

"For five hours. He was handing out free gifts and such for us, out front."

"How long have you known him?"

"About five hours."

Lieutenant Morgan's eyebrows arched upward.

"I never saw him before he showed up today at eleven. I hired him through the Stewart Entertainment Agency in Baltimore."

"He lives and works right here in Abbotsville. You never saw him before?"

"I'm new here, Lieutenant. I know very few people so far. No, I never saw him before, although I understand he does some acting at the Abbotsville Playhouse."

"You knew that."

"Yes, he mentioned it as I was writing his check." Why was she starting to feel very uncomfortable? Was it this man's dark eyes, boring into her as if trying to read her mind? Jo slipped her hands into her pockets, then pulled them out, realizing as she did so that she was fidgeting.

"He was here until the end of the day?"

"No, just until four."

"What did he do after that?"

"I thought he left. I was very busy around that time. He took his check and I assumed he left soon after."

"You never noticed if a man in white face paint and fuzzy red hair walked out your front door?"

"No, I didn't." Jo's discomfort flared into anger. What was he implying? "He told me he wanted to change in the back. If he had, he would have walked out looking like anyone else. I never noticed that he hadn't left."

"And when was the last time you went into your storeroom?"

"Besides when I found him dead?"

41

"Yes." Lieutenant Morgan stared hard at her. Jo glared back just as hard, ready to spit out her answer, then realized she didn't have one.

"I don't know," she admitted. "I went in this morning, before we opened up. I'm sure I ran in a few times during the day, but I can't remember just now when the last time was."

"You closed up when?"

"At six."

"You didn't go into the back room at that time?"

"No. Carrie — my coworker, Carrie Brenner — and her husband, Dan, whisked me away for dinner. It was an exhausting day. Lieutenant, tell me, please. What happened to Cudd—, I mean, to Kyle? What killed him?"

The lieutenant's eyes bored into her once more, but Jo stood her ground, waiting. It was a reasonable question, she felt. She had every right to know before someone — Kyle Sandborn's mother? or wife? — slapped her with a million-dollar lawsuit for wrongful death. The lieutenant didn't seem to see it that way, however.

"We're looking into that," he said. "Now, this Carrie Brenner. Is she here?"

Jo sighed. This wasn't going to be easy.

Jo flopped into her bed after what felt like days since she'd left it. She had been right after all, she thought as she punched up her pillow, although being right wasn't offering any satisfaction. Never get too optimistic, no matter how great things seem to be going. It only sets you up for the fall. Expect the worst, and maybe it won't be such a shock when it slams you in the face.

Except, how in the world could she have even halfway expected what slammed her today?

A less-than-grand opening — that she had been prepared for. Things going wrong, nobody showing up — those she knew were all possibilities. Even catastrophes like floods or fire — forget famine, Carrie would always have food around. But natural catastrophes one's mind could deal with. They happened. Finding dead bodies in one's back room, however, didn't happen, or wasn't supposed to.

Why, oh why, had she ever hired that man in the first place? He was a headache for her while he was alive, and now dead — Jo caught herself. What was she thinking! This man, Kyle Sandborn, was dead. Whether she'd liked him or not, whether he'd been a major pain the whole day or not wasn't important anymore. The guy was dead! After what he'd probably expected to be a normal, boring, *safe* job, he was dead!

Yes, her grand business venture, her new life start had probably gone down the tubes. But shouldn't she still put it in perspective?

Jo tried. She tried to think of Kyle Sandborn as a man deserving her sympathy, but his whining, grinding voice kept slipping through, grating at her. She tried reminding herself that he was dead, whereas she was alive and well. But thoughts of the horrendous bills she still had to pay off, the inventory that would sit unsold in her stockroom, the workshop registrations that would be cancelled faster than you could stamp the words *NO WAY!* crowded everything else out.

Who would ever want to step into her shop again after what had happened? Her cozy Craft Corner had turned into a shop of horrors that would be shunned by all the decent, safety-conscious people of Abbotsville. She would never ring up a sale again.

Poor Kyle Sandborn, she tried to think, but it kept detouring into *what am I going to do now!*

CHAPTER 4

Jo stood outside her Craft Corner, watching mournfully as the crime-scene cleanup crew, gear in hand, invaded her store. The police had informed her that this was a necessary step, as they turned the store back over to her after having finished gathering their evidence.

"But I'm perfectly capable of washing things up," she had protested, thinking of the expense.

"No, ma'am. I'm afraid the blood from the scene is a biohazard, and this is a place open to the public. It's required." The officer gave her the names of a couple of firms in the area and left, leaving Jo to worry where she would find the money for it.

Dan came to the rescue with his advice to check with her insurance. "This kind of thing is probably covered, though nobody ever expects to have to use it."

He had been right — on both counts.

Thankfully, her insurance would pay, and Jo arranged to have a crew come out the next day. She had envisioned, though, the usual housekeeping or janitorial-type workers, quietly doing their job with mops and buckets and such. What arrived was a huge van — bright yellow — which the driver parked smack dab in front of the store. The crew that emerged from the van suited themselves up in spacemanlike outfits complete with breathing apparatus, and unloaded high-tech-looking equipment, which they dragged into her store.

Crowds quickly gathered, of course, eyes wide with curiosity, heads together exchanging whispers and pointing fingers, all of which caused Jo to groan. This was not the way she ever wanted to draw a crowd. Her cozy Craft Corner, she feared, was doomed to be forever known as the house of death.

Hold on, she instantly chided herself, don't be so quick to give up. Yes, things had come to a bad state, but shouldn't she be looking at this cleanup as a turnaround? She had been a take-charge person in the past. Wasn't this an opportunity to put things back on track?

"Hi, Aunt Jo."

Jo turned to see Charlie, hands jammed deeply into pants pockets and shoulders hunched. She was glad to see him, and said so. "Are your folks here too?"

"They went to Amanda's soccer game, but Mom's not staying long. She said I should come over and see if you need some help."

Charlie, unlike what Carrie had bemoaned in the past, didn't look as if this time he had to be pushed very hard. As he spoke, his neck craned to see what was going on inside the store.

"So it happened back there, huh?"

"Yes, it did."

"So, will they let us in, do you think?"

"No, Charlie. I'm sorry, they won't. They have those biohazard suits on because it's considered dangerous."

"Oh." Charlie's face fell, and Jo moved to console him.

"But once they give us the all-clear, you can come in and help me move things back where they should be. That should give you the chance to look around." Jo didn't add that by the time they went in, all that would be left to see would likely require much work by Charlie's imagination.

What she said seemed to satisfy Charlie, and he hung around, watching with Jo as the crew trudged back and forth from the back room. They sometimes carried sealed bags, and Jo guessed they might hold cleaning utensils that came in contact with the blood. As they had suited up, the lead man of the crew had explained about some of the concerns with blood-borne pathogens, such as HIV or hepatitis. Who knew if Kyle Sandborn's blood actually contained anything dangerously contagious? But no one, apparently, could take the chance that it didn't. Jo, on reflection, was grateful not to have to deal with it herself. But, she thought, glancing back at the gawking crowds, she did wish this crew could have somehow handled it more discretely.

Carrie showed up as the crew packed away the last of their gear.

"How did it go?" she asked.

"The professional's are done," Jo said. "Looks like just some tidying up to do."

"Good. I'll help you straighten up in the storeroom. Charlie," Carrie said as she turned to her son, "I'd rather you stay out of there, okay? There'll be plenty to pick up in the front part of the store."

Jo smiled to herself, thinking that was probably as hopelessly wishful as trying to hold back tidewater. Charlie would manage, one way or another, to get an eyeful of the crime scene, and Jo was also sure that at fifteen he would be okay with it. She settled up with the cleaning crew and watched them drive away. She, Carrie, and Charlie then slipped into the store. As she locked the door firmly behind her, Jo saw the last stragglers from the crowd outside wander away. The show was over.

"Well," Carrie said, looking at the floor, "I guess tracked-in dirt isn't considered bio-harzardous."

"No. They focused on the back," Jo said, making her way to the storeroom. "The fingerprint powder is cleaned up," she said, poking her head in, "and the floor looks good. But the stock is all over the place. We have a lot of reorganizing to do."

As she said it, Jo slipped once more into wondering if it would be worth all the effort. She had the depressing feeling that her budding craft business faced an insurmountable obstacle in trying to recover from its disastrous opening day. She avoided saying so to Carrie, though.

Carrie and Dan had helped her so much and had been pulling so hard for her, that, although the Craft Corner's failure would be Jo's loss, she worried as well about the effect it would have on them. So she tried her best to push away thoughts of the likely futility of it all, and plugged on.

As she and Carrie sorted through the stock, Jo realized she had not lost as much as she had feared. Though greatly disarrayed, her sealed boxes of supplies had remained sealed, and the crime-scene techs had thankfully restricted their powdering to surfaces that would reasonably retain a fingerprint. Unlike most of the flat surfaces, it would have been difficult, if not impossible, to thoroughly clean her heaps of Christmas greenery and trimmings. A few items that had been close to Kyle's body had been carried off, presumably for further testing at the crime lab, but Jo had been given a receipt with some vague hope of either return or reimbursement.

As she moved about the room, visions of the dead Cuddles/Kyle lying there continually intruded, and Jo struggled to keep them down. Charlie might be excited over the idea of violent death, but his fascination, she knew, came from the movies, not reality. Jo, however, had come face to face with reality, finding a person lying dead who had been alive and well just a short time before. There was no fascination to it for her, only shock and a fervent wish never to have seen it at all.

"We'll have to dump some of these yarns, don't you think?" Carrie asked, breaking into Jo's thoughts. She held out two skeins that had been in open cartons and showed signs of dark powder having drifted through. A few others had been knocked onto the floor.

"Right," Jo agreed. "There are also things over here that either got stepped on, or mashed by something heavy being set on top. No use trying to salvage them either."

They grabbed trash bags and began to fill them, setting them at the doorway for Charlie to carry out to the Dumpster. He managed several good looks around the back room in the process, as Jo had expected, which seemed to satisfy him, despite the missing gore.

Charlie filled his own bags with broken items from the front and swept up excess dirt before Jo came out and wet-mopped. Little by little the place returned to order. After a couple hours, Carrie leaned her own mop handle into a corner one last time and plopped down on a chair.

"I think that's it," she said, with a tired sigh. "Jo's Craft Corner is back in shape and ready for customers."

"Well, back in shape, anyway. Thanks, Carrie." Jo turned to Charlie, who was returning from carrying out the last of the trash. "Thanks a whole lot, Charlie," she called out. "We couldn't have done it without you."

Charlie shrugged, causing Jo's first smile of the day. A young man of few words, she thought with amusement, though his eyes, and probably his imagination, had been busy.

Carrie pulled herself out of her chair. "Time to get on home, I guess. There's homework waiting to be done. See you tomorrow, Jo. I can open up if you like."

"No, don't bother. You might as well sleep in."

"But —"

"Oh, I'll come down and open up, but I don't expect to have much to do. Jo's Craft Corner, I expect, will be quiet as a — forgive the word — morgue."

The next morning, Jo woke early, despite her tired body. She spent the extra time dawdling about the small house, sipping coffee as she sporadically watched the morning news shows, restless but enervated. Finally, she could put it off no more, and she showered and dressed, then drove glumly to the store, prepared for a day of dreary emptiness.

Jo turned the corner at tenth and Main, and looked down the block to her store. A small crowd seemed to be gathered. More police? Reporters? Jo groaned softly.

Shouldn't that be over with by now? She pulled into an empty parking spot just beyond the group and had barely switched off her ignition when she heard her name spoken sharply.

"Jo McAllister! You're late!"

Jo stared at the wrinkled face that appeared at the open passenger window of her car.

"Huh?"

"I said, you're late! The sign on your door says you open up at ten. It's now ten-oh-three."

"You've been waiting for me to open?"

The tall, gray-haired woman pushed up the sleeves of her navy velour warm-up suit. "Our power walk winds up at nine-thirty. I told the girls all about your place, and we powered on over here, hoping you might let us in early. Instead, we had to cool our heels, waiting!"

Jo looked around, feeling dazed. Nearly a dozen women milled about, actually champing at the bit waiting for her to open her store. It was unbelievable, or nearly so, since here, in fact, they were. Jo pulled out her keys and worked her way to the door through the gaggle of chattering women, apologizing for her lateness as she went. They poured into the store behind her and spread out, barely waiting for her to flick on the lights.

Jo dropped her bag behind the counter and unlocked the cash register, still feeling somewhat out-of-body. The gray-haired woman came up to her.

"Ina Mae Kepner," she said, holding out her hand. Jo shook it, feeling the strength. Despite the age evident on her face, Ina Mae was clearly in great shape.

"I figured you might need a little boost today, after what happened on Saturday."

"A boost?"

"Why, yes. I can pretty well imagine what you must have been going through. There it was, your big day, and it ends up with police and ambulance people tramping all over your place." Ina Mae glanced around. "Looks pretty much back to order, by the way. Must have been a job and a half."

"Yes," Jo admitted. "As a matter of fact it was. I had help, though."

Ina Mae nodded. "Carrie Brenner. She's a good woman. Coming in today?"

"A little later."

"Good. I'd like her help picking out some yarn for a project I have in mind."

The bell on Jo's door jingled as more customers arrived. Ina Mae wandered off toward the knitting section as someone asked Jo for a particular fabric paint. Then another woman wanted help tracking down all the materials Jo had used to make "that lovely autumn wreath you have hanging on the door. I just have to see if I can duplicate it." That pleased Jo, but she realized she'd better call Carrie fast and hope she could get down in a hurry. She still felt befuddled, trying to cope with the fact that instead of morguelike, her business was lively and bustling. But why should that be?

Little by little, she began to understand. With every purchase of paint, or dried flowers, or picture frames, came variations of the same questions: *How terrible was it finding that poor man? Was there an awful lot of blood? What actually happened?*

Jo fielded the curiosity as best she could while ringing up the sales, but one eager face was quickly replaced by another. Then they came in twos and threes, all waiting wide-eyed for the answers that she didn't particularly want to give, that she hemmed and hawed over to find the vaguest response, while it sank in that the big draw today was not Jo's lovely craft items, but Jo's horrifying yet — to the customers, at least — exciting story.

Carrie showed up soon, and Jo saw her encountering the same problem. *How did he look? What did the police say?* Carrie seemed to be handling it better than Jo, but Jo could see it begin to wear on her as well. The upside was they were doing terrific sales. The downside was wondering how quickly these customers would fade away once their morbid curiosity was satisfied.

Ina Mae was the only one, Jo noticed, who didn't probe for information. She even pulled a customer off when Jo was being particularly hard-pressed.

"Deirdre Patterson," Ina Mae exclaimed at one point, "let this poor woman do her work! She's had enough talking about this unfortunate business."

Deirdre Patterson was obviously not one of Ina Mae's power walkers. A forty something woman who looked dressed for lunch with the girls in a green silk pant suit complete with pearls and pumps, she bristled at Ina Mae's words, protesting, "I was only trying to offer my sympathy for a very unfortunate occurrence. Many people find it helps, you know, to talk about stressful things. Don't you find it so?" she turned to Jo, beaming an encouraging smile.

Jo was rescued from having to answer by Ina Mae, who simply but firmly changed the subject. "Carrie thinks this blue tweed

56

wool will work for the sweater I want to make for my ten-year-old grandson. What do you think, Jo?"

Jo, who knew little about yarns, picked up the skein and held it out speculatively, turning it about with several studied "hmms."

"Well, I'll just be on my way," Deirdre said, and grabbed her package. As she left, Ina Mae leaned closer to Jo. "Deirdre's married to our state senator, Alden Patterson. She quit working when she married him, but she could probably use a few more things in her life to keep herself occupied. Things besides other people's business."

Jo checked the sign-up sheet Deirdre had just returned to her. "I see she signed up for our wreath-making workshop, so I guess that's a start."

"Did she? Well, I never figured her for a craft person, but sometimes people surprise you. I'm coming to that one too, along with one or two of my friends. Looking forward to it."

Jo smiled at this no-nonsense woman. Until now, Jo had been wondering how many registrants would actually show up. Now she pictured Ina Mae personally rounding them all up and hustling them into the shop like a mother hen with her chicks. What did Jo ever do to deserve someone like her? More important, how could she keep her around?

Traffic slowed down around lunchtime, and after Jo finished ringing up a sale for a man whose wife sent him to pick up refills for her glue gun, she called across to Carrie, who was straightening up a display of wreaths.

"Hungry yet? How about I run out for subs and sodas?"

"I've decided to try and lose a few pounds. Again. If I'd thought of it, I would have packed up a salad for myself."

"The sub shop has salads. At least I think they do." As they debated the question, a uniformed police officer entered the store.

"Mrs. McAllister?"

The hairs on Jo's neck stood on end. The patrolman himself looked harmless enough, red-cheeked and young enough to be, well, not her son yet, thank goodness, but at least a much younger brother. But the fact that he had come specifically looking for her set off alarm bells.

"Yes?"

"Ricky, my gosh, is that you?" Carrie interrupted. "Remember me, Coach Brenner's wife? I haven't seen you since you were on that fantastic soccer team. You all won the trophy that year, didn't you?"

"Ricky" paused, apparently struggling between a chatty reminiscence with Carrie and maintaining his official presence. "Yes, ma'am," he finally answered. "That was a great team. It's good to see you again."

"So you're all grown up and with the police department now! How time does fly."

"Yes, ma'am." He turned back to Jo. "Uh, Mrs. McAllister? Lieutenant Morgan would like you to come down and talk with him."

"Now?" Jo frowned. "If this is about filling out more forms I'd rather wait til I close up, if you don't mind."

"It's not about filling out forms, ma'am."

"I assume it's about the accident we had here on Saturday. I've already told him everything I know about it."

"Ma'am, there's been some further developments on that case, which Lieutenant Morgan would like to discuss with you. Would you come with me, please?"

From the serious look on Officer Ricky's face, Jo realized the "please" was just a courtesy. He wasn't asking, he was ordering. Jo felt her empty stomach sink.

"Well, I guess I'd better." She turned to Carrie. "Mind holding down the fort?"

Carrie shot a reproving glare toward the patrolman. As the coach's wife, Carrie must have served gallons of Gatorade and orange slices to this former soccer player, but she didn't look eager to offer any refreshments now. Both elbows jutted out as Carrie braced her hands on her hips. Her brows lowered in righteous indignation.

"Ricky!"

Ricky's eyes turned downward, abashed, but he quickly recovered and looked up at Jo.

"Ma'am?"

Jo sighed. "It's all right, Carrie." She picked up her purse and turned toward the young officer, not quite holding out her hands to be cuffed, though the image crossed her mind. "I'm ready."

CHAPTER 5

Jo sat facing Russ Morgan, second in command of the Abbotsville Police Department. Officer Ricky had ushered her into Morgan's office, deep within the building that served as Abbotsville's Police Headquarters, and he rose from behind his utilitarian gray metal desk to thank her for coming. His tone told her, however, that this was not a social visit, though he did offer coffee. She accepted and sipped it, hoping her grumbling stomach would be pacified until she could find something more substantial.

Lieutenant Morgan got right down to business. "Mrs. McAllister, I thought you should be informed that the death of Kyle Sandborn has been ruled a homicide."

Jo had been in mid-swallow and she sputtered, immediately setting down her mug to avoid spilling coffee all over her white jersey.

"What did you say?" she managed to croak once her coughs subsided.

"I said, the death has been ruled a homicide."

"But, but, that means murder, doesn't it?"

Russ Morgan looked at her as if she'd just asked, "Water means wet, doesn't it?" which annoyed her greatly. What did he expect? Maybe *he* was used to talking about homicides, but she certainly wasn't. Why should he act as if he expected she were?

"Yes," he answered stone-faced, "it means murder."

"But, how could that be?"

"I was hoping perhaps you could tell us."

"Me? How would I know? I thought something in my stockroom fell on him, or whatever. I was worried to death that I might be sued."

"Being sued might be the least of your worries."

"What do you mean?"

"Mrs. McAllister, do you carry size-two Coyle knitting needles in your store?"

Jo remembered seeing Morgan, the night she had called the police, checking over the stock in her knitting section. She was sure he knew exactly what kind of needles she carried. She only wished *she* did.

"We carry several brands of knitting needles, but offhand, I can't say for sure."

"You can't?"

"Lieutenant Morgan, you saw the immense variety of stock I carry. I'm not a walking computer, so, no, I'm not sure I carry those particular needles. Carrie Brenner would know, better than I. What in the world does that have to do with Kyle Sandborn's death anyway? He wasn't sitting in my stockroom knitting when someone did him in, was he?"

"No, he wasn't." Her flip response didn't bring even the hint of a smile to the man's lips. Jo could see a slight resemblance in Lieutenant Morgan to Mike, with his dark, even features and thick-lashed eyes, a thought that produced a familiar pang deep down. Mike, however, would never be making her feel this uncomfortable, staring at her as if he had photographic evidence of her running all the red lights in Abbotsville. Mike would have —

The lieutenant cleared his voice, jarring Jo back to the present. "Mr. Sandborn was in fact stabbed to death with a size-two Coyle needle."

"What!"

He simply stared and waited.

"Stabbed with a knitting needle? How can that be? Knitting needles aren't meant for stabbing."

"Things sometimes are used for purposes for which they were never intended."

"But . . ." Jo's thoughts flew as she tried to picture this absurd method of murder. Bad enough the poor guy had to die in his clown suit. But by a knitting needle? How was it possible? "But he was in our back room, while we had a store filled with customers. Surely he would have fought back somehow. Someone would have heard something."

"We found evidence of a sedative in Mr. Sandborn's blood. He had been drinking a lot of your punch that afternoon, hadn't he?" Jo heard a slight emphasis on the words "your punch." and didn't like it.

"*My* punch," she said, jumping to its defense, "was served to scores of people that day. There was nothing whatsoever in it that should not have been there. I saw your evidence people take away leftover samples. They must have tested for that."

Morgan maddeningly wouldn't confirm that, though Jo was sure it must be true. What he did say was, "Things can be slipped into individual cups."

Jo sighed. "And you don't have Kyle's cup, of course. It was one of dozens of paper cups, all crumpled up and thrown away."

"We don't need it. We know he ingested this sedative," he looked down at a paper on his desk, "temazepam, also known as Restoril, an hour or so before he was killed. The exact time he was at your shop."

Jo thought back, remembering that Kyle *had* seemed tired at the end of his session, drooping over her counter as he waited for his check. But, busy as she was, she had barely given it a second thought, and if she had, would have attributed it to the heat and stress of his day.

"Could he have taken this tem . . . uh, this sedative himself?"

"That's something we're checking in to. But it doesn't seem likely, does it, that he'd take medication to slow himself down while on a job that called for a lot of energy?"

"No," Jo admitted. "It doesn't."

"Mrs. McAllister, I understand you're a widow?"

Jo's head jerked up. "Yes, I am."

"I'm sure the loss of your husband was a very stressful thing to go through."

Jo nodded, frowning. What did that have to do with anything?

"Many people who have suffered a loss such as yours have trouble sleeping. Was that the case with you?"

Jo caught where he was going and was even less happy with it than she had been with his insinuation about her punch. "Yes, it *was* the case with me, Lieutenant, for a certain length of time. But no, I don't need or take sleeping pills now, nor do I go about slipping them into the drinks of people in my employ!"

"I'm sure —"

Jo jumped up from her chair. She'd had enough. "*I'm* sure you've made up your mind that I've come to Abbotsville to set up shop and start killing off your citizens one by one. Well, Lieutenant Morgan, you're going to have to come up with a lot of proof for that crazy idea. Good luck finding it. And if you want to talk to me anymore, you're going to have to talk to my lawyer first!"

With that, Jo spun around and marched out of the office, the heels of her imitation leather shoes pummeling the linoleum floor. Heads bobbed up curiously as she stomped her way through the maze of desks, calling Morgan and the Abbotsville Police Department every miserable name she could think of under her breath. By the time she reached her car, however, other emotions managed to slip in, namely worry and fear. Did he really suspect she had murdered Kyle Sandborn? And if so, what was she going to do about it?

Morgan was right about one thing: being sued was the least of her concerns. She had tossed out brave words in his office, even throwing up the roadblock of a "lawyer" as if she really *had* a lawyer, as if she could really *afford* a lawyer. But she didn't feel very brave right now, as she climbed behind her wheel, her legs suddenly rubbery and her fingers trembling as she fumbled to insert the key.

"What rubbish!" Ina Mae Kepner sat at the workshop table, a jumble of greenery, pinecones, and ribbons before her. She wasn't referring to her materials.

"Why should that man think for an instant that you could have killed the Sandborn boy? I don't believe you ever saw him before Saturday, did you?"

Jo smiled gratefully at the older woman who had huffed scornfully as Jo related her experience at the police station. Ina Mae had bustled in promptly at seven with two other registrants for the Christmas wreath workshop, looking every inch the retired third-grade teacher that she was. Jo half expected her to take over the class, but instead Ina Mae sat down quietly with the others and waited patiently for Jo to get herself organized. It wasn't until Jo apologized for the third time for bungling her instructions that Ina Mae asked her what was wrong. Then the whole story came tumbling out.

"No, I certainly didn't know him. How do I prove that, though? Besides, my not having a motive might not matter. Kyle was killed in my stockroom, with an item from my stock. Means and opportunity, isn't that all they need?"

"Yes, you're probably right," Loralee Phillips, a diminutive, soft-spoken woman to Ina Mae's right, agreed, nodding. She picked up a holly sprig and held it speculatively against her wreath. "And you certainly look strong enough to jam a knitting needle into someone, I'd have to say."

"Loralee!" Javonne Barnett, the slim African-American woman across from Loralee, protested.

Loralee glanced up from her work with mild eyes. "I was only looking at it from the lieutenant's point of view, Javonne. If Jo is going to defend herself, she'll need to know exactly what from."

"Loralee's right," Carrie agreed, calling

out from the beginner's knitting session she was conducting at the other end of the shop. She had obviously been listening to the conversation with one ear. She left her ladies practicing their cast-ons, to come over. "Jo needs to look out for herself. She shouldn't just trust that the police will discover she's innocent."

"What do you suggest?" Jo asked. "Some subtle bribery with teddy bears for every police officer's desk? Beadwork frames for their badges?"

"Russ Morgan's single, isn't he?" Javonne grinned slyly. "How about an 'accidental' encounter at the Brass Parrot. I've seen him hanging out there sometimes. Got any sexy red dresses in your closet, Jo?"

The ladies shrieked and cackled, and Jo rolled her eyes at Carrie. "Lieutenant Morgan didn't strike me as someone who lets emotions get in the way of his work."

"Lieutenant Morgan strikes *me,*" Ina Mae said, "as an overly busy man, with a very small staff at his disposal. He obviously needs help to look a bit farther than his nose for solutions. Perhaps you can provide it, Jo."

"Oh, that's a great idea," Loralee chimed in.

"I wouldn't know where to start," Jo protested.

"Start by getting to know Kyle, why don't you? Does anyone here know anything about the young man?"

"I know his regular job was working the tennis desk at the country club," Javonne said. "My Harry recognized that picture they put in the paper. Harry plays doubles there Wednesdays when the office is closed." Javonne's Harry was a dentist. She had arrived for the class a few minutes late, explaining that her husband needed her help assisting with an emergency tooth repair. She had then gazed speculatively at Jo's own smile and casually mentioned Harry's office location and hours.

Loralee added, "Kyle was in a lot of the playhouse productions. I saw him in their last show, *Biloxi Blues*. He played the older brother, and was very good, I thought."

"Bob Gordon wanted to talk to me about setting up a craft show at the country club," Jo said. "If he hasn't changed his mind, I suppose I could talk to some of the people that worked with Kyle when I go over there."

"Oh, Bob is a great friend of ours!" Deirdre Patterson spoke up for the first time. Jo remembered her as the silk-suited woman

Ina Mae had edged off that busy morning. She had been silent until now. "I could ask him to take you around if you like." Deirdre wore a pink cashmere sweater set, and Jo feared for its life as Deirdre fumbled around with the wire and glue guns.

"Maybe it's best if Jo does it on her own," Carrie said. "People might open up more if their supervisor isn't standing there listening in, don't you think?"

The other ladies nodded. Jo was amazed to see how quickly they all assumed she would begin snooping around, searching out possible murderers. But she was just as surprised to realize how she was warming to the idea. It was, after all, much better than sitting around waiting for the handcuffs to be slapped on, and Jo had always thought of herself as a person of action. Unfortunately, her actions hadn't always led to the best results.

Like that time in New York, when, after learning her usual delivery service was backed up, she decided to hand-deliver an order of her specialty jewelry to a town in New Jersey, and ended up lost, in a broken-down car, needing to check into a Bates-like motel on a foggy night. Mike, to say the least, had not been happy when she'd called to explain the pickle she'd got herself in, and she eventually promised him to never again jump blindly into uncharted territory. Was that, however, what she was contemplating doing?

Mike, she explained silently, somehow feeling the need, this is different. I'll just be asking a few simple questions. It'll be perfectly fine, I promise. One of Mike's exasperated looks flashed into her mind, and she quickly turned back to her class.

"Now ladies," she said, seeing them puzzling over the arrangement of their wreath decorations, "to get back to our workshop. I want you to be creative in how you place your trimmings since I think that's half the fun of putting it all together. My suggestion, just to get you started, is to cross and attach these two curly willow branches at the base of your wreath, on a slight angle, then make and attach the bow onto it like this." Jo demonstrated. "Then you can add your bird's nest, the pinecones, and these other lovely items about the wreath to brighten and balance everything out. But play around with it before you glue anything in place. Rearrange until you're happy with the design. You'll see. Little by little it'll all come together."

You'll see, Mike. It'll be all right.

The women dug in, and Jo watched with

satisfaction as their wreaths developed. She offered help here and there, and was about to compliment Loralee on her work when a wail snapped her attention to the opposite end of the worktable.

"Jo, help!" Deirdre cried. "I've glued my fingers together!"

CHAPTER 6

Jo stepped back and looked at the box she had filled with various craft items. It was the second of two. If she didn't stop soon she'd have half her stock packed up to show to Bob Gordon at the country club.

"Charlie, I'm so glad you're able to help out. There's no way I could haul this stuff by myself."

"It's okay, Aunt Jo. I've got nothing better to do."

That was the truth, Jo realized, with an inner sigh. Carrie had been confiding of late her continuing worries about her son and his apparent lack of drive. Since dropping out of baseball eighteen months ago, Charlie had done very little with his free time beyond the household chores his parents required of him. And those he had to be pushed and dragged through, according to Carrie, which only caused more tension between him and his father. Dan, once he'd accepted Charlie's lack of interest in team sports, had tried to get him involved in some way in Dan's home improvement business. But Charlie, while showing some budding skills in carpentry, had been such a source of aggravation with his reluctance to follow Dan's precise directions that Carrie had insisted, for the sake of preserving what was left of their father-son relationship, that Charlie lay down his hammer.

That had left, however, large chunks of unfilled time in Charlie's after-school hours, chunks that he had been occupying, when his parents weren't around, with television and video games. Carrie feared his brain, which was capable in the past of generating *A*s and *B*s in school, was slowly turning to mush.

Jo, though not totally delighted with this current manifestation, was fond of Charlie and wanted to do what she could to bring back the brightness she felt sure still lurked there. His showing up to help with the store cleanup the other night, though it was at Carrie's instigation, had at least got him moving. It gave Jo the idea to ask Carrie what she thought of paying him a modest sum to help out now and then with store-related things. Carrie was all for it, and Charlie, characteristically, neither cheered nor groused, but simply showed up. Jo decided to take that as a positive sign and put him to work helping transport her things to the club.

"Do you know much about the country club?" she asked Charlie as they drove out of the small parking lot next to the Craft Corner and onto the street.

"Uh-uh. My folks don't belong. Too expensive. Some kids I know have part-time jobs there, though."

"Really? That might come in handy."

"For what?"

"After I finish with the club manager, I want to talk to people who worked with Kyle Sandborn, the guy who was killed in my shop. See what I can learn about him."

"Uh-huh."

"If you see anyone you know, maybe you could help me out there. You think?"

"Mmm." Charlie's enthusiasm was underwhelming.

The rest of the drive passed in silence until Jo pulled up to the entrance of the Abbotsville Country Club, marked by an ornate sign that hung from the arch between two open, wrought-iron gates. Jo drove in, and as she progressed up the long drive, she sized up the main building. The clubhouse had been built in the antebellum style, with tall white pillars and a second-story veranda. However, the white vinyl siding gleaming in the sun signaled its age was closer to 5 than 155 years.

Pseudo-historical had sprung up a lot in southern — and northern — Maryland, with developers aiming to appeal to the growing sector of nouveau riche. Carrie told her the country club had been flooded with applications within days of its opening, its high membership costs apparently not a problem for certain segments of Abbotsville and some of its newer, high-end suburbs.

Jo parked and climbed out of the car to open her trunk. As she did so, she heard the *thunk* of tennis ball against racquet that came from the high-fenced courts to her right. Golf carts creeping along the path leading to the distant greens gave off a soft *whirr.* She pulled out one of her boxes and looked around. So this was where Kyle Sandborn had spent his days. It was certainly an agreeable spot. What, though, had made him so particularly disagreeable? Well, Jo thought, as Charlie reached for the second box and slammed the trunk closed, that was one of the things she aimed to find out. But first she had to track down Bob Gordon and convince him she could put together a proper craft show. Even snoops, after all, had bills to pay at the end of the month.

Bob Gordon didn't need much convincing. He positively beamed at having found someone willing to organize and set up the craft show, and seemed unconcerned with exactly how she went about it. A portly man of about fifty, he looked like someone who spent more time behind his desk or in the club dining room than utilizing any of the fitness or sports activities his club offered. He barely glanced at the various items Jo had so carefully packed up, and quickly bustled her over to the terrace, which held tables for outdoor dining.

"This is where you can set up," he said. "We can rearrange these tables any way you like, take away the chairs, bring in larger, folding tables, whatever. If the weather gets damp, we can pull down the awning or, if worse gets to worse, move it all inside."

Jo took in the spacious area, which faced the golf course beyond. "This will be perfect," she said, delighted. She could hardly believe her luck, having half expected to be squashed into a dark corner near the gift shop.

"We like to include the ladies' groups from our local churches and such too. They raise a few dollars selling their homemade cakes and doilies, and it draws more people to the show. Your task, besides setting up and selling things from your store, of course, would be to coordinate those groups, as well as bring in a few other types of professional craftsmen. You know, maybe decoy carvers, or potters, things like that. It means a lot of time on the phone and can sometimes seem like herding cats. Think you can do it?"

"No problem. Just give me your list of names, and I'll get right to work on it. Thank you so much for this opportunity, Mr. Gordon."

"Call me Bob. And it's my pleasure. I've had to oversee this in the past, and it's just not my kind of thing. The board, however, feels it's good community relations for the club, and the members enjoy it."

"It'll be great exposure for my new shop too. Plus, in a setting like this, all the items can't help but look amazing. Your grounds and facilities are beautiful."

Gordon's smile broadened. "We try our best. Look around some more, Mrs. McAllister, if you like. Get familiar with the layout. I'd take you myself, except I have prospective members coming. I'll have someone get you a copy of our file — names, phone numbers, lists of things we did in the past. If you have any questions after you look it over, just give me a buzz."

With that, Bob Gordon trotted off, surprisingly light on his feet for his size and clearly delighted to have delegated away a necessary but somewhat burdensome task.

Jo turned to Charlie, who had shadowed her mutely the entire time. "Guess we didn't need to bring all this stuff after all, huh? Let's drop it back in the car and take up Mr. Gordon's carte blanche." At Charlie's puzzled look she rephrased. "Let's look around."

From the car they headed toward the tennis area, with Jo remembering what Javonne Barnett had said about Kyle working at the tennis desk. She led Charlie along the winding walkway past the tennis courts and found the door to the tennis shop. On entering, they encountered several women of various ages in tennis togs milling about, apparently gathering for scheduled matches. The young woman behind the desk, wearing a green polo with the country club's logo, was showing a new racquet to one, and a college-aged boy knelt on the floor farther back, unpacking cans of balls.

The players heads swiveled toward Jo and

Charlie, but not recognizing prospective opponents, quickly turned back to chatting with each other. Jo sensed Charlie's reluctance to wind through this unfamiliar, overwhelmingly feminine scene, and encouraged him with a smile. "We can hang around the apparel shop over there," she said, "until things clear out a bit."

They lingered over tables stocked with visors, sweatbands, and tennis socks, Jo fingering idly through racks of tennis shirts, shorts, and warm-ups, Charlie shifting from foot to foot, until finally the lively group drifted out to the courts and the prospective racquet customer left. Jo headed over to the desk as the young woman there was re-hanging the demo racquet. She turned and flashed Jo a smile.

"Hi. Can I help you? Need to reserve a court?"

"No, we're kind of just looking around."

"New members?"

"Actually, I'll be handling the fall craft show here this year for Bob Gordon. I'm Jo McAllister. I own Jo's Craft Corner."

Jo paused, watching as the young woman, whose name tag identified her as "Tracy," connected the dots. Her pale complexion flushed. "Jo's Craft Corner. That's where Kyle . . . ?"

"Yes, I'm afraid it was."

"God, that must have been awful."

Jo nodded. "It was."

Jo gave the girl a moment. As Tracy's cheeks faded back to her normal shade, Jo noticed the fellow working on the tennis balls looking over at them.

"Were you a friend of Kyle's?" Jo asked the girl.

"Um, yeah, I mean, he worked here and all. We weren't always here at the same time, though. But I knew him. Not real well, though."

"I met him for the first time on that day," Jo said. "He didn't seem very happy to be working a clown gig."

Tracy smiled. "No, I wouldn't think so. Kyle, I think, was planning to be the next Johnny Depp or Leonardo DiCaprio, or something. He was always talking about his latest role at the playhouse and how it was going to be a springboard to a career in New York or Hollywood."

"So working here was pretty much a stopgap for Kyle?"

Tracy's coworker behind the counter snorted loudly. "You could say that," he said, picking up the now-empty packing box and sauntering over as he compacted it. "That is, if you could call it working at all."

"Ryan! Kyle's dead!"

"Yeah, and it's too bad and all. But it doesn't make him any less of a jerk when he was alive."

Tracy winced at the harshness of Ryan's words, but Jo noticed she didn't correct him.

"You didn't care for Kyle, I take it."

"Who would? He was a pain in the butt most of the time, always talking like he was some big-deal actor getting ready for his next role, putting up with all us little people. He only actually worked when Mr. Gordon happened to be around."

"That's not true," Tracy protested. "I know for a fact he stayed late sometimes when he didn't have to, if the mixed doubles teams finished late."

"Yeah, and you know why?" Ryan planted one elbow on the counter and leaned toward Jo. "He was spying on them."

"Spying?"

"He called it 'doing character studies,' which was a load of crap. He was sneaking around, eavesdropping on everyone's conversations."

"For future roles?"

Ryan laughed. "Yeah, right. Plus he dramatized everything, turning the stuff he picked up into some kind of soap opera plot, like he was directing a movie or something, and everyone around him were actors in some screenplay."

"Yeah, actually, that's right," Tracy joined in. "Kyle tried to convince me once that a couple of the mixed doubles people were having an affair. I couldn't see it. These were two really nice people who just happened to need partners to play in the league. They liked *tennis,* not each other. I mean, not in that way. It seemed pretty over the top."

Ryan grinned, nodding. "He once told me Mr. Gordon must be embezzling funds from the club, and you know why?"

Jo shook her head.

"Because he showed up one day driving a new Lexus. Like Gordon couldn't afford it? He makes, well, I don't know what he makes. But it must be enough to afford a Lexus. Kyle said he was keeping an eye on him."

"Did any of these people realize he was, ah, studying them?"

"Probably not," Ryan said. "He could be pretty smooth about it. But who knows?"

Indeed, Jo thought.

The phone rang. As Tracy reached for it, a player rushed in from the courts holding up a racquet with a broken string. Jo could see their discussion about Kyle was at an end, and she drew Charlie away from the desk and out the door.

They walked a few feet down the path before Jo turned to the teen. "What did you think?"

"About this guy Kyle?"

"Uh-huh."

"Sounds like Ryan didn't like him much."

"I got that too. Did Ryan sound believable to you, or did he seem to be putting it on a little thick about what Kyle was doing around here?"

"I don't know." Charlie looked down at his shoes for a few moments. "That girl Tracy is pretty hot." Charlie flashed an embarrassed grin. "Maybe Ryan was trying to impress her. Or maybe Kyle was always hitting on her and it ticked Ryan off."

"Ah, I hadn't thought of that. Some good points, Charlie."

Charlie threw Jo a hint of a smile, then gazed back at his shoes, his hands stuffed in his pockets. "But I don't know," he said. "Maybe Kyle really was a jerk."

Jo could confirm that part, at least from the way Kyle had behaved at her grand opening. But were his actions here at his job as over the top as Ryan claimed? And if so, who else might have noticed?

They reached the car, and Jo searched

through her pockets for her keys. As she unlocked the passenger door, she noticed Charlie looking off toward a small group of grounds workers walking toward the golf course with a cart of tools, a couple of them probably high schoolers.

"Anybody you know?"

"Yeah."

"Like to go over and talk to them?" she asked, feeling on a roll from the tennis shop and eager to keep it going.

Charlie shrugged. "Uh-uh," and climbed into the car.

Jo looked back at the group longingly. She weighed her chances of success at strolling over, commenting on the weather, and casually turning the topic to Kyle Sandborn. The scale tipped heavily toward "not good." She sighed and slid behind the wheel, deciding what she learned from Tracy and Ryan would have to do for now.

CHAPTER 7

Jo settled in the cubicle she called an office the next morning, eager to start working on the craft show while Carrie handled the customers. Bob Gordon had sent over a thick packet containing information on the club's past craft shows. She started by calling Phyllis Lenske, head of the Ladies' Sodality at St. Adelbert's, who had hosted a high-grossing table last year.

"Another show? Oh, how nice," Phyllis responded. But Jo's hand, which had moved to pencil the group in, halted as Phyllis quickly qualified her interest, saying, "Let me check with Mary Louise, first. She's having knee replacement surgery, but I really can't remember if it's this month or next. And we would definitely need Susan Crosby to pitch in, but I'll have to find out when she and her husband are taking that cruise to the Bahamas," as well as several other problems that stood in the way of a definite answer.

Jo got an enthusiastic response when she called the office of the Abbotsville United Methodist Church, but then she was given the numbers of several more women to call who "may or may not be available for the project. And thank you *so* much for thinking of us."

Even the professional craftsmen she contacted left her hanging, some describing their schedules as in flux and saying they would therefore need to hold off on a definite answer for a bit, "but really, what a nice opportunity it sounds like." Others responded only with messages on their answering machines that promised to get back to the caller "very soon." It quickly became clear why Bob Gordon had been so happy to give her the job.

"Arrgh!" Jo cried after hanging up from possibly her twentieth unproductive call. "Herding cats is right. Gordon must be dancing in his office right now."

"I thought the phrase was 'herding chickens.' " Carrie looked over from the stamping section where she stood, filling out an order sheet.

"No, it has to be cats. A chicken might at least gift you with an egg for your efforts. Cats give you nothing, and the harder you try, the more they secretly laugh at you. These people are cats, and they're all rubbing their paws beside their phones right now, saying, 'Hee, hee, she thinks she's actually going to get cooperation from us, snicker, snicker.' "

"Spoken as one who never owned a cat, of course."

"There's a good reason for that." Jo got up from her chair and stretched her tired back. "And as soon as I think of it, I'll let you know. What's on our agenda for tonight?"

"The scrapbooking workshop. But you're on your own for that. I'm going to 'Parents' Night' at the school."

"Oh, yeah. Guess I better bone up on scrapbooking some more. They never taught it at art school, you know, mostly because it didn't exist at the time."

"We all kept scrapbooks as kids. Mine were always a mess, though, just pages with everything I wanted to save thrown in — awards certificates, school pictures, dried corsages. This is a lot different, isn't it?"

"Absolutely. This is a real art form, Carrie. Each page is decorated according to the theme of the entry, snapshots are trimmed to set off the subject, and everything is arranged on layers of beautiful papers. It can be quite elaborate. And the range of tools available," Jo moved over to the scrapbooking section, pointing out the stock, "embossers, calligraphy pens, paper punchers, special paper trimmers —"

"Sounds like a great hobby to encourage," Carrie said with a grin. "The more enthusiastic the scrapbooker, the better your business."

"Right! Tonight's workshop, though, is for beginners, of which I still consider myself one."

"Oh, I know your wheels will start turning as they always do, as soon as you see those blank pages before you. Who's signed up for it?"

Jo found the sign-up sheet and laughed. "Ina Mae, for one. She seems determined to learn everything our little Craft Corner can offer."

"It's the elementary school teacher in her. All those years of decorating bulletin boards. They can't stop."

"And Deirdre Patterson's coming too. She signed up at the end of the wreath workshop."

"Even after the glued fingers? You must have really stirred up the hobbyist in her. I never thought she'd be inclined toward arts and crafts, what with the damage that can do to one's manicure."

"I don't know. She's clearly never done much of it before. Maybe it's the novelty, or she might just like the camaraderie. Could she be feeling lonely?"

"I wouldn't think so. As Mrs. Alden Patterson, I'm sure her social calendar is well booked."

"Well, whatever it is, I'm glad to have her. Maybe she'll pull in a few of her many friends and acquaintances if she keeps it all up."

That evening, after Carric took off for a quick dinner with her family before Parents' Night, Jo watched her scrapbooking students file in. Ina Mae was first, right on time, with white-haired Loralee Phillips trailing behind, carrying the large tote Jo had noticed the other night. Nearly half the size of the petite woman, it seemed to be her way of staying prepared for any and all things. The other night when Javonne mentioned having rushed over from the dental office for the wreath-making workshop without supper, Loralee had reached into her tote, pulled out a box of trail mix and a perfectly ripe banana, and passed it over without a word.

Jo had learned that both Ina Mae and Loralee were widows, but that's where any similarity seemed to end, what with Ina Mae's power walking and active volunteerism versus Loralee's quieter interests. But Jo suspected Ina Mae's strong personality complemented Loralee's gentler one. Also, she remembered her Great-aunt Martha once explaining why she regularly lunched with a highstrung, chronically giggling neighbor. "I find," she'd said, "the older I get, the less picky I am about my companions." There was something to be said for that.

Mindy Blevins, who held the distinction of being Jo's first customer ever, arrived next, carrying a box filled to overflowing with photos of her toddler twins. Jo speculated they would fill quite a hefty scrapbook if she intended to incorporate them all. The youngest of the group at about twenty-five or so, Mindy wore her medium brown hair pulled back in a time-saving pony-tail style. The oversize shirt she wore seemed designed to cover a few extra pregnancy pounds, which no doubt, with twins to chase after, she would eventually lose.

Deirdre Patterson brought up the rear, dressed more sensibly this time in dark T-shirt and jeans. She clutched a much smaller box than Mindy and wore an expression that struck Jo as more determined than eager. Deirdre clearly was still out of her element and would need help to discover that crafting could be relaxing and fun. She greeted Jo cordially, however, as well as her fellow students, as she joined them around the worktable.

Once they settled down, Jo went over the basic idea of scrapbooking with the group and then displayed the various tools available. "You don't need a lot of these at first, and if you have basic things like a pair of sharp scissors you'll have a good start. But these tools can help with wonderful special effects as you progress, like crimping and embossing. The first thing you need to do now, though, is decide on a theme for your scrapbook, or perhaps a separate theme for each page."

"I can't decide if I should do a separate book for each twin, or keep them together," Mindy said.

"Oh, keep them together," Loralee cried. "I've always loved to see identical twins in their matching outfits."

"Separate books," Ina Mae countered, in a firm teacher-to-parent tone. "Each child should retain his own identity."

"You have so many photos," Jo said, "you could probably do both. One for each of the twins and one focusing on their twin-ness."

"Oh, I like that!" Mindy upended her box, creating a huge mound of photos. "I'll get started on sorting them out."

"My goodness, you do have a lot," Deirdre said, the expression on her face saying, "Far better you than I."

"What kind of scrapbook are you going to do?" Loralee asked Deirdre.

"I want to put together a book for Alden, to record his career in the state senate. I plan to surprise him with it for his birthday."

"How nice." Loralee smiled sweetly but said no more, leading Jo to wonder if her vote during the last election might have been for Alden Patterson's opponent.

The ladies got busy, and Jo wandered around, offering a suggestion here and there. Ina Mae, she saw, planned to do scrapbooks on her vacations, starting with a recent one to the Southwest. When Jo eventually returned to her own station, Ina Mae, barely glancing up from her work, asked, "So, what have you learned about Kyle so far?"

All the heads around the table popped up, faces full of interest. Jo wasn't sure if she should feel touched or pressured. Either way, they were obviously not going to let her off the hook.

Loralee explained to Mindy, who had not been at the wreath workshop, "We've encouraged Jo to do a little side-investigating, to supplement what the police might be doing."

A diplomatic way of putting it, Jo thought, since what they had really hinted was that she needed to save her own skin.

"Well, I did talk to two of Kyle's coworkers at the tennis desk," Jo said.

"And?" Deirdre asked.

"And, neither seemed to find Kyle very likable, which was pretty much my own opinion, though I thought he might just have been having a bad day."

"Coworkers often have the clearest view of a person," said Ina Mae. "The best and worst of one's character come out at the workplace."

"Oh, I agree," Mindy jumped in. The sorting of her photos was going slowly, as Mindy couldn't seem to handle any snapshot without taking a long, loving gaze at it. "I once took a job working for a friend of mine in a bridal shop, more as a favor to her than anything else. Whooo, was that a mistake. I saw a side of her I never knew before. Talk about 'bride-zillas,' she was definitely boss-zilla. When she —"

"What," Ina Mae interrupted, "exactly did Kyle's coworkers say about him?"

"They claimed he spent more time spying on the clientele than working, and turned every situation into a soap opera. He apparently felt his job there was beneath him and that he was just marking time until his acting career took off."

"That must have annoyed them. Do you trust their judgment?"

"I'd like to talk to a few more people at the country club and see if I get similar stories."

"Good idea," Deirdre piped up. She had edged away from Mindy and her spreading project. "But since Kyle was so interested in acting, I'd check with the group at the playhouse too."

Mindy agreed, nodding. "I know they were starting work on their next production at the playhouse, some kind of fairy-tale story, I heard. Kyle must have been part of it. I bet you'd get a lot of dirt on him there."

"Absolutely," Deirdre said. "And," she added, as if anticipating Jo's question of how to approach the playhouse group, "you could offer to do a little set designing, or costume accessorizing, or something as a way in."

"Wonderful idea, Deirdre." Loralee fairly

bounced on her seat with approval.

Jo looked at the group, dryly noting how ready they were to send her off on more expeditions with no thought as to how she was going to fit this all into her already bulging schedule. Between minding the store, craft classes, and now the craft show to set up at the country club, Jo barely had time left, lately, to eat and sleep. But then, she reasoned, if she didn't find a way to stretch her time now, she might have nothing to fill it with later on.

Except, she thought wryly, making license plates.

The group made a good start on their scrapbooks and were packing up their materials for the night, when Jo heard Deirdre cry out in exasperation, "Shoot!"

"What's wrong?"

"My bracelet. I took it off tonight so it wouldn't get in my way, and now, when I tried to put it back on, I see the clasp is broken. Darn! I wanted to wear it to a lunch tomorrow."

"Oh, what a shame," Mindy said.

"Let me see," Jo said, reaching for it and looking it over. "I can fix that if you like. But my jewelry tools are at home. If you want to follow me there, I can have it done in two minutes."

"That would be so nice! Are you sure you don't mind?"

"Not at all. Just give me a minute to close up the shop."

The others said their good nights, and Deirdre helped Jo do a final straightening up before turning out her lights and locking up. When they left, Jo pointed out her Toyota, then led the way to the house, waving Deirdre, once she'd parked her Mercedes, into the garage.

"I've set up my jewelry bench in this little built-in workroom," she explained, pulling out her keys and unlocking its door. "I think one of the owners used it for a photography darkroom. It has good lighting and a lock, so I feel safe leaving my things in it."

"How very handy. What a cute little place you have here," Deirdre said, referring to Jo's house.

Jo smiled, aware of her house's shortcomings but satisfied with the rent. "It's comfortable," she said. She took Deirdre's bracelet out and got to work, removing the broken clasp and replacing it with a new one. As promised, she finished the job quickly.

"Wonderful!" Deirdre cried when Jo

handed it back to her. "What do I owe you for this?"

"Never mind," Jo said. "It was my pleasure."

Deirdre protested, but Jo waved it away. "Just bring a few friends to the craft show if you like. I want Bob Gordon to be happy with the turnout."

"I surely will, then." Deirdre paused, looking around. Jo got the feeling she hoped to be invited into the house.

"Like to stay for a minute, for coffee perhaps?"

Deirdre lit up. "Maybe just a minute, if it's not too late for you?"

It had been a long day, and Jo was feeling tired. But it wouldn't kill her, she thought, to be a little hospitable. "We can go in through here." Jo indicated the connecting door between the garage and her kitchen. Deirdre followed as Jo flipped on lights.

"What a charming place," Deirdre said, and Jo smiled once again, this time at the word "charming." By now she was familiar with the buzzwords real estate people used for various properties. "Cozy fixer-upper" often translated as "run-down shack," and "charming," Jo thought, was code for "cheap but livable." She hadn't seen Deirdre's house but could imagine something worthy of hiring a full-time housekeeper to manage. Jo made no apologies for her own living situation, though. It was within her means, it kept her out of the rain and cold, and, hopefully, it was temporary.

"Regular or decaf?" Jo asked, going to her coffee cupboard.

"You know, if you have something cold, that would be great."

"Sure." Jo pulled open her refrigerator and looked in. "Iced tea?"

"Great. Mind if I look around? I love old places like this."

"Not at all." Jo poured out two glasses of tea and handed one to Deirdre. She led her to the living room.

"Oh," Deirdre cried, "you're making a new wreath." Jo had left her work-in-progress on the coffee table, her supplies scattered on the floor about it.

"I'm working on a prototype for the next wreath-making class. This one's a spring wreath, and I'll probably hang it on the Craft Corner's front door next March or so, to freshen up the seasonal look of the store."

"Wonderful idea. And I love what you've done so far with those pretty flowers — you're so creative! I'll have to sign up for that class, definitely."

Jo walked her about the rest of the house, and they chatted about some of the interesting features — at least Deirdre seemed to find them interesting — of the small house, such as the built-in bookcases in the living room, still mostly bare, and the stained-glass window in the powder room. Jo did like that but would have traded it in a flash for a rust-free sink.

Jo began to wonder once more if Deirdre might be feeling a little lonely. Wasn't her senator-husband around to go home to and chat with? Or perhaps Deirdre really did enjoy older houses. Maybe she was considering a career in real estate, or home makeovers, to fill her time. But then Deirdre glanced at her watch and gulped down the last of her iced tea.

"This has been great, Jo, but I'd better run. Thank you so much for the tea and especially for my bracelet repair." She set down her glass on the kitchen counter and headed for the connecting garage door. "Good luck at the playhouse, whenever you go. I wouldn't put it off, though. I'm betting you'll find out some very helpful things about Kyle Sandborn while you're there."

"We'll see." Jo walked Deirdre to her car and waved her off, watching the Mercedes drive smoothly away. At worst, Jo thought spending some time at the playhouse might help her understand Kyle a bit more, and that certainly couldn't hurt. She wondered if she should have invited Deirdre to come along with her but decided there was someone else in greater need of having time filled.

CHAPTER 8

Jo pulled up to the Abbotsville Playhouse with one of the boxes she had taken to the country club now repacked with samples of her jewelry and tucked snugly on the back-seat floor. She had asked Charlie to come along on this Sunday afternoon, explaining that she appreciated having an extra pair of eyes and ears with her, as well as valuing his particular viewpoint. In typical Charlie fashion, he had been shruggingly agreeable.

"I spoke to the director, Rafe Rulenski, on the phone," Jo said as she cut her engine. "Besides directing this latest production, he seems to be the guy in charge, overall. Anyway, he's interested in looking over my costume jewelry, and maybe we can learn a few more things about Kyle while we're at it."

"What's the show?" Charlie asked after glancing over at the theater and seeing its poster windows were blank.

"It's a musical version of *Rumpelstiltskin,* with a twist. It's aimed toward adults, not kids. I got the impression Rulenski wrote it himself."

Charlie snorted, but Jo was unsure if that was a comment on the show's subject or Rulenski writing it. Since neither particularly concerned her, aside from the fact that fairy-tale characters such as kings and queens offered an opportunity for her to load them up with sparkly jewelry, she reached for her sturdy traveling box and climbed out.

Rulenski had told her the theater would be unlocked, rehearsals would be in progress, and she could find him somewhere down front. Jo, therefore, headed for the front doors, Charlie close behind, and made her way through the small lobby, following the sound of voices. As they pushed through the inner doors, they entered a scene of organized chaos.

Actors recited their lines on stage while scenery builders hammered away behind them and a soloist struggled through an odd, rambling melody. Jo stood in place for a moment, letting her eyes and her brain adjust to take it all in. Then she spotted a man likely to be Rafe Rulenski standing at the edge of the orchestra pit.

"Genna, sweetie, for the tenth time," he called up to a woman on stage, "it's Alo-WISH-shus, not A-LOY-shus."

"I'm sorry, Mr. Rulenski. I just never heard that name before, and I keep forgetting."

"That's the whole point, darling, that it's an unusual name. This odd little man *needs* an unusual name. You wouldn't expect it to just be Harry, would you?"

"No, Mr. Rulenski."

Jo motioned to Charlie with a jerk of her head and started down the sloping aisle, keeping an eye on Rulenski, a trim, fortyish man in a black T-shirt and Levi's. His thinning hair had been cut close, and, as he turned to consult with a young assistant, Jo saw he sported a day's growth of beard. She had often seen that look in New York, mostly among actors, and occasionally in her and Mike's world of artists, and had always puzzled how the beard was maintained at that level. Mike had been either clean shaven or not, with the in-between period fairly limited. How much effort, she wondered, did it take to work out the timing? Did Rulenski, for instance, have to set his alarm for 3 A.M. to get up and shave in order to have a five o'clock shadow by noon? These irrelevant thoughts ended when Rulenski caught sight of her and waved her over with a directorial crook of fingers.

"Mrs. McAllister?"

"Yes. And this is my assistant, Charles Brenner."

Rulenski gave Charlie a cursory glance and graced him with a nod. "Have a seat, please. I'll be finished here in a minute."

"That's fine." Jo slipped into a row nearby and set her box on the seat beside her. She glanced over at Charlie, who gazed at the stage, openmouthed, as he settled in. The female soloist at the rear seemed to have finally caught on to her song's melody, since she now kept pace with the accompanist. The song itself, though, hadn't improved, at least to Jo's ears.

She listened for a while, then whispered to Charlie, "What is that she's singing? Is it, 'She spins, she's cold,' or 'She wins the gold'?"

"I dunno. I thought she was singing in Russian." Charlie grinned lopsidedly, and Jo stifled a laugh.

The dark-haired girl named Genna finally delivered her lines correctly, and Rulenski clapped, whether encouragingly or with sarcasm, Jo couldn't say. He dismissed Genna and her fellow actor, then turned to Jo with world-weary eyes.

"Well, thank you for coming by, Ms. McAllister. Let's see what you have there."

"Call me Jo." Jo reached for her box. "I brought several styles, since I wasn't sure just what direction you were going."

"At this point, I'm open to suggestions," Rulenski sighed. "My costumers haven't come up with anything the least bit interesting so far. Perhaps you can lead the way."

"Well, I presume, since your story has a king, and the young girl who spins his flax into gold becomes his queen, you'll want some sort of crown, or tiara. Now I have —"

"Is it okay," Charlie asked, half-rising, "if I look around? I've never been backstage."

"Go ahead," Rulenski barely looked over, "just watch your step."

Charlie wandered off, and Jo pulled out a few items from her box. "Now these would look nice and glittery on stage, and the gold and silver is actually brass and nickel, of course, to keep them affordable. I can add 'jewels' of any color, to catch even more light, and we could go with one color theme for your king — say, the deeper colors of ruby and sapphire — and maybe keep to the lighter hues for your miller's-daughter-raised-to-queen, to symbolize her newness to royalty, her innocence and naiveté."

"Hmm, yes, that might work."

Jo pulled out a few chains and demonstrated how they could be variously wrapped around the waist or hung from the neck, then reached for her sketch pad and drew out a few more ideas. Rulenski seemed receptive, especially as she emphasized the low cost of the items, and how easily they could be retooled for future productions. If the Abbotsville Playhouse was like all other small theatrical groups, it operated on a shoestring and had to cut corners mercilessly in order to survive.

Jo reeled him in further by saying, "Since I'm anxious to establish my new shop, I'd be happy to reduce my usual fees substantially for a prominent mention in your playbill." Rulenski scratched his bristly cheek, as if weighing the thought carefully, but Jo had caught the flash of interest in his eyes.

They went on to discuss possible set decorations that Jo could contribute, including flowers and greenery — now that Rulenski knew her services would come cheaply his needs had suddenly expanded — until the young female assistant Jo had seen earlier scurried up. "Mr. Rulenski, the accompanist wants to know if you got Kyle's copy of the score back yet."

"Tell him, yes. I've already passed it on to Doug, who's been studying it."

As the girl hurried off, Jo asked, "Kyle Sandborn?"

"Mmm. He was to be our male lead. Most unfortunate."

Jo searched Rulenski's face but was unable to tell if he meant unfortunate for Kyle or unfortunate for Rulenski to have lost one of his actors in the midst of rehearsals.

"I understand Kyle was really into the theater, that he aimed to make a career of it."

Rulenski sighed. "They all think it's so easy. Just show up in New York or L.A. and the jobs will be waiting for them. They assume playing the lead in a place like Abbotsville means they are star material."

"Kyle wasn't?"

"Oh, don't get me wrong, he wasn't bad. And he had the drive. Who knows, perhaps if he'd enrolled in some good acting classes, along with a lot of luck, maybe . . ."

"Did you direct him in all the plays he did here?"

"Lord, who knows?" Rulenski rubbed at his eyes with long-suffering patience. "Yes, probably. I do remember him auditioning that first time. What was it? I think we were attempting to do Tennessee Williams that year. A disaster. Anyway, I gave him a small part then, a walk-on. After that, like most of our troupe, he worked his way up to the bigger roles but rotated into small ones if that's what fit him best in a particular play."

"So he cooperated well, you'd say? Got along with everyone?"

"Far as I know. At least I never witnessed any fistfights," Rulenski said, grinning. "What happens between these people off-stage is the least of my concerns. Now, about some of those designs we talked about, how soon do you think you can get them to me?"

Jo took the hint and got back to business. Since the soloist had returned to practicing her nerve-grating song, she was just as happy to finish up and move out of hearing range, although Jo couldn't help but feel disappointed at gleaning so little from Rulenski. That feeling, however, disappeared when she reunited with Charlie.

"How did you learn all this, Charlie?" They were back in the car, and Charlie had filled her in as she pulled away from the play-house.

110

Charlie shrugged. "Nobody notices kids like me. They think we're part of the scenery or something, and they talk as if there's nobody around."

"So, let me get this straight," Jo said. She slowed at the intersection and signaled a left heading toward Charlie's house. She had promised Carrie she'd drop him off in time to study hard for tomorrow's Spanish test. "A blond girl named Kerry asked Genna, the one who has trouble with names, if things were better between Genna and Pete now that Doug was Genna's leading man."

"Uh-huh. And Genna said yes, but that it still felt weird doing a love scene with her cousin, even though he's her second cousin. Plus he's a lot older than her."

"And cousin Doug is playing the part that had been Kyle's."

"I guess."

"That I know, since Rafe Rulenski said he gave Kyle's copy of the score to Doug to study." Jo's voice grew excited. "It sounds like jealousy on boyfriend Pete's part to me. Does it to you?"

"Yeah, probably."

"Then that's great information and de-serves a high-five!" Jo held up her hand to slap Charlie's, who looked surprised but pleased as he returned the congratulatory slap.

"Charlie, you may have learned something very important, something I didn't get even a hint of by spending all that time trying to pump the show's director. If Genna's boyfriend was jealous of Kyle doing love scenes with Genna, that's the first hint of danger in Kyle's life we've found so far. And you dug it up!"

"So you think it's important?"

"It could be. We won't go jumping to any conclusions, but it bears further investigation, wouldn't you agree?"

"Yeah, I guess."

"I knew it was a good thing to bring you along."

"It was better than studying Spanish anyway." Charlie paused, then admitted, "Actually, it was pretty neat looking around that theater. I wouldn't mind going back. If you want me to."

Jo looked over at Charlie, seeing something new in his eyes.

"To find out more about Kyle, or about the theater?"

"Both," Charlie replied. "I'd just like hanging out there. Maybe I could get some kind of job. Then while I'm around, I might, you know, hear things, like today."

"That might be a good idea, Charlie. Let's run it by your folks and see what they say." Jo turned back to her driving, thinking she could pretty well predict what Carrie would say. Dan, though, might be another thing altogether. Well, they'd have to wait and see. Jo crossed her fingers for Charlie that it would work out the way he hoped.

CHAPTER 9

Jo pulled up to Charlie's house, the fixer-upper Carrie and Dan had bought when they first moved to Abbotsville more than fifteen years ago to set up Dan's home improvement business. The house looked fine from the curb, but every time Jo walked through it she was reminded of the saying "the cobbler's children go without shoes." The essential renovations in the house had been done over time — the kitchen and bathrooms, and finally the family room. But Carrie's living room sat as it had from day one, looking as if a crew were expected the next day to work on the floor, replace moldings, and paint walls.

Dan had great plans in mind, which included adding hardwood floors, and when he finally got around to it, the living room would look fantastic. But working on his own home had a low priority next to working on other people's — clients who would pay him for his services, which in turn would keep the family finances in the black, and his children shod. For the time being, therefore, Carrie's living room remained in the white — white dust sheets over furniture sitting on white drop cloths. It was fortunate her friend had a sense of humor, and was able to joke about changing the colors of the sheets with the seasons, as some people changed their slipcovers, or perhaps stenciling bright designs on them for decoration.

As Charlie climbed out of the car, Carrie appeared at the door, waving Jo to come in.

"I made a big pot of chili," she called out. "Stay for dinner."

Jo grinned. Carrie knew her weakness — hot, spicy chili, usually accompanied by Carrie's homemade biscuits. "If you insist," she called back, and fairly leaped from the car.

Amanda was already setting an extra place. "Hi Aunt Jo," she said, clinking down the tableware. Amanda wore her red and black soccer uniform, which reminded Jo that Amanda's team, which Dan coached, had played that afternoon.

"How was the game?" Jo asked.

Amanda scrunched her face. "We lost. Christy, our best goalie, was out with a sore throat."

"But Amanda scored the only point, against one of the top teams in the division," Dan added.

"Hey, Amanda! Way to go!"

Amanda grinned and curtsied, stretching her soccer shorts out like a skirt. "Next time, if Christy's in, we'll beat them. Right Dad?"

"Absolutely. Ten to nothing." Dan pulled the extra chair up to the table. "Well, how did it go at the playhouse?" he asked.

Charlie's head was in the refrigerator as he searched for something to drink, so Jo answered. "Pretty interesting." She glanced at Amanda, not sure how much to say about Kyle's murder in front of her, so she simply said, "They're putting together a musical version of *Rumpelstiltskin*. Rafe Rulenski, the director, seems to like my ideas for costume accessories and such."

Carrie brought two steaming bowls of chili to the table, and said, "Sit down, everybody. Amanda, come get the biscuits for me, first." She dished up more bowls, and said, as Jo and Dan slid their chairs into place, "I don't imagine this will be terribly lucrative, will it? The playhouse just barely scrapes by as it is. The town council talks about subsidies for them every so often, but nothing ever comes of it."

"What's 'lucrative' mean?" Amanda asked, setting down the plate of warm biscuits, the sight of which made Jo's fingers twitch as she resisted the urge to immediately reach out for them.

"What, haven't you reached the *L*s yet in English?" Charlie asked. Less restrained than Jo, he had already stuffed half a biscuit into his mouth. This turned out to be a bad move when Amanda made a face at him, which produced a snicker followed by a choke on inhaled biscuit crumbs.

"Don't talk with food in your mouth, Charlie, and 'lucrative,' Amanda, means well paid." Carrie joined the four of them at the table.

"I'm working out an arrangement," Jo said, "to get some free advertising out of it."

"Well, good. That's the least they should do," said Dan. He had helped Jo considerably in understanding the financial end of running a small business.

They all dug into Carrie's chili, and Amanda shared the highlights of her soccer game for most of the meal, chattering animatedly between spoonfuls. About the time Dan was pouring cups of coffee for the three grown-ups, the phone rang.

117

Amanda bounced up to answer it, then said, "It's Lindsey. May I be excused?"

Carrie nodded, and Amanda took the phone out of the room to talk to the girl, who, Jo knew from having heard the name many times, was her current best friend.

Charlie scraped at the last of his rice pudding. As soon as Amanda left the room, he said, "That playhouse today was pretty neat."

Jo knew what he was leading up to and added, "Charlie was great today, picking up information while I was tied up with the director."

"Really?" Carrie looked at her son, pleased.

"Yeah, I was kind of wandering around backstage, and people were going every which way, nobody paying attention to anyone else. It was like I was invisible. I could have held a tape recorder under their faces and they wouldn't have stopped yakking."

Carrie grinned. "So what did you find out?"

Charlie shrugged. "Oh, not that much, really, but Aunt Jo —"

"Aunt Jo," Jo interrupted, "thinks it's 'that much.' " She told Carrie and Dan about the conversation Charlie had overheard between Genna and the blond actress. Dan nodded politely, trying, but obviously not terribly impressed, while Carrie beamed.

"Good going, guy! That's the first lead you've gotten so far, right Jo?"

"That's right. I think it's really worth looking into."

"That's what I was going to ask you, Mom, Dad . . ." Charlie hesitated, his voice deadpan but his eyes flashing with eagerness. "I'd really like to spend more time down there. At the playhouse. It might help Aunt Jo, and, uh, I'd kinda like to learn something about, like, uh, how they put on plays and all."

Jo glanced from one face to another. Both seemed a bit stunned, but Jo guessed that Carrie's surprise was more from the fact that Charlie was actually interested in something, whereas Dan seemed stuck on the "something" itself.

"Plays?" he repeated, as if he'd never heard the word before.

Carrie recovered first. "I think that might be very nice, don't you, Dan?" She glanced at her husband's frozen face and quickly looked away. "But what about helping out at Aunt Jo's store? Didn't you promise you'd do that first?"

"He can probably do both, actually, that

is, if it's all right with you two. Helping me at the store was going to be an 'as needed' kind of thing. I don't think you planned on a lot of time at the playhouse either, did you Charlie?"

"I talked to Mr. Rulenski's assistant, that girl with the big glasses? She thought he could use someone around on the weekends mostly. Maybe once in a while during the week." Jo saw Charlie's knees bouncing nervously, even as his face remained calm. He wanted an okay on this badly.

"You want to be an actor?" Dan asked, still clearly dumbfounded.

"No! I mean, I don't know. I just want to be there, to be able to watch everything. You've been telling me to get out of the house, to do more stuff. This is what I want to do." Charlie's chin began to jut forward, and the knee bounces had accelerated.

"Yes, but . . ."

"Let Dad and me think it over a bit, okay, Charlie?" Carrie said before Dan could say any more. "We'd have to be sure you still have time for your studies, for one thing."

"I'll study. I promise."

"That would always have to come first. And speaking of studying —"

Charlie jumped up. "My Spanish test, I know. I'm on top of it right now." He pushed back his chair with more energy than Jo had seen in a long time. "Bye, Aunt Jo." He turned back to Carrie. "It'd be okay, I promise."

With that he hurried out, and Jo heard him take the stairs up to his room two at a time. She turned to Dan, whose face showed that the more he turned the idea over in his mind, the less he cared for it, somewhat like a baby tasting mashed asparagus for the first time. He turned to Carrie, his brows lowered to a puzzled scowl.

"Acting?"

CHAPTER 10

Jo, having opened up the craft shop herself the next morning, took advantage of Carrie's arrival a half hour later to start work on some of her *Rumpelstiltskin* jewelry. She spread out her supplies and tools, which she'd brought from home, on the workshop table.

When Carrie came over to watch, Jo asked, "So, what did you and Dan decide?" Jo had taken early leave from dinner the previous evening to let them discuss Charlie's proposition in private. Jo reached for her chain nose pliers and squeezed them over a micro crimp to separate a grouping of three softly colored crystals on her chain.

Carrie didn't answer directly, instead commenting, "That's pretty. Which character will it be for?"

"The miller's daughter. I think she's called Annalisa in Rulenski's version."

"Mmm."

Jo looked up.

Carrie sighed. "Dan eventually agreed to let Charlie give it a try, especially after I pointed out his school doesn't really have an active drama department. I remembered that Mrs. Pettibone, one of the English teachers at Charlie's school, is part of the playhouse troupe, and that helped. But you would have thought he had agreed to let Charlie volunteer for experimental drug trials or something."

"I'm sorry if I brought about a problem."

"No, no. I really think this will be good for Charlie. Did you see how he ran upstairs to hit the books? It's the first time in ages I've seen him so motivated."

"I agree." Jo slid three more ice-blue crystals onto her strand of beading chain. "If it lasts, this might be just what Charlie needs."

"I guess Dan just finds the whole thing completely alien, since his main interests all his life were sports and woodworking."

"He'd like his son to enjoy the same things, of course."

"Mm-hmm. He sees Amanda learning how to knit from me, and enjoying experiments with cooking and baking. I know Dan likes coaching her soccer team, but he still probably wishes Charlie wanted to do more things with him. I've pointed out that Amanda's interests are very likely to move on as she grows older. She seems keen on her science subjects at school, for one thing, so who knows? She might want to go to medical school later on. And you remember how I nearly fainted in biology when we had to dissect those awful frogs."

Jo smiled. She did indeed remember Carrie's face draining of color, and the biology teacher, Miss Erdmann, rushing over to catch her before she fell off her stool. Carrie had been highly embarrassed, and the fifteen-year-old Jo highly amused.

"I just wish," Carrie said, picking up a stray crystal from Jo's worktable and fingering it, "I wish Dan could be more open to the idea."

The door jingled as a customer came in, and Carrie left to take care of her. Jo continued to work at her jewelry, enjoying the craft that she had neglected of late, with the all-consuming busyness of setting up the store. The phone rang, and seeing Carrie occupied, Jo set down her pliers and picked it up.

"Jo's Craft Corner."

"Mrs. McAllister?"

Jo tensed as she recognized the voice. "Yes?"

"Lieutenant Morgan here. There's something I want to discuss with you. I'd like to see you today, if you please."

If I please? And if I say no, Lieutenant, what then?

Morgan added, "You may bring your lawyer, of course."

Her lawyer? Was he laughing at her, calling her bluff? Or did he really think she had one?

"What time?" she asked, as smoothly as she could manage.

"Within the hour would be good."

"Fine. I'll be there."

Jo, with great effort, replaced the phone carefully, then sat gripping it and staring into space. She caught a concerned glance from Carrie, who was bagging her customer's sale. Carrie came over as soon as the woman left the store.

"Something wrong?"

"He wants me down at the station again."

"Lieutenant Morgan?"

Jo nodded.

"What about?"

"He didn't say. But he said I could bring my lawyer if I liked." Jo laughed grimly.

"Oh, Jo, maybe it's time you did get one."

Jo didn't answer.

125

"Dan and I would be more than glad to chip in."

"No, absolutely not."

"Then what about a public defender?"

Jo sighed, and got up. She pushed her chair into place, keeping hold of its back. "I already checked into that. I'm not eligible."

"You're kidding, right?"

"No, really. It seems I don't meet the poverty guidelines. Although I sunk nearly every penny I had into the store, it now counts as an asset. And, even if I'm not yet drawing a measurable income, it seems they can go by what I'm expected to produce with a business like this. I'm simply not poor enough." Jo laughed. "Of course, they haven't seen the threadbare, secondhand furniture in my rented house, nor my Mother Hubbard pantry."

"That's outrageous."

"No, it's simply your government saving your tax dollars. You probably should be glad."

Carrie looked at Jo glumly. "Then let Dan and me —"

"No, Carrie. No way." Jo reached for her purse and started for the door.

"Wait, Jo," Carrie said, stopping her. "Let me make a couple of calls. There's a lawyer you might be able to afford. I can't think of his name, but I've heard he's sort of semire-tired. You really need *someone.*"

Jo hesitated. "Well, see what you can dig up. If he's available, and cheap, maybe." She spread a large cloth over her jewelry work-place, as Carrie made her calls, to a neigh-bor, a fellow soccer mom, and then, appar-ently, the affordable lawyer's office. She handed Jo a slip of paper with Earnest C. Ainsworthy's address on it.

"His office is on the way to police head-quarters. And he's very reasonable."

"Okay, thanks Carrie. I'll give him a try."

Jo sat in Lieutenant Morgan's office, Ear-nest C. Ainsworthy beside her. He had pat-ted her hand paternally after they had been ushered in by the uniformed young woman who informed them Lieutenant Morgan would be with them shortly.

"Don't you worry, now, little lady. Every-thing will be just fine."

Jo managed to smile back, but she wasn't so sure about that. She had located Ainswor-thy's office, expecting something modest, which it was. Situated above a real estate office, the law office consisted of a tiny, unmanned reception area, then a small in-ner office occupied by Earnest C. However, being told he was semiretired led Jo to expect a white-haired, elderly gentleman. Earnest was a pot-bellied man in his fifties at most, with more dark hair than white, and, rather than the wise, elder statesman she had hoped for, seemed more interested in locating his missing tie clip than listening to her story. Not altogether reassuring, but she assumed he would be better than nothing, and, considering his modest fee, retained him.

As they drove together to the police headquarters, however, Jo caught the alarming whiff of alcohol emanating from him. Now that they sat side by side, waiting for the appearance of the lieutenant, Jo was not feeling entirely bolstered by the presence of this counselor.

She glanced around the room as they waited for Morgan to appear. Giving us time to stew, she thought, as she half-seriously checked for the spotlight Morgan might turn on her face while demanding her answers. She found only fluorescents, high on the ceiling and useless for zeroing in on guilty suspects. Surely Earnest C. will prevent any attempts at bullying, Jo assured herself. And Morgan wouldn't unnerve her because she wasn't hiding anything.

She looked around for signs of the lieutenant's personal life, such as family photos, but then remembered Javonne Barnett had said he was single. Single-divorced or single-never-married? Either way, she saw no photos of children. If he had none, weren't there nieces and nephews he might care about? What about friends? The walls were bare of softball team photos and even awards. The room contained nothing beyond essentials, and the effect was cold. Probably, she thought, exactly what he intended.

The door opened, and Morgan strode in. "Sorry to keep you waiting," he said.

Jo's lawyer stood up and held out his hand. "Earnest C. Ainsworthy, representing Mrs. McAllister." They shook hands, and both sat down, the lieutenant behind his gray metal desk.

"Okay, then," Morgan said. He opened a file he had brought in with him and scanned it for a few moments before looking up.

"Mrs. McAllister, your husband, Michael McAllister, was killed in an explosion."

"Yes, that's right." Jo said it calmly, though the familiar pain sucked at her heart to think of that day.

"What exactly happened?"

What was this about? Jo wondered. She glanced at Ainsworthy, but he offered no advice, so she answered as evenly as she could, "We don't know precisely, but Mike worked with acetylene tanks. He did metal sculptures. Something malfunctioned and caused the explosion. That's all we know."

"Something malfunctioned." Morgan looked at her as if expecting more.

"Yes."

"Was that a highly unusual thing? I mean, I presume there are safeguards against that kind of thing happening."

"Yes, I thought so too. As I said, after looking into it, no one could tell me what went wrong. The explosion and fire destroyed nearly everything, so it was impossible to determine. Why are you asking me this?"

"So there was an investigation? The authorities in New York City searched for a reason for this explosion?"

"Yes, of course." From his frequent glances at the file, Jo was certain he had copies of the reports before him. But why?

"You and your husband shared this loft that was destroyed."

"Yes, we did."

"For how many years?"

Jo thought back. "I believe, about five years."

"And your husband worked at his metal sculptures, with acetylene tanks for those five years?"

"Yes, he did."

"There was no problem before this?"

"Obviously not."

"How did you and your husband get along?"

"Lieutenant Morgan, what does all this have to do with Kyle Sandborn?" Jo could feel her temper rising. Was that what Morgan wanted, though? The thought unfortunately ratcheted her anger even higher. She looked at Ainsworthy for help, but he made no objection to Morgan's line of questioning, his hands folded calmly over his high mound of belly. His eyes seemed focused on the front edge of Morgan's desk.

"Did you and your husband have marital problems?" Morgan asked.

"No!"

"You received payment of his life insurance, and shortly after that, you moved here."

"Yes, and I'm sure you know exactly how much that payment was, and how thinly it had to be stretched in my efforts to start a new life. I did not set up my husband's death, a husband I dearly loved, in case you care, in order to live a life of luxury here in Abbotsville."

Morgan simply looked at her for a few

moments, then turned a page in the file before him and began a new tack.

"Mrs. McAllister, did you, when you lived in New York, have dealings with a Niles P. Sandborn?"

Jo's shock must have shown, since Morgan looked gratified.

"Niles? Where did you dig him up?" Why was her life suddenly being examined? What was going on?

"You had business with him?"

"Yes, at one time. He is a dealer. He bought jewelry from me, for a while."

"Was your relationship amicable?"

"As a matter of fact, no, it was not, at least not always. When I got tired of his late payments and other finagling, I put an end to it."

"*You* put an end to it?"

"Yes."

"It wasn't the other way around?"

"Oh, Lord. What did he tell you? Yes, I know Niles tried to sue me for breach of contract. But it came to nothing. Our 'contract' was quite flexible, allowing either of us to end it easily, and he knew it. He was just blowing smoke."

"I suppose you never threatened him either?"

"Lieutenant Morgan, what is going on

here? Does the fact that a crime happened to take place in my storeroom give you the right to invade my privacy? Does it automatically make me the prime suspect? The only suspect? For heaven's sake, look for someone who actually knew the victim, why don't you? I never even saw Kyle before he showed up at my store in his clown suit."

"Didn't you?"

"No!" Jo nearly shouted it. She drew a breath to say more, but something in Morgan's face stopped her. "What?" she asked.

"You never encountered the victim, Kyle Sandborn, in New York, during that entire period you dealt with his uncle, Niles Sandborn?"

"Niles Sand . . ." Jo's voice died in her throat. "His uncle? I, I never made the connection. We seldom used each other's last name. I barely remembered what it was."

"You barely remembered the name of the man who threatened you with a lawsuit?"

"Yes," Jo answered weakly, acutely aware that Morgan didn't believe her. She looked desperately to Ainsworthy whose eyes were now closed. To her horror she heard a soft snore rise from him.

Morgan drilled on. "Kyle Sandborn went to visit his uncle in New York regularly. He stayed with him so he could go on auditions, and occasionally helped him in his business. Niles Sandborn is positive you met his nephew."

"If he says so, perhaps I did. But I doubt the man was in clown makeup at the time, don't you, Lieutenant?"

"So you admit you did know him?"

"I said 'perhaps,' didn't I?"

"I'm wondering why you never mentioned this to us, Mrs. McAllister, this prior connection to the victim."

"I'm wondering why I bothered to come here and listen to these outlandish insinuations, Lieutenant Morgan. In fact I refuse to listen to any more. If you have something to charge me with, you know where to find me."

Jo stood, exchanging glares with the man behind the desk, holding her breath at the same time to see if in fact he *would* slam her with some ridiculous, trumped up charge of murder, or manslaughter, or whatever he thought would hold water. When he remained silent, she shook Earnest C. Ainsworthy, who woke with a series of coughs and snuffles.

"Come on, let's go," Jo said, dragging him upward.

She heard Ainsworthy stumbling through

his "good days" to Morgan, but she reached for the door, unwilling to look at Morgan and see the sneer that was likely gracing his face. Their exit wasn't as forceful as her last one, as Ainsworthy seemed unable to negotiate the maze of desks with any rapidity. Eventually, though, they made their way out, Jo's emotions swinging between relief — at actually leaving — and anger and amazement over the whole unbelievable situation.

What the heck, she wondered, was going on?

CHAPTER 11

Jo dropped Ainsworthy back at his office, struggling through gritted teeth to remain civil to her so-called lawyer as he mumbled inanities laced with legal jargon. Delighted to see him finally stumble out of her sight, she began to drive back to the Craft Corner, her foot heavy on the gas pedal, until she realized there was no way she'd be able to calmly resume work on her jewelry. Nor did she want to face Carrie's questions. She needed time to cool down and gather her thoughts. She turned toward the little park she had passed often on her drives between home and work, and hoped that in the middle of a school day it would be unpopulated and quiet, offering her a few moments of peace.

Her hopes rose as she pulled into the parking lot and saw only two cars in an area that could hold twenty. Jo got out and began to walk rapidly, following a paved lane that wound past rhododendron and azalea plant-ings, all long past their bloom times and readying for the cold weather that was to come. A cool breeze hinted it was already on its way, and Jo pulled her light cardigan together more tightly and brushed back the dark bangs that had blown into her eyes. She came to a statue of a man in Civil War uniform and paused to check out the en-graved sign at its base, while slowing down her breathing as best she could.

A white-haired man in gray shorts and T-shirt jogged by, puffing out a breathy "mornin'." Jo returned the greeting, manag-ing a stiff smile, then turned back to the bronze soldier. Brigadier General Jeremiah Boggsworth, she learned, scanning the sign, was a native son of Abbotsville, born in 1811. He had died during the War Between the States in 1862, not in a blaze of glory on the battlefield, unfortunately, but of infection caused by a rusty horseshoe nail. Poor General Boggsworth, Jo thought. Done in by an ignominious puncture. Not unlike Kyle. It was just her miserable luck that Kyle's occurred in her craft shop.

Jo sighed, and pushed her hands into the pockets of her sweater. She moved on, run-ning over the previous hour spent enduring Russ Morgan's near-accusations. They continued to make her blood boil, but she realized her situation had grown even more serious. Morgan seemed determined to find that final link that would let him charge her with murder. She could almost hear the prosecutor's words to the jury, as she sat trembling behind the defendant's table:

"Ladies and gentlemen, I put it to you that what we have here is a cold-blooded murderer. This woman allowed nothing to stand in her way — not a husband whose death would bring her riches, nor a poor, struggling actor who happened to be witness to her . . ."

Her what? What did Russ Morgan think Kyle knew about her that she would be willing to murder him for? What was Niles hinting about her? Jo knew Niles could be unconscionable in his business dealings, but what would he stoop to, what lies would he tell or maybe even half-believe in a misguided attempt at family revenge? Did *he* truly believe Jo was guilty of his nephew's murder?

Whatever was going on, it was clear Jo needed to find out the truth of what happened in her storeroom before some wild, devious theory was devised and then believed by one and all. Until now, she had been dabbling at investigation, humoring her crafting ladies and reassuring herself that she was doing something active. Now the stakes had been raised. Jo needed to find out who actually killed Kyle Sandborn, and find out fast, while she was still a free woman.

What exactly had she managed to dig up about Kyle? His coworkers at the country club hinted that he liked to poke into other people's business and imagine wrongdoing on little evidence. Not unlike his Uncle Niles, Jo laughed grimly, then wondered: *had* she met Kyle in New York?

Jo thought back to her few visits to Niles' consignment shop, on Broadway, north of Houston. There had always been people around such as sales clerks and customers looking for bargains. Occasionally he had introduced her as a jewelry designer, but she didn't recall ever meeting a nephew. If it had happened, it had been a nonevent, a quick introduction in passing, something neither of them would remember. It boggled her mind that Niles was suddenly making such a point of it.

She moved on to the people at the Abbotsville Playhouse. Genna, the actress who would have played opposite Kyle if he'd lived, had a boyfriend who seemed to have been unhappy with that fact. This definitely bore investigation. Jo needed to talk to Genna.

A high-pitched screech jarred Jo out of her thoughts. She looked up, startled, and realized she had come to a small playground. A young mother stood beside her toddler, who was strapped into a baby swing, laughing delightedly. The mother's arm pushed automatically as she simultaneously carried on a conversation with another young woman whose baby sat in a stroller.

How contented they look, Jo thought, feeling a flash of envy for those who appeared to have uncomplicated lives, filled with simple joys. She and Mike had occasionally discussed having children, but always ended up putting it off to some undefined time when things were "right." Had that been the right or wrong decision, considering the turn her life had taken? She had since tried not to agonize over it. What was done was done, or perhaps not done, and she directed any surfacing maternal feelings toward Carrie's two as the need arose.

The woman at the swing looked over and smiled, and Jo strolled in that direction, having wearied of her solitude. The toddler wiggled and pointed, along with more screeches, clearly signaling "I want out!"

His mother complied and watched him dotingly as he ran to a nearby jungle gym and grabbed onto its lower bars, sidestepping on the packed mulch beneath.

Jo sat down on a nearby bench, tucked between two spruces and somewhat protected from the hair-tossing breeze. The toddler, apparently constitutionally unable to stay in one place for more than a minute or two, suddenly came careening toward Jo, and she caught him as he stumbled on a tree root.

"Whoops! Here you go," she said, setting him back on his feet.

"Thank you," his mother, a pretty blond-haired woman, called. She hurried over and sat on the other end of the bench. "Cory, when are you going to tire yourself out enough for a nap?" she asked with mock exasperation. She pulled a small bottle of apple juice out of her tote and handed it to her son, who immediately sank to the ground to suck at it.

"Hi, I'm Dawn," she said, turning to Jo.

"I'm Jo. Looks like he keeps you pretty busy," Jo said, glancing at Cory, whose round blue eyes gazed at her over his bottle.

Dawn nodded, grinning. "And to think I could hardly wait til he started walking. I don't think I've seen you here before."

Jo hesitated, glancing over at the second mother, who was placing her baby in the swing Cory had vacated. Should she identify herself as not only new in town but also proprietor of Jo's Craft Corner? Would it worry Dawn to have her child so near a, a what? A murder suspect? No, word surely wouldn't have gotten around yet. At worst, Jo was still only the unlucky woman who had found the body. If that frightened Dawn away, so be it. She enlightened her new acquaintance, whose eyes widened only briefly with recognition.

"I heard they still don't know who did that to him," Dawn said, quickly getting down to what interested her most.

"No, they don't."

"It's so weird, a thing like that happening to someone you know."

Jo's gaze, which had wandered to Cory, darted back to Dawn. "Oh?"

"Well, not *knew* him, but, you know how it is. In a town this size, you always know someone who knows someone, so you feel connected."

"Who do you know who knew him?"

"My cousin, Genna."

"Really." Jo tried to muffle signs of her

interest. "Is she the girl I saw at the play-house?"

"Yes! See what I mean? Everyone knows everyone here, one way or another. What did you see her in? *Biloxi Blues*?"

"No, I was at the rehearsal for the show they're working on now, something to do with Rumpelstiltskin."

"Oh, is that their next one? I didn't know. What's Genna's part in it?"

"She has one of the leads, playing the spinner who pledges her firstborn to Rumpelstiltskin."

Dawn grinned, and rolled her eyes at Cory. "Tempting idea, sometimes! Good for Genna, though, getting a part like that. Last time she played a prostitute." Dawn giggled. "My aunt wasn't delighted with that. Does she get to sing in this one?"

"There's some music in it." Jo thought back to the peculiar song she heard being rehearsed, and hoped whatever else there might be would fit the word "music" better. "I didn't hear Genna sing, but I guess she might."

"I hope so. She has a really nice voice." Dawn reached over to button her son's jacket, which the breeze had started to flap.

Jo asked, "Was Genna terribly upset over Kyle? I imagine they must have been close,

I mean as fellow members of the playhouse troupe."

"Well," a cautious look crept over Dawn now, and she seemed to choose her words carefully, "she was upset, of course. I mean, it's a horrible thing to happen to anyone. But she has plenty of support. There's her family and friends. And Pete, her boy-friend."

Jo noticed that Dawn looked away when she mentioned Pete, as though regretting having brought him up. "Does Genna live at home, then," she pressed, "or do she and her boyfriend —"

"No, they don't live together, not that Pete hasn't tried to talk her into it. Genna has a roommate. They share a two-bedroom in those new Wildwood apartments, a really cool place." Dawn began talking faster. "I wish they had been built when Jack and I were first looking for one. We'd move, but they cost more than where we are now, and we're saving for a house. You know those houses over on . . ." Dawn chattered on, clearly much more comfortable with the new subject.

Jo waited for a pause, and, when Dawn drew a breath, jumped in with, "Yes, they do sound very nice. I was wondering, though, about Genna's boyfriend. Did he —"

Dawn suddenly leaned down and grabbed her son's bottle, pulling it from his mouth with a pop. Cory reacted with an indignant wail, and Dawn picked him up, explaining to Jo, "I can't let him drink too much right now. I don't have any extra diapers with me." She consoled the toddler with a quick pat on his back, then turned him away from Jo. "Oh, look, Cory, there's a squirrel!"

Cory's wails stopped, and he wiggled to get down, taking off after the gray squirrel as soon as his feet hit the ground. Dawn picked up her tote, and turned to Jo.

"It's been real nice talking to you," she said, then hurried after Cory.

Well, that was interesting, Jo thought, her eyes still blinking with surprise as she watched her potential source distance herself.

She laughed ruefully. Wouldn't it be handy to have a Cory to take along with her the next time Russ Morgan wanted to talk? Jo stood, giving up on any further conversation, and headed back toward her car, mulling over what had just happened. Something about Pete certainly made Dawn very uneasy. But what exactly? The only real information Dawn had shared was that Pete had tried to talk Genna into living with him. Which implied Genna had resisted for some reason. Hints and innuendoes. That seemed to be all Jo was able to gather. But then, that was also all Lieutenant Morgan had gathered on her.

Being reminded of her uniformed adversary began to stir the anger Jo thought she had managed to dispel, and she drew a deep breath. This would not do. If she had learned anything over the past year it was that emotions needed to be kept under control if she expected to accomplish anything. She came to the azalea plantings and snapped off a twig, rolling it rapidly between her hands in an effort to cool down, then began to pluck off its small leaves, one by one, until she realized what she was doing: the daisy petal game. He loves me, he loves me not.

Not quite appropriate here, she thought grimly, tossing the twig. There was certainly no question. Morgan loved her not, and she returned the feeling, in spades. Lieutenant Morgan obviously saw her as a cold-blooded murderer, and she in turn viewed him as the man working to send her to prison for life, or worse. With all those leading questions about her marriage, and their terrible implications, Morgan had shown himself to be a cold, callous, hardheaded man, and nothing whatsoever like her warm, open-hearted Mike.

Why, then, she wondered, the thought bringing her to a stop, did she find herself so often thinking of one along with the other?

CHAPTER 12

Jo's gaze swept over her ladies, gathered together for a stamping workshop. She was growing quite fond of them. Beyond their ongoing interest in crafts, she sensed a deeper concern for her and her dicey situation.

Once again Ina Mae sat directly across from Jo at the worktable, with Loralee right beside her. Javonne Barnett had arrived in a rush again, from her husband's dental office, and Deirdre Patterson waited expectantly next to Loralee. Mindy Blevins was absent, presumably still sorting through her mounds of "twin" photographs back home.

"What are you going to teach us tonight, Jo?" Javonne asked, pulling off her multicolored silk scarf and tucking it safely into the handbag at her feet.

"Tonight, ladies," Jo said, "you will enter the fascinating and endlessly creative world of stamping." She caught Carrie's eye, who was guiding her beginning knitters through their first sweater on the other side of the store, and grinned. "Our first project will be a beautiful, handmade thank-you card."

Ina Mae hmmphed. "Maybe I'll send it — self-addressed — to a certain relative who has yet to mention that gift I sent six months ago."

"Oh, I know," Loralee commiserated. "Thank-yous are just too much trouble for some people. Some *young* people."

"I've always been extremely meticulous about thank-you notes," Deirdre insisted. Jo wasn't sure which age group Deirdre, a fortysomething, was putting herself in with that statement. "And I never, never send one by e-mail."

"Oh, e-mail!" Ina Mae rolled her eyes. "I'd be drop-dead grateful for that at least. But we're digressing, Jo. Please go on."

Jo displayed and explained the basic tools of decorative stamping — rubber stamps, stamp pads, plain and novelty scissors, paper cutters, and more.

"I'm going to show you how to make this lovely card," she said, holding it up and pausing as Loralee oohed, "and in the process teach you some of the skills to create your own designs. Now first, we will cut our dark blue paper, which has the delicious name of "Night of Navy," to fit in this standard envelope when folded."

The women watched as Jo measured and cut hers using the paper cutter, then followed suit. Jo next demonstrated how they could create a window effect by cutting a smaller white rectangle of paper to center over the dark blue, then four yet-smaller squares of blue to top that, two over two with the white framing them all, like window panes. All layers would be attached using double-sided tape.

"But first, before we cut the smaller blue squares, we will stamp them with these individual tree stamps, using white craft ink, which is a little thicker and whiter than regular ink. And when it's all put together it will look like a view through a window on a snowy night."

"Oh, I love it," cried Javonne.

"Wait, what do I do with the white paper?" Deirdre asked, looking thoroughly befuddled.

Jo explained the process once more, and then a third time to Deirdre alone as the others got busy on their own cards. As Deirdre seemed to catch on, Jo strolled around the table, looking over shoulders as stamps thumped and papers were cut, ready to answer questions.

As she completed the round, Ina Mae looked up to ask, "Find out anything at the playhouse?"

Once again, four pairs of eyes looked up, curious for the answer. "Well," Jo said, smiling, "I learned Rafe Rulenski doesn't write very good music."

"Jo-oh," Javonne prompted.

"It's true! He might be a good director, but I really think he has a tin ear."

"Will you be doing anything for the production?" Deirdre asked.

"Yes, some of the costume jewelry, and maybe some odds and ends for the stage sets."

"Great!"

"At cost. Or nearly so. But I'll get a bit of publicity from it."

"What did you learn about Kyle Sandborn?" Ina Mae persisted.

Jo shrugged, warning them it was very little, then told them what she and Charlie had picked up concerning the jealousy of Genna's boyfriend, Pete. "It may turn out to be nothing, but it's the strongest motive I've come across so far for Kyle's murder. Genna's cousin didn't actually confirm the jealousy when I talked to her in the park, but I suspect she might have. She definitely didn't have good feelings toward the boy-friend."

"I think you're on to something," Deirdre said. "I remember, now that you mention it, that Rafe Rulenski once complained about someone who might have been Pete. This was a few weeks ago at the fund-raising Thespian Ball. Alden and I were chatting with Rafe about the amount of scenery needed for *Biloxi Blues,* and he nearly turned purple. He said he had to have an entire section of a flat replaced because of damage caused by an actress's boyfriend. The boyfriend claimed it was an accident, that he had lost his balance somehow and fallen through, but Rafe said the damage looked more like someone had kicked through it in a rage."

"Oh my," Loralee cried. "And that was Pete?"

"Rafe didn't give a name," Deirdre said as she carefully pressed her tree stamp on the blue paper, "but he did say this man didn't like his girlfriend acting like a," Deirdre hesitated, glancing over at Loralee and Ina Mae, "like a w-h-o-r-e."

"Oh!" Loralee's hand flew to her mouth.

"He must have meant Genna's part in the play," Jo said. "Her cousin told me she

152

played a prostitute in the last show."

"This boyfriend sounds jealous and controlling," Ina Mae said, "and definitely someone worth looking into."

"I agree," Javonne put in.

"I'll try to talk to Genna at the next rehearsal."

Carrie left her two knitting students and came over for one of the sodas she and Jo kept stocked in a cooler. "Tell them about the police lieutenant, Jo," she urged, popping open a diet Dr Pepper.

"What? Did he pull you in again, Jo?" Javonne asked.

"He firmly invited me in for a talk," Jo corrected. She described what she had endured at the hands of Abbotsville's finest, leaving out mention of Earnest C. Ainsworthy because of Carrie, who felt awful enough as it was over the disastrous result of her attempt to help. The group's faces reflected much of the same indignation Jo had felt with Morgan.

"That's outrageous," Ina Mae pronounced, thumping down her stamp hard enough to make the others jump.

"He actually brought up your poor husband's accident, as if there were some connection?" Loralee asked. Jo nodded.

"I'm going to have Alden talk to that

man," Deirdre declared. "This sounds awfully close to harassment to me. Something should be done about it."

Jo smiled gratefully at Deirdre for the sentiment, though she wasn't sure what effect, if any, Deirdre's state senator husband would have on a police investigation. Perhaps Lieutenant Morgan deserved a bit of harassment himself, though. The thought cheered her.

"What do we know about Russ Morgan?" Ina Mae asked. "He's been with the Abbotsville Police Department for only a short time, as far as I'm aware. Where did he come from? Anyone know?"

"He came," said Javonne, "from some big-city police department, I forget exactly where, but some place in the Midwest. Chicago? Or maybe Cleveland? My Harry heard this from Merle Snipes, who's in his tennis group. Anyway, Merle thinks he's being groomed to take over as captain when Joe Meloni finally retires."

"So he probably wants to look good on his first big murder case in our little town," Ina Mae said. "He's single. Ever married?" She looked around, waiting.

"One of the ladies I lunch with," Deirdre offered, "did say she was sure he was divorced. She hinted it was a bitter one. I don't know if there were children or not, but if so, he obviously lost custody since we've never seen him with any."

"Maybe he's full of anger toward women," Loralee speculated, "and he's taking it out on our poor Jo."

"Well," Ina Mae said, "it might help Jo to know where he's coming from. As far as what he's been throwing at her, the man is on a fishing expedition. He might be able to prove Jo knew Kyle before he showed up at her grand opening and that could be hurtful, but he'd need more. A lot more."

"Which is why Jo should present him as soon as possible with all she can find out about this jealous boyfriend." Deirdre looked at Jo as if she were ready to push her out the door and in the direction of the playhouse. No matter that it sat empty tonight. She should take her sticky tape and tweezers and immediately start crawling about the dark stage searching for clues.

"I will do my best, Deirdre," Jo promised, before quickly adding, "tomorrow."

"Maybe I can track down Pete's last name, in case you run into a roadblock," Javonne offered. "He might be one of Harry's patients, or a friend of one. People tend to get chatty in a dentist's chair, trying to postpone the inevitable."

"I'll talk to my hairdresser," Loralee said. "She's about that age; she might know something about him."

"I'll check with my power walkers," Ina Mae put in, "see what I can come up with on both this Pete and Lieutenant Morgan."

Jo looked from one to another, touched by their readiness to help. What it would ultimately produce remained to be seen. But at worst, Jo felt reassured she would not lack visitors should she eventually find herself behind bars.

Nor would mail be sparse, she predicted as she watched them gradually return to their projects. Each day would likely bring one or more beautifully stamped "missing you" cards.

How comforting.

CHAPTER 13

Jo walked into the Abbotsville Playhouse, Carrie at her side. They had agreed that the shop could be closed early on an evening when no workshops were scheduled. The lost business would be minimal, Jo reasoned, and she wouldn't have insisted for the world that Carrie stay behind. Charlie had started working there, and Carrie wanted to get a feel for the place with which he was involved.

"It can be so frustrating getting any details out of him," she groaned to Jo. "The larger his vocabulary grows, the fewer words he actually uses."

Though Carrie never admitted it, Jo was sure the idea of her son being involved in an acting group was as alien to her as it was to Dan. But seeing the energy and enthusiasm reappear in Charlie, easily won her over. As his mother, though, she wanted reassurance that the playhouse was no den of iniquity, and it helped that the first person they encountered was Mrs. Pettibone, Charlie's English teacher.

"Hello, Mrs. Brenner," she called out, as Carrie and Jo made their way down the semidark aisle. Mrs. Pettibone, a plus-sized woman of fifty or so, stood below the stage, holding what Jo assumed was an open playbook. "Here to see Charlie?" she asked.

"Oh, not really. I'm just tagging along with Jo," Carrie said, with less than convincing nonchalance. She introduced the two.

"Oh, yes," Jane Pettibone said to Jo. "Rafe told me you'll be sparkling up the costumes and sets for us. Terrific! We can use a lot of help in that department."

"She's been putting together some great stuff," Carrie said.

Jo noticed Carrie's eyes scouring the area as she spoke. Apparently Jane Pettibone did too, for she pointed to a large piece of still-unpainted scenery. "Charlie's been working on the back of that castle wall there. They're reinforcing the braces."

Carrie smiled. "That's fine. I won't interrupt him."

"Is Rafe around?" Jo asked, holding up the box she carried. "I'd like to show him a couple of samples I've put together and see what he thinks of them."

Jane Pettibone turned about, searching through the shifting groups. "I don't see him right now. But I'm sure he'll pop up soon. Why don't you have a seat and watch the rehearsal? But don't expect too much." She smiled. "We're still in the early stages."

She called up to the stage. "Okay, guys. I want Annalisa and the King stage front."

Jo saw Genna, the person she most wanted to speak to tonight, step forward. A slim man in his thirties, apparently Kyle's replacement, took his place by her side.

"Let's start from, 'Annalisa, tell me you care for me.'"

The actors turned toward each other and recited their lines, somewhat woodenly, it seemed to Jo. Whenever they faltered, Jane Pettibone prompted, her role apparently being only to see that they got the lines right. How they were finally projected, Jo assumed, would be decided by Rafe.

Jo found herself enjoying the scene, even with its rough quality. Rafe had written with wit, telling the story of Rumpelstiltskin with tongue-in-cheek humor. She also noticed a flair in Genna begin to appear as she warmed up. The king remained stiff, though that might be attributed to his needing much more prompting. Jo reminded herself he had stepped into the part only recently.

When the two started again from the top, Carrie whispered to Jo and slipped off in the general direction of Charlie's work area. Jo saw Rafe walk out from the wings, then trot down toward Jane Pettibone to observe the rehearsal of his two leads. At the conclusion of their second run-through, he had a few words with them on their delivery and then told them to move on to their next scene, before turning it back to Jane. He came over to Jo.

"You've brought things to show me already?" he asked. "You work fast."

Jo pulled out her samples, and he seemed pleased, even interrupting the pair on stage to run up and drape one of the necklaces on Genna, then step back to gauge the effect.

"Lovely!" Jane cried. "Oh, that will be lovely."

"Hmm, yes, I think it will do," agreed Rafe. He slipped it over Genna's head, causing an "ouch" as it caught a strand of her hair, and handed it back to Jo.

"Yes, I think we're heading in the right direction with these," he said.

"Good." Jo accepted the faint praise, suspecting that from Rafe Rulenski it was close to a rave. She described what she would do next, Rafe nodding until his attention suddenly flew back to the rehearsal.

"Genna, dear, put some *life* into it when you tell this man you'll marry him. For God's sake, you're the miller's daughter, and he's the king! You should be ecstatic."

"Yes, Mr. Rulenski."

Jo packed up her jewelry, aware that the moment Rafe was willing to spare of his precious time was over. Jane Pettibone threw a rueful smile in her direction, as though saying, "That's all we can expect from a temperamental artist." Or perhaps it was more like, "Yes, he can be a pain, but we put up with it." Whichever, Jane, at least, seemed content to roll with it for the reward of being part of the community playhouse team.

And it was fascinating teamwork, Jo had to admit. She was beginning to understand just how many pieces went toward putting together an entire production, and how much talent was involved. She heard the sound of hammering and wondered if Carrie had found Charlie, and what all was going on behind that flimsy castle wall.

Other actors were summoned stage front to run through their lines, and Genna and her romantic lead left the stage. Seeing Genna trot down the steps and up the aisle toward the back of the theater, Jo left her sample box and followed, catching, as she entered the lobby, a glimpse of the door to the ladies' room swinging closed. She waited a couple of minutes, then walked in to find Genna at the sink, washing her hands.

Jo paused in front of one of the mirrors and fluffed her hair, an action that did nothing to improve it but gave her a moment to catch the young woman's eye. She smiled.

"Hi. You're our star, aren't you?"

Genna laughed, but looked pleased. "Not hardly." She was quite pretty, Jo thought, with dark brown hair framing an oval face. She was also more petite than Jo had realized while looking up at her on the stage. Barely five-two, Jo guessed.

"I just have the lead this time around," Genna said.

"Well, I'd call that being a star. I was watching the rehearsal. You were very good."

"Thanks." Genna peered more closely. "Are you the one who made the necklace?"

"Uh-huh, and don't worry, I'll fix the hair-catching links."

Genna grinned. "Next time I won't let Mr. Rulenski pull it off."

"Probably a good idea." Jo turned serious. "I understand Kyle Sandborn was your original costar."

Genna's smile vanished. "Yes, he was." She reached for a paper towel and wiped at her hands. "That was so awful, what happened."

"No one can understand why he would be attacked like that. I imagine you knew him pretty well. Would you say he was the last person you'd expect that to happen to?"

Genna tossed her towel in the wastebasket, frowning. "I don't know about the last person," she said. "But who expects that to happen to anybody that you know? I mean, we're in *Abbotsville,* for gosh sakes, not in D.C. or Baltimore, where you might be used to things like that. I don't mean *used to* it, 'cause I don't suppose anyone gets used to such awful violence, do they? What I mean is maybe it's not such a *surprise.*"

Genna was babbling, and Jo sensed her nervousness. Was it simply the subject of murder causing it, or this particular murder?

"Can you think of anyone in particular who might want to murder Kyle?"

"No! Absolutely not! And, you know, I'm sorry, but I really don't like talking about this. I've gone over all of it with the police, and I couldn't help them at all."

"It's not pleasant, I know. I've had to talk

to the police quite a lot. It was my craft store where it happened."

"Oh! I didn't realize."

Jo nodded. "I'm the one who found him that night. It was quite a shock."

The actress's face softened. "How terrible."

"Yes, but the worst thing now, at least for me, is that the police think I must have had something to do with it, because of where it happened."

"Oh, gosh."

"So I'm really not just prying. I need to find out what did happen."

"I wish I could help you," Genna said, "but I don't know anything about it."

Jo drew a breath. "I've been told your boyfriend Pete didn't much like the idea of Kyle playing your romantic lead. Is that right?"

Genna slumped back against the tiles. She didn't seem surprised to hear her boyfriend's name brought up, and Jo figured she knew where this was leading. "Pete gets upset easily," Genna said, "but he's not a bad guy. Not at all." She looked at Jo, her eyes asking for understanding. "He's had it rough, growing up, that's all. Yes, he tends to get too possessive, but we're working on that. He would never, never do what you're thinking. Never."

Jo asked gently, "He has gotten violent, before, though, hasn't he?"

Genna nodded. "I've told him I won't put up with that, and he's promised me it won't happen again. He can be very, very sweet sometimes. I've been tempted to break up once or twice, but I just think he's worth hanging in there for. I really do."

Jo looked at the girl, wondering if she was kidding herself and if Pete was simply a good manipulator. The door swung open, and Rulenski's assistant poked her head in, her heavy glasses sliding down her nose.

"There you are, Genna! They want you on stage again."

Genna straightened up. "I'll be right there." She looked at Jo, worry lines puckering her brow. "I know you probably want it to be Pete. But he's not like that. Not underhanded, I mean. Pete gets mad, yes, but when he blows up it's in front of everyone, then it's over. He's the kind of guy who might punch someone in the face, but he'd never lie in wait to catch them off guard." She laughed ruefully. "That might not sound like the greatest endorsement, but it's the truth."

She left the restroom, and Jo listened to her footsteps click across the lobby and fade into the theater. She pulled open the door and followed.

Jo returned to where she had left her things, and not seeing Carrie, settled down to watch the rest of the rehearsal. Genna ran through a scene with another actor, and not surprisingly, seemed distracted. When it ended, Jo saw her disappear into the wings.

A small chorus gathered to practice a song, and Jo found herself wishing Carrie would return so she could leave, especially since the music was not much improved from her first visit. She was on the verge of going on a search when her friend reappeared.

"Ready to go?" Carrie asked. She looked satisfied with whatever she had encountered behind the castle wall.

"Absolutely," Jo replied, and led the way up the aisle.

Back at the car, Jo had just straightened up after dropping her box on the backseat when she caught sight of two people walking away from the theater. One looked like Genna. Was the other her boyfriend?

"I'll be right back," Jo said hastily to Carrie, who had been buckling herself in and looked up in surprise.

The sidewalk was fairly dark, with large trees shading much of the light from the streetlamps. The couple walked rapidly, and Jo had to hustle to catch up with them. She was thankful that she had worn her sound-muffling soft-soled shoes. What would she do, though, if Genna suddenly looked back and saw her?

That didn't appear likely as Jo soon saw the two were fully absorbed in their discussion.

"I just don't like the way he keeps holding on to you," the man said, his voice low and grumbly, almost sulky.

"Pete, he has to. He's supposed to be in love with me. With my *character.* And you know he's my cousin."

So this was Pete, a tall, burly man who towered over his petite girlfriend. He was someone who could be described as a big teddy bear with the right personality, or intimidating with the wrong one.

"He's your second cousin," Pete countered.

"So what? I've known him since I was a kid. I went to his wedding, for gosh sakes, when I was twelve."

Genna spoke in a light tone, clearly wanting to coax Pete away from his worries.

A man walking his beagle approached from the other direction, and Jo dropped back as the couple slowed and gave him room to pass. The dog then veered toward Jo, sniffing upward hopefully. Another time she might have reached down with a pat, but tonight she stepped nimbly out of its reach. When she caught up again, Genna and Pete's topic seemed to have switched.

". . . not right, that kind of thing," Jo heard Pete say.

"I know," Genna agreed. She sounded sad, but resigned.

Jo didn't catch all of what Pete said next with his low-pitched voice. What she did hear was, ". . . don't like you being there."

Genna responded with, "I guess that should be my decision." She said it evenly, but she dropped hold of Pete's arm and edged slightly away.

Pete jammed his hand into his jacket pocket, looking, from his posture, angry. The two picked up their pace, but said no more, and Jo saw Genna gesture toward a convenience store up ahead and mutter something about needing milk. Jo turned and trotted back to the car where her patient friend sat waiting, a quizzical look on her face.

"Sorry about that," Jo said as she slid behind the wheel. "A bit of spontaneous sleuthing." After describing it quickly to Carrie, Jo wondered what, if anything, she had managed to learn. Bits and pieces, once more. She could only hope they would soon fit together to fill a complete picture. There was still too large a hole in this flimsy tapestry she was trying to weave together.

Where would she find those essential threads she needed to fill it in?

CHAPTER 14

Phyllis Lenske of St. Adelbert's called Jo at the shop to confirm that the ladies of the sodality would be able to do a table at the country club's fall craft show.

"Mary Louise's knee surgery won't be done until November," she explained meticulously to Jo, "and even though I know the poor thing's in pain, she insists she can do it. And Susan and her husband are leaving for the Bahamas tomorrow, but she'll be back in plenty of time."

Phyllis promised she could round up several ladies from the group who did things like needlepoint eyeglass holders and hand-painted Christmas ornaments. "We'll do a beautiful table, don't you worry."

Jo thanked her profusely and added Phyllis to the list. One professional craftsman had finally agreed to come from the Eastern Shore with his array of hand-carved waterfowl. And the group from the Methodist church was gradually coming together too. That left several "maybes," including a basket maker who had run a highly successful table last year, and Jo planned to make a few nudging phone calls today. She needed a nudge herself. She hadn't yet considered what her own table would hold, what with all that she'd been dealing with lately. This was a great opportunity to give her struggling shop a new image and help erase pictures of Jo's Craft Corner surrounded with police tape and crime-scene cleanup crews from people's minds. She needed to make the most of it.

Since business had been slow that day, possibly due to the sporadic rain, Carrie had taken the opportunity to make a quick run to Sears and pick up some new work clothes for Dan that were on sale. Jo looked up as her friend came in, arms full of bags, appearing triumphant.

"Good luck?" Jo asked.

"Not only," Carrie crowed, "did I get two new pairs of work pants and a new flannel shirt to replace that ratty blue one he keeps wearing, all at one-third off, but I stocked up on underwear and socks for Dan and the kids at *half* price."

"Woo-hoo!" Jo hooted. "But nothing for yourself?"

"Oh, I don't need anything," Carrie said, then grinned slyly. "But I did see one or two things that Dan might want to get me for Christmas. He tends to need very precise suggestions for his gift lists. Including exactly which end of which department of which store to find the thing."

"It's only a kindness to give him such help," Jo replied.

"That's how I feel." Carrie set down her bags and looked around. "Any activity here while I was gone?"

"A little," Jo said. "That woman who dithered back and forth on the yarn for her sweater after asking your opinion over a dozen times came in and bought the yellow acrylic."

Carrie grinned. "My advice was to go with the navy worsted, but, oh well."

"And Javonne Barnett stopped in to give me the full name of Genna's boyfriend. It's Pete Tober. She tracked it down through Genna's friend's mother, who came in for a teeth cleaning." Jo grinned. "Nothing like a small town, is there?"

"Tell me about it."

"And not only that, but remember Dawn, the girl I spoke to in the park? Javonne's pretty sure she's Dawn Buchmann, which means she has a reason not to want to bad-mouth Pete. Dawn's husband, Jack, has a sister married to one of Pete's brothers."

"Ah, family ties."

"Exactly, with tangled family loyalties."

"So," Carrie asked, "now that you know who Pete is, what will you do?"

Jo frowned. "I don't know yet. Genna was so anxious to convince me Pete was incapable of such a crime. But her eagerness tends to make me more suspicious since it tells me the thought already occurred to her and that she's been trying to convince herself of its impossibility."

"The conversation you overheard came across as controlling on his part, wouldn't you say?"

Jo hesitated. "Yes and no. It sounded like Pete's *attempt* at control, but Genna didn't sound all that compliant to me. She was standing up for herself. I wish I had been able to hear more, though." Jo laughed at herself. "I can hardly believe I'm saying that, or doing that. Tiptoeing up to listen in on conversations. Next thing I'll be sending away for my super-duper lock-jimmying set."

"Whatever it takes," Carrie said, and Jo saw she was only half joking. The front door jingled as a customer walked in and Jo got up to wait on her as Carrie lugged her Sears bags to the back.

When they picked up their conversation again, Carrie's thoughts had turned to Charlie and how good she felt watching him at work at the playhouse.

"He was, like, electrified, Jo," she said, rephrasing much of what she had already related the night before. "I mean, all he was doing was fetching and carrying tools and such for the scenery crew, and once in a while he turned the screwdriver on a couple of braces. But he was having a ball doing it! His eyes were going every which way, drinking it all in."

"He liked the camaraderie, maybe?"

"That could be part of it. He's drifted away from a lot of his old friends when he stopped doing sports, mostly because they were still busy with practices. But there also wasn't that mutual interest anymore. He made a few new friends, but there didn't seem to be much enthusiasm. That's what I was seeing in him again. Enthusiasm."

Jo saw the same thing in her friend's eyes at the moment. Carrie was delighted with the new interest that was making her son happier.

"I presume you shared all this with Dan?"

"Yes, of course." Carrie's glow dimmed a

bit. "He's still not great with it. I wonder if he worries this might be taking Charlie off in a strange, new direction."

"What, like to New York, like me?"

Carrie grinned, and Jo remembered how her announcement that she was moving to New York had astonished Carrie and Dan, whose idea of a life-altering change was relocating from the town they had all grown up in to Abbotsville, a mere twenty miles away.

"You and Dan tried your best to talk me out of it at the time. You probably thought you'd never see me again, that I'd disappear altogether into the bowels of the big city. But that didn't happen, did it? We stayed friends the whole time, and I got to do what I loved."

"Yes, of course. And I see that, but maybe Dan still thinks you would have been better off, safer perhaps, to stay near home."

Jo thought about that. Would she have given up ever knowing and loving Mike, who she had met and married in New York, to avoid the final pain of losing him? Tough choice, because that pain was the worst. But no, she wouldn't pass on the time she had with him. Only someone outside her shoes could think it might have been better not to have had the good in order to avoid the bad.

"Charlie's only fifteen," Jo pointed out. "He's not going to be making any life-changing decisions for a while. I hope Dan will see that this might be only one of many things Charlie wants to look into."

"I hope so too."

As if their thoughts had mysteriously drawn him to them, the door jingled as Charlie bounced in, his school backpack hanging from one shoulder.

"Hi Mom! Hi Aunt Jo."

Jo heard a liveliness in his greeting that had been missing before. Carrie was right. Even now, coming from a day spent at school, Charlie seemed energized.

"Charlie! Is it that time already?" Carrie looked up at the clock. "How was your day? Are you hungry?"

"Nah, I stopped at McDonald's with some guys. Got some fries."

As he swung his heavy backpack onto the counter, Jo caught the aroma of fried burger grease still lingering on his clothes, and, though she had cut down on such high-fat treats some time ago, it triggered a hunger pang. She wondered what Carrie might have around to nibble.

"That's why I came here," Charlie explained. "Aunt Jo, remember those guys I knew who worked at the country club?"

"Yes?"

"Well, they had a lot to say about Kyle Sandborn, the guy that got offed here."

"Charlie," Carrie automatically admonished, but mildly.

"Tell me," Jo urged.

"I was cool about it," Charlie said, clearly pleased with himself. "I mean, I didn't just come right out and say, 'Give me all you know about this guy.' I acted like I might be interested in getting a job there, which I *might*," he said defensively. "You never know."

"So I asked them what it was like working there, and this one guy, Garth, says it's okay except for having to work for the grounds supervisor, Hank Schroder. Schroder's an old guy but an ex-Marine who runs the crew like a drill sergeant. Garth said everything has to go exactly his way, and he won't let you dig a hole without making sure you've got exactly the right shovel and measured everything ten times. He drives them all crazy."

"How does this fit in with Kyle, honey? Kyle didn't work for him, did he?"

"I'm getting there, Mom. Then they start laughing, Garth and these other guys, 'cause they're remembering how Kyle used to play tricks on Schroder."

"That's interesting," Jo said.

"Uh-*huh!* Kyle used to do things like sneak over and turn off the sprinklers after Schroder walked away. He'd do this over and over until Schroder thought something was broken and took the whole system apart, checking it out. When he didn't find anything, he'd set the sprinklers up again, watch it til he was okay with it, then, when he finally relaxed, Kyle would turn them off again.

"Schroder would accuse the guys, but they could always prove they were nowhere near. So he'd take it all apart again and go crazy when he couldn't find a problem."

"That's kind of mean, isn't it?" Carrie said.

"Yeah, I know. These guys, Garth and the others? They're not the brightest bulbs, if you know what I mean, but they wouldn't snitch on Kyle because of all the guff Schroder gave them.

"Then," Charlie paused dramatically, "Kyle changed the timer on the sprinklers without Schroder knowing, and they all went off when a bunch of bigwigs were on the golf course. It soaked them, and they were jumping up and down, they were so mad. And Mr. Gordon," Charlie said to Jo, "you know, the manager? He really chewed Schroder out and said things like maybe Schroder was getting too old for the job."

"Uh-oh. How did Mr. Schroder take this?"

"He was steaming. Garth said his skin under his gray buzz cut turned bright red."

"That's sounds awfully immature for someone Kyle's age," Carrie said doubtfully.

"Yeah I know, but Garth also said there's a guy married to Kyle's older sister who might want Schroder's job. They live in Virginia and want to come back here. He thought Kyle might be trying to open up the job for him, but he was having a ball at the same time, doing it."

"Did Schroder figure out what was happening?" Jo asked.

"I don't know. These guys started acting stupid, so I couldn't get to that."

The phone rang, and Jo reached for it. It was Loralee.

"Jo, how are you today?" she began. Jo sensed Loralee had called for reasons other than to check on Jo's health, but Loralee, ever the soul of old-fashioned courtesy, was not one to rush into things. Eventually, though, after a comment or two on the weather, she got down to it. "Jo, dear, Ina Mae asked me to tell you that she found out through that walking group of hers that the young man we were discussing the other night, Pete, works over at Hanson's Garage. Ina Mae would have called you herself," Loralee explained, "but she had to rush out for another one of her meetings, book club this time, I believe."

"Hanson's Garage? Thank you for calling me with this, Loralee."

Loralee had a question about her scrapbooking project, which Jo discussed with her for a couple of minutes. After hanging up, she shared with Carrie and Charlie what she'd learned.

"This is the boyfriend," she explained to Charlie, "that you overheard mentioned backstage."

"The guy who was happy Kyle wasn't going to be the lead with his girlfriend?"

"Uh-huh. I overheard him talking to Genna as they were leaving the theater last night, mad about something else. I'd like to find out more about him and maybe talk with him, but I'm not sure yet how to go about it."

"I can do it," Charlie quickly offered, clearly buoyed up by his recent success.

"What? How?"

"Guys like me hang around garages all the time. It'd be no problem."

"No, Charlie," Carrie said, her expression

firm. "I don't think that's a good idea at all."

"Mom!"

"I mean it. I don't want you hanging around someone who might be dangerous."

"Your Mom's right," Jo agreed. She wasn't about to start sending her only godson out alone into unknown territories.

Charlie looked ready to argue, his jaw beginning to jut, but then he gave in. Jo figured he might have been thinking he already had one precarious situation going — his time spent at the playhouse — and didn't want to jeopardize it.

"Okay," he said, picking up his backpack, "but I still think it's a good idea."

As the door jangled closed behind him, Jo turned to Carrie. "Well, Charlie's come up with another suspect for us — Hank Schroder of the country club."

"I know," Carrie said, looking pleased but also concerned.

"I'm sorry, Carrie. I shouldn't have let Charlie get involved at all, should I?"

"But he is involved, Jo, just for caring about you like the rest of us. Don't worry, he's a sensible kid. He won't do anything foolish."

Carrie smiled confidently and wandered away to tidy up the yarns. But Jo noticed her glancing out the window often, as if her thoughts were following Charlie on his way home.

CHAPTER 15

Jo had mixed feelings as she pulled up to Hanson's Garage. She'd called ahead to arrange for an oil change and recognized Pete's voice on the phone. It gave her an odd feeling as they spoke, knowing his thoughts were on one thing — garage business — while hers were on the much less prosaic notion of murder.

What would she accomplish by coming here? Part of it, she was aware, was simply heading off Charlie, in case he decided he knew best after all. It was getting hard to remember the old Charlie, the one who had to be dragged away from his mind-numbing Game Boy. Jo was happy to see his new energy but feared it might push him too far toward playing private eye.

But after her intriguing evening at the playhouse, Jo wanted to get a better understanding of Pete Tober, and to do that she had to talk to him face-to-face, and watch him with others. Was it a foolproof way of judging if the man was capable of murder? No, but it was a start.

A large man in oil-stained overalls came over, and she realized it must be Pete, whom she had previously seen only from behind and by mottled streetlight. His face was that of a boxer's: broad, with blunted features. Only his friendly smile saved him from looking intimidating.

"Mrs. McAllister?"

"Yes."

"Pull over to the first bay there, will you? Leave your keys in the ignition, and I'll drive your car onto the lift."

Jo followed Pete's direction, wondering at the same time what he must think of her rusty old Toyota. Some might have dumped a wreck like hers before putting any money whatsoever into it. But hey, it was only an oil change, a bit sooner than she needed it, but it wouldn't break her. The noises she was beginning to hear in her transmission were something else, but she wasn't going to think about that now.

"You said something about coffee, when I called?" Jo asked, as she climbed out.

"Yes, ma'am. Right there in the office. There's magazines to read too, while you wait."

"I'd like to watch, if you don't mind."

Pete hesitated. "I don't know. It's pretty dirty, and there's no place to sit."

"I don't mind, really. I promise to stay out of the way."

Pete glanced over at an older man nearby — Mr. Hanson, Jo guessed. The older man nodded. "All right. Sure."

"Great." Jo got her coffee and carried it out to see her car rising several feet into the air. She saw its battered underside for the first time and prayed that it would hold together for a few more months.

Pete had been polite, but she would have expected that. He wouldn't last long in the business if he weren't. She chose a spot and stood quietly, trying her best to disappear into the background, watching his interaction with the other workers. His banter with them seemed easy. She knew she had been forgotten when cusswords slipped in, not in anger but in usual guy talk. This was a far different world from her craft shop, and the testosterone floating about was nearly palpable.

Gradually Jo caught on that Pete was second in command, under Hanson. Pete didn't do her car's oil change, but oversaw a younger guy working on it, as well as checking out an engine job on a Ford pickup in the next bay, and making occasional phone calls for parts.

As she watched, Jo formed an impression of an efficient, conscientious mechanic. But then she remembered Genna's admission of Pete's temper, even as she had defended him for at least not being underhanded. Did he have a Jekyll-Hyde personality? Could he turn on the charm or turn on a foe as easily as the twist of a faucet? So far, Jo couldn't say.

The wall phone jangled, and Pete reached for it, barking, "Hanson's." He had his back to Jo, but she was only a few feet away and could hear him well, even as his voice dropped.

"Yeah, I'm glad you called back. I can't talk long, but I wanted to tell you I found a place."

Pete shifted his weight as he listened, then apparently interrupted the speaker, saying, "No, wait, wait, wait. I *know* all that. But I'm telling you it doesn't matter." Pause. "No, it doesn't! I'm telling you it's not good, and you've got to get out of it."

Pete's tone had risen, growing demanding and agitated. Then it suddenly softened. "Baby, look —" Was he talking to Genna? "I'm only thinking of you, of what's best for you." Pause. "Yes, I do know that." Pause. "No, I don't think that. Genna, for God's sake, use some common sense!" He had escalated to shouting. "Fine! Great!" He slammed the phone on its hook and stomped out of the bay, disappearing from Jo's view, and she soon heard the sound of something metallic and hollow being kicked. Hard.

A few heads in the garage turned at the noise, but no one commented, although glances were exchanged. When a young mechanic walked near Jo to get a tool, she commented, "Sounds like your boss is upset."

"Ah, it's nothing," he said, smirking. "Woman problems." This thrown out with an air of worldliness by a guy who, Jo guessed, still needed a shave only every *other* day.

"We should be done here in just a few minutes," he said.

"Great. Thanks." Jo sipped at her coffee and wandered to the bay's open doorway. Pete was nowhere to be seen. After a few minutes, however, he returned to the garage, looking calm, though grim, and jumped right back into his work.

Before long, Jo's oil change was finished, and Pete came over to check on the job.

"Looks like your oil wasn't too dirty, which is good. You might want to think about replacing that muffler and exhaust pipe pretty soon, though. We could do it while you're here, if you like."

"I guess I'll wait on that."

"Okay." Pete nodded agreeably. "No pressure."

He directed the car to be lowered, and guided her into the office, where he wrote up the bill. As he waited for Jo to sign the credit-card slip, the young mechanic who had spoken to Jo earlier poked his head through the door.

"Hey, Pete, is it all right if I run over to the vet's for a minute?"

"Yeah, sure, Del. Not too long, though, okay?"

Del ducked back, and Jo glanced up at Pete.

"His dog's been real sick," he explained. "Kid had him since he was in kindergarten."

"That's a shame," Jo said. She picked up her receipts and tucked the papers into her purse. "A friend of mine has a cat who's in a bad way, but she can't bring herself to put it out of its misery yet."

"Yeah, it can be tough. Del's going to be all broke up when the time comes. Might have to give him the day off." Pete opened the door for Jo. "Let me know if you decide on the muffler and exhaust pipe. I wouldn't let it go too long, if I were you. And don't worry, we'll give you a real fair price."

"Thanks." Jo looked into a face that, at the moment, appeared as open and honest as any she'd ever seen. And likeable. Was it a salesman's mask, though, or a true reading of the man within? As she drove off, Jo realized meeting Pete face-to-face had raised as many questions as it had answered. She had seen his temper, but how far would it carry him? Was he capable of murder? At this point, after spending a good chunk of her afternoon in a garage watching the man at work, Jo knew only one thing for sure: he had given her possibly the cheapest oil change she'd ever had in her life.

And the coffee wasn't bad either.

CHAPTER 16

"Ooh, I do like that melon-colored paper around your picture," Loralee said, glancing at the page Ina Mae was working on. "It brings out the beautiful sunset streaks in your photo."

"I took that shot at Red Rock Canyon," said Ina Mae. "We had a wonderful time hiking through the area."

"You weren't worried about snakes?" Deirdre asked. She sat on the other side of Ina Mae tonight, well away from Mindy and her piles of twin pictures.

Jo doubted there was much at all that Ina Mae worried about, a fact the older woman confirmed by the look she threw Deirdre. "I try not to interfere with their lives, and they don't interfere with mine. Jo," she said, turning away, "you suggested we decorate our pages to the theme of the photo. Do you have any stamps with a southwestern look, like maybe a cactus?"

"I think we just might. Let me check. And, for another idea," Jo reached for a raffia bundle, "you might like to attach a few strands of this, artfully, to your page to add a desert feel."

"Oh, I like that," Mindy chimed in. "What can I do to this page I'm putting together on the twins at the Fourth of July picnic?"

Jo helped Mindy look through several possibilities until she found a combination that satisfied her. At least for the moment. Jo had seen Mindy change her mind, and her pages, dozens of times, so progress on her scrapbook was moving at glacial speed — which didn't seem to worry her in the least. Mindy clearly enjoyed the process as much as the result.

Deirdre had finished a page or two on her scrapbook. Looking them over, Jo noticed that though the scrapbook's stated purpose was to memorialize her husband's career, the photos she had chosen so far all had Deirdre in them as well: Deirdre smiling beside Alden as he received an award from the local chamber of commerce; Deirdre at his side as he shook hands with the Governor. Right now Deirdre had pulled out a couple of photos of the two of them dressed formally — Alden in a tux and Deirdre in a knock-out red gown — possibly for a charity ball. The theme of the scrapbook certainly seemed to be turning into "Deirdre and Alden's Excellent Adventure" rather than "Alden's Career," but Jo wasn't about to comment on it.

"Oh, Jo," Deirdre said, "I spoke to Alden about the way Lieutenant Morgan treated you. He promised to talk to Russ about it."

"Thanks, Deirdre," Jo said, not hoping for any miracles to come from that but appreciating the effort.

"Have you had any luck looking into this jealous boyfriend, Jo?" Ina Mae asked. She was experimenting with the looks of a few western-style stamps Jo had found for her.

"Yes, I have," Jo said. All hands around the table collectively paused as the workshop women waited for Jo's latest report. She recounted her talk with Genna, followed by her eavesdropping on Genna and Pete's conversation outside the playhouse.

"That sounds like a problem boyfriend to me," Mindy stated firmly.

"Definitely," Deirdre agreed.

Jo then told them about going to Hanson's Garage, and the phone argument she overheard between Pete and Genna.

"What do you suppose he meant about 'finding a place'?" Loralee asked.

"I'm guessing, since Genna's cousin

mentioned Pete has wanted Genna to move in with him, that it was about that."

"That he found a place for the two of them?" Ina Mae asked, her raised eyebrows signaling both absorption of the information and disapproval of it.

"I assume so. And it sounded like Genna wasn't going for it, so Pete got pretty mad and stomped around kicking things."

"A violent temper." Deirdre nodded, sounding convinced.

"Violent enough for murder, though?" Ina Mae asked. "Was he jealous enough of Kyle to kill him?"

"That's the question I'm struggling with," Jo said. "From what I overheard outside the playhouse, his jealousy of Genna is easily inflamed. Genna, however, insisted Pete would never fight unfairly, or catch an enemy off guard, which is what happened to Kyle. Kyle was drugged, remember? So he was woozy by the time he was stabbed in my stockroom."

"Are you sure, though, that Kyle didn't take this sedative himself?" Deirdre asked.

"No, but it just doesn't seem likely, does it, when he's on a job that needed lots of energy? So if it was the killer who slipped it to him, I can't see Pete doing that. I see him confronting Kyle head on, out in the open, and giving Kyle a fighting chance."

"I don't know about that sedative," Mindy said. "Maybe Kyle *would* have taken it himself. Think about it. He hated playing a clown; he probably felt stressed with all the kids coming around him — and believe me, I know how aggravating kids can be sometimes, even when you love them like crazy — so maybe this sedative was something he felt he needed to keep from snapping."

"That's very possible," Loralee agreed, excited. "And Pete came along — maybe he just had an argument with Genna and was all fired up — and he saw his opportunity and took it."

"But to stab Kyle with a knitting needle?" Jo asked, skeptically. "And wouldn't there have been an argument, something loud enough that we would have heard?"

"You said the store was very busy by then, didn't you, Jo?" Ina Mae put in. "They might have had words, but it wouldn't necessarily have to be shouting. Sometimes the angriest, the most dangerous words will be muttered so low as to scarcely be heard. Then, the knitting needle was at hand, grabbed in the heat of the moment, and . . . there you are."

Her ladies nodded, agreeing with the

scenario. Jo, however, was not ready to join them. She found it difficult to picture the man she watched and conversed with at Hanson's Garage acting that way. Perhaps she had been just one more woman charmed by a skilled manipulator, but at this point she didn't think so. She saw the respect the other workers had for him, and the way he treated them while she was there. She just wasn't convinced he was someone capable of such artifice.

"Maybe, Ina Mae," Jo said. "Maybe. But I have a lead on someone else too, which bears looking in to, before I focus only on Pete." Jo explained about Hank Schroder and what Charlie had found out.

"Oh, my, now *there's* a motive," Loralee cried, ready, apparently, in an instant to switch her vote on suspects.

"It does sound serious," Ina Mae agreed.

"But Jo, would someone like this Hank Schroder be likely to show up at your craft shop opening?" Deirdre protested.

"He might if he knew he'd find Kyle here," Mindy pointed out.

"But that's ridiculous. He can find him right at the country club!" Deirdre argued.

"Nobody said murderers are always logical!"

"Ladies, ladies, first things first. Let Jo

look into this Hank Schroder situation and see what she finds out. Then we can argue about what he might do."

"You're quite right, Ina Mae," Loralee said.

Deirdre, Jo thought, looked a bit miffed, and she moved to soothe any ruffled feathers. "I really appreciate all your input on this," she said. "It helps more than you know, to hear discussions of all sides of a point. I planned to go to the country club anyway, to talk to Bob Gordon about the progress on the craft show plans. Hank Schroder will be only one of the people I'll be looking into while I'm there. I want to dig a little more deeply into some of the things Kyle was doing in the tennis area."

"Good idea, Jo," Ina Mae said. "I wouldn't be surprised if there's quite a bit still to be found out."

"Goodness, look at the time," Deirdre exclaimed, tidying up her work area. "I promised Alden I'd be home when he brings back one of his colleagues after their business dinner."

"How are you keeping your scrapbook a surprise?" Mindy asked.

"Oh, I stash everything in one of the cupboards in the laundry room. Alden never goes in there."

"I used to hide Martin's birthday and Christmas presents in the basement," Lora-lee said. "The easiest way to make sure he stayed out of there was to suggest it needed cleaning up." The ladies laughed, adding their own husband stories, and Jo was glad to see Deirdre smiling along with them, her little snit apparently forgotten.

Deirdre took off, and the others began to pack up their things too. As Loralee slid photos and papers into separate compartments of her huge tote, she commented, "You know, all Deirdre needs to do to hide her scrapbook is to keep it wherever her dogs are."

Mindy grinned. "I know, she told me she has a special room just for her two Afghan hounds, because Alden doesn't care for them much. She really dotes on them, though. Have you seen those dogs? They're gorgeous."

"Yes, I've seen her walking them. Or maybe they were walking her, they're so big. And all that long fur. She must have to get them groomed constantly."

"Humph. Expensive pets." Ina Mae sniffed. Jo knew that Ina Mae volunteered at the local SPCA and had heard her once or twice comment negatively on buying dogs from breeders when so many were available for and needful of adoption.

"Yes," Loralee agreed, "but of course, that might be their appeal to Deirdre."

Jo looked at Loralee, whose normally sweet face seemed to have turned just a bit sour. Was there some history between Loralee and Deirdre that Jo wasn't aware of? Perhaps Carrie would know. And if Jo ever got to the point of having enough leisure to look into the finer details of her workshop ladies' lives, she just might ask. There was still so much to learn about this newly adopted home of hers.

"Thanks, Jo," Mindy called, on her way out. "Another great night." Ina Mae and Loralee followed, and Jo soon turned off the lights, locked up, and headed to her quiet home. She planned to heat up something from her freezer, watch a bit of late-night TV, and try to sleep, before tackling another day of "keep Jo out of jail" activities.

Jo woke early the next morning, restless dreams pulling her out of the deep oblivion where she would have preferred to remain, for at least a while. She had vague memories of Russ Morgan arresting her for a rusted tail pipe, Mike trying to fix it with his acetylene torch, and Kyle, in his clown suit, running with an umbrella through the sprinklers on the golf course.

The thought of sinking back into that mess with all the emotions they stirred outweighed any lingering urge to remain curled around her pillow, and Jo crawled out to face the day. Wrapped in her terry robe, she padded into the kitchen and started coffee, then pulled out orange juice from the refrigerator. She debated over bagels or cereal until she remembered how her newish black slacks had begun to bag at the waist. She reached for the bagels and grabbed a tub of cream cheese along with them.

Jo never remembered having a problem with keeping *on* weight before — quite the opposite, in fact. But the recent stresses piled atop the older ones were taking their toll. That, plus hating the bother of cooking for one, had the pounds slipping away. She would have to do something about that, or the face that looked back at her from the mirror would soon turn haggard. In other words, it would reflect more accurately how she felt inside, lately.

Enough of that, she ordered herself briskly, a vision of Ina Mae surfacing as she did so, and dropped a split bagel into the toaster. She clicked on the small television to chase away the gloomy thoughts with cheery news anchor chatter, and poured out a glass of juice.

Jo carried her breakfast into the living room, set her coffee on an end table, and bit into her cheese-slathered bagel as she settled into the sofa. A spring in the cushion of her secondhand sofa poked uncomfortably at her, and she wriggled over, wondering how she had failed to notice the wayward wire at purchase time. Had it possibly been those artistically arranged pillows clustered so densely as to prevent her sitting there? And that couple had seemed so nice.

A voice on the screen talked about traffic tie-ups in the Baltimore area, as graphics depicted roadways, and flashing red arrows pointed to trouble spots. What a relief, Jo thought, to at least not have to face that kind of daily commute. She swallowed the bagel bite and took a careful sip of her hot coffee. The TV station went to commercial, and Jo worked the remote to switch stations.

A navy-suited African-American man appeared on the screen, welcoming her to the Channel Four newsbreak, and Jo set down the remote and picked up her bagel. She listened to his smooth voice announcing the day and time, then moving on to talk of Mayor Phelp's latest battle with his Washington, D.C., city council members. With barely a pause for breath, the newsman moved on to his next story.

"Police are looking into the death of a young woman in Hammond County last night."

Jo dropped the bagel to the plate.

"The woman's body was discovered around 11 P.M. at the base of a rocky cliff, as her dog's frantic barking caused a neighbor to investigate. Police are uncertain at this time if the death was accidental, saying only that they are investigating. This is the second violent death in less than two weeks in the small town of Abbotsville. The woman, twenty-two-year-old Genna Hunt, was . . ."

Jo could hear her phone ringing, but barely. She knew she should be moving, reacting, but all she could do was stare at the television screen, which had changed in a flash to show a weather map. No rain was predicted, and the temperature at Reagan National, it seemed, as well as much of the surrounding area, was presently 61 degrees and climbing. Not an unusually chilly morning for this time of year.

But Jo felt cold, very cold.

CHAPTER 17

Jo took another sip of coffee. Her shivering had finally stopped, some time after Carrie had arrived at her place and insisted on bringing her back to her house. The kids had been sent safely off to school, unaware of the latest incident, but Dan was home.

"Dan knows people in fire and rescue," Carrie had explained. "He might be able to find out more than was on television."

"I just keep seeing her face," Jo mused, setting down her cup, "that delicate face. And it keeps asking me, 'Why didn't you do something?' "

"Jo, there's nothing you could have done. Don't do that to yourself." Carrie edged a plate of oatmeal muffins closer to her friend, although Jo had already refused them twice. When at a loss for what to do, Carrie seemed to say: eat.

"What did you find out?" Jo asked Dan, who came back to the kitchen after making his phone calls.

"Not too much. She was found at the base of the Highpoint Road cliff, which is a pretty steep drop down to Abbot's Creek, about thirty, forty feet, and rocky. It's not far from the Wildwood apartments, where you said she lived. It's a nice area, and a lot of people walk their dogs there because of the view, plus there's plenty of grass and shrubs."

"She walked her dog at eleven o'clock at night?"

"She was found then. We don't know when she actually went out. They only found her because a neighbor came by and recognized the dog, which was barking frantically. An odd thing, though . . ." Dan rubbed his chin.

"What?"

"Her dog was tied to a tree near the edge."

"Tied that way when they found it barking?"

Dan nodded.

Jo looked at Carrie, who seemed to be having the same thought. If there had been any faint hopes that this had been an accident, the secured dog erased them.

"I have to talk to Lieutenant Morgan," Jo said.

Carrie nodded, but Dan looked surprised.

"What? Why?"

"I have to tell him what I know about Pete Tober. I hate to, because I still hold out the hope that he's a decent guy, but this is just too coincidental."

"Wait a minute, you lost me. Who's this Pete Tober and what does he have to do with this?"

Jo hesitated. Obviously Carrie hadn't told Dan about Pete. She glanced at her friend who shrugged somewhat guiltily.

"Jo's been checking out Pete," Carrie explained, "who is Genna Hunt's boyfriend. She had heard that he was pretty possessive, had a temper, and didn't at all like Genna playing love scenes with Kyle. He was just one possibility that showed up as someone who might have, ah, killed Kyle."

"I wasn't convinced Pete was capable of that," Jo hurriedly put in. "But Genna's death, I'm afraid, puts things in a whole different light. I have to talk to the police about it, although I hate throwing Pete to the wolves." Even though it might help clear me, she thought, but didn't say. She found herself hoping, in spite of herself, that Pete would have a solid alibi.

Dan's face began taking on a dark, burgundy color. He looked from Carrie to Jo, and back to Carrie. "Charlie's been hanging around a place filled with people like this?"

"Dan, that's not fair!" Carrie protested. "There's plenty of decent people —"

He cut her off with a wave of his hand. "No more! He's out of there."

"Dan, we should at least wait until we know —"

"I know all I need to. He doesn't go there anymore. The whole thing was a stupid waste of time anyway. Tell Charlie when he gets home, Carrie. No more."

Dan pushed a kitchen chair on his way out of the kitchen, and Jo soon heard the front door slam behind him. She looked at Carrie, who leaned her face into her hands and then spread her fingers to look at Jo. She didn't have to say anything. Jo knew what she was thinking. This was going to really hurt Charlie.

Jo had difficulty getting in to speak with Lieutenant Morgan. For once he didn't seem anxious to talk to her. Not that she was all that happy to see him, but she knew she had to. The thought of dragging Earnest C. Ainsworthy along — he was still on retainer — crossed her mind, but only long enough to produce a pained laugh.

The Abbotsville Police Department

bustled with activity and tension, but, unlike at Hanson's Garage, Jo was not allowed to simply blend in and soak up what was going on. She was kept, and watched over, in an outer area where all she could see were stone-faced patrolmen hurrying in and out, and all she could hear through the briefly opened doors were sounds of phones ringing and the babble of raised voices. Finally, someone ushered her into Morgan's office.

"Thank you for seeing me," Jo said, noting that Morgan looked as though he hadn't slept overnight.

"You had something to tell me?" he asked, a busy man getting right to the point.

"It's about Genna Hunt."

Morgan's tired eyes flashed alertly. "Yes?"

"I thought you should know about Pete Tober, her boyfriend. He's shown signs of a violent temper along with jealousy and possessiveness of Genna. I hate to say it, but I'm very concerned he might be involved in her death."

"You're saying you think Miss Hunt didn't fall, but that Pete Tober pushed her?"

Jo winced. It *was* what she was saying, but it didn't mean she liked it. She nodded. "It could have been accidental. Perhaps they were arguing and he grabbed her too hard.

She might have pulled away and rushed off blindly, plunging over the edge in the dark."

"Tober would still be responsible, though, wouldn't he?" Morgan was examining her intently.

Jo nodded.

"How do you happen to know so much about Tober and Miss Hunt? As a newcomer to this town, I mean?"

Jo had anticipated this question, wondering how best to answer it without sounding like a stalker.

"I've been to a couple of the playhouse's rehearsals, since Rafe Rulenski asked me to work on part of the costume and set designs. I've spoken with Genna during breaks. She confided a bit about her problems with Pete."

"Oh? So you were a friendly shoulder to cry on?"

"There was no crying. We just talked."

"I see. And Tober, did he talk with you as well? Tell you his side of it?"

"No, Lieutenant Morgan. I didn't mean to imply I was an intermediary of any kind. I simply learned a few things about Pete from Genna. Plus I overheard them argue, and he certainly came across as a controlling boyfriend. Others have mentioned his temper, and I've seen it myself."

"He threatened you?"

"No."

"You heard him threaten Miss Hunt?"

"Not exactly. But I heard him argue with her on the phone and insist on her agreeing with him. When she didn't, he was visibly upset, kicking things around and such. You can ask his coworkers at Hanson's Garage. They saw it too."

At Morgan's questioning look, Jo explained. "I was there for an oil change on my car."

"I see."

Morgan was silent for several moments, and Jo waited uneasily. What was going through his mind? Did he believe her?

"I hoped it might have been an accident," she continued, "but her dog being left tied to a tree didn't make any sense for that scenario."

Morgan, who had been focusing on his clasped hands, snapped his head up. "How did you know about the dog?"

"I, ah, from a friend. He knows people who had been at the scene. Why?" Jo recognized that look, the one that said he was one step away from putting her behind bars. "Look," she said, standing up, "I just thought you should know what I learned about Genna. What you do with it, I guess, is up to you."

"We've already questioned Pete Tober. It was difficult to fully understand him through the high degree of grief he seemed to be suffering. But we did learn he was working late last night, at the garage, and he wasn't alone. That's been verified."

"Oh!" Jo felt a mix of surprise and relief wash over her. "Well, I'm glad for that, at least."

"Now, I have a question for you." Morgan's eyes bored into hers, oddly stirring up feelings of guilt in Jo where she knew there should be none, which quickly made her angry and extremely sorry she had come. She braced for his question, knowing what to expect, but it still stung like a slap when it came.

"Mrs. McAllister, where were you between 9:30 and 11 last night?"

CHAPTER 18

Jo hurried from the stockroom, her arms full of Christmas greenery to replace what had sold out that day from the shelves out front.

"Oh, and do you have any more spools of red velvet ribbon?" her customer called out.

"Just a sec," Jo said, reversing her steps to add velvet ribbon to her load. The craft store was bustling, nearly reaching her grand-opening level, and had been keeping both her and Carrie hopping. Jo could hardly complain, especially after the few slow, rainy days she had experienced. But she was not thrilled, once again, with the reason behind it.

"Here you go," she said to her customer, dropping the jumbled pile on the counter.

"Wonderful." The pleasant-faced, middle-aged woman picked out several pieces to add to her other items and said, "That should do it."

As Jo totaled the purchases on the cash register, she also counted the seconds to herself: one-one thousand, two-one thousand. She only had to reach four-one thousand before the question came, a record so far.

"So, wasn't that a terrible thing that happened to the poor Hunt girl? Have you heard anything more about it?"

Jo tried hard to keep from gritting her teeth. What has Jo's Craft Corner become, she wondered? Crime Information Central? Since Kyle's murder in her stockroom, was she now the unofficial source of grim news? This woman was not the first to come searching for creative materials with a side of gossip. And Jo knew she would not be the last. She had heard people in the aisles discussing Genna's death as they picked out sweater yarns or card stock. Perhaps it was a small way of reaffirming that life goes on, but, beneficial though it might be to her business, Jo wished it would all stop.

However, when she saw Ina Mae and Loralee enter the shop, Jo was glad to see them, even knowing what they likely had come to talk about. There was a huge difference, she felt, between gossip and discussion, the first causing her stress, and the second having at least some purpose. The two women greeted her, and, seeing her occupied with customers, wandered off to browse the stamping shelves.

Carrie replaced Jo at the cash register, chatting genially with her customer about the embroidery project she planned, but it wasn't long before the questions turned from floss to fatalities. Carrie handled it smoothly, but Jo could see it was bothering her too. Happily, the busyness eventually calmed, at least for the time being, and Ina Mae and Loralee emerged from their nook, each having picked up a few items for their scrapbooking and stamping projects.

"Terrible goings-on," Ina Mae said.

Loralee nodded, her face a picture of sadness. "That poor child."

"Sally Hardesty said she saw you going in to talk to the police. Did you tell them about Pete Tober?"

"Yes." Jo sighed, thinking about her latest spar with Russ Morgan. "I could have spared myself the trouble. They've already talked with Pete, and he's been cleared."

"An alibi?" Ina Mae asked.

Jo nodded. "He was at the garage, working late. A coworker was with him."

"Hmmm." The older woman scowled, mulling this over.

"I don't believe it," Loralee declared, her

eyes flashing.

Jo looked at her. "You don't?"

"Not for a minute. He could have snuck out easily, while that other person was occupied. Or, maybe they're in cahoots!"

What surprising things came out of Loralee, Jo thought. Behind that sweet grandmotherly face seemed to lurk the mind of a Mickey Spillane.

"You mean this coworker might have helped Pete kill Genna?"

"Don't you think? Or, if not, maybe he's lying about Pete having been there the whole time. If his crew likes him, they could be closing ranks to protect him."

"That would be a very risky thing to do," Ina Mae said. "However, I've seen this kind of blind loyalty, especially among young males."

"I don't know," Jo said. "I mean, I agree his crew might very well be inclined to defend him, but I'm just not sure he needs defending. Lieutenant Morgan indicated Pete was extremely upset. He may have been overly controlling, but I had the impression he truly cared for Genna."

"Maybe he did," Ina Mae acknowledged. "But could what he was feeling be regret? Over what he had done in a moment of rage?" Ina Mae asked.

"Yes, absolutely!" Loralee firmly agreed.

Jo had to admit they had a point. Even if the police had crossed Pete off their list of suspects, she probably shouldn't. Not yet.

Two customers walked in, putting an end to the discussion. "Did you want me to ring these up," Jo asked, indicating the items Ina Mae and Loralee each held in their hands.

"Please," Ina Mae said, setting hers down on the counter.

"Oh, I forgot the double-sided tape," Loralee exclaimed, and rushed back to the shelves she and Ina Mae had been scouring. Jo totaled it all up and packed their items into bags.

"Thanks for coming by," she said, handing them their purchases. "It's been a difficult several hours. You've helped clear some of my thinking on this."

"Terrible happenings," Ina Mae said, repeating her earlier comment. Jo looked at her, detecting more feeling behind that comment than she would have expected.

"Did you know Genna?" Jo asked gently.

"Taught her, back when she was in the third grade," Ina Mae said. "A sweet girl, but too concerned, even back then, with trying to please everyone." Ina Mae shook her head sadly. "It never works."

■ ■ ■ ■

Things quieted down at the shop by dinnertime, and, with no workshops scheduled for the evening, Carrie went home for dinner with her family. Jo took the downtime to try to catch up on some bills, nibbling at a sandwich as she worked. She had just written a large check for an order of plastic bags, amazed once again at how much the simple act of packing up a customer's purchase could cut into the store's profits, when the front door's bell jingled. Jo looked up to see Charlie march in.

Uh-oh, she thought, he got the word about Dan's injunction. Jo slipped her check into the envelope and got up to face the agitated teen.

Charlie glared silently at Jo, then turned to pace the front of the store, hands in the pockets of his jacket. When that continued for a while, with still no sound coming from his tightly pressed lips, Jo said, "If you're just here to pace, let me put a dust mop in your hands to drag back and forth while you're at it."

Charlie stopped. "He said I can't go back there. Just like that! No listening to my side of it at all."

Jo nodded.

"He thinks I'm a kid! A three-year-old who can't take care of himself."

"No, he knows you're his fifteen-year-old son, whom he loves and worries about."

Charlie glared and went back to pacing. After a turn or two, he stopped once more. "I was just starting to learn the soundboard. You can't believe how incredibly cool that was. They would have let me be the assistant on it, if I'd had time to get into it."

"Charlie, I think things at the playhouse have come to a stop. There won't be any soundboard work, or scenery building, or rehearsals for now. Their lead, Genna, is dead."

That stopped Charlie in his tracks. The look on his face changed to guilt as he realized his self-absorption — not abnormal for a teen, Jo was sure, but still guilt-producing. Charlie's own problem suddenly looked minuscule compared to the graver issue.

"Yeah, that's right," he said, shamefacedly.

"If you can just hang in there until all this is cleared up, your Dad just might look differently at your going back to the playhouse."

Charlie's gloom lifted somewhat. "Do you think they'll find that her falling off that cliff was just an accident?"

Jo frowned. "I don't know, Charlie. The situation sounded suspicious." She told him about the dog tied safely to a nearby tree. "You know I've wondered about Genna's boyfriend, Pete, with his controlling ways and bad temper. Several people I've talked with are highly suspicious he may have caused Genna's fall. But I already found out from Lieutenant Morgan that Pete has an alibi for the time involved." Unlike me, Jo thought, but didn't say. "It might not be ironclad, though."

Charlie scowled. "So you're thinking this Pete might have killed Genna out of jealousy? And Kyle too, because he was getting too close to Genna?"

Jo nodded.

"But Aunt Jo, Kyle was a major jerk, remember? Nobody's going to get jealous over someone like him."

"We don't know exactly how Pete would have felt about him. Maybe he saw only the onstage side, the more attractive side of Kyle. Maybe his thinking was blurred."

"Maybe," Charlie said, but his voice dripped skepticism. "But since he has an alibi, why not look into the guy I told you about at the country club. The landscaping guy."

"Hank Schroder?"

"Yeah. I know the kids who work under him, remember? We could go over there and pretend I'm interested in a job and you're my aunt helping me get it."

Jo had almost forgotten about Schroder, with what had happened lately. She agreed he was a strong "person of interest." Charlie would be a perfect cover, a way to question Schroder. Would it be dragging Charlie back into dangerous waters, though? Perhaps not, as long as she made sure to always swim alongside him. She'd check with Carrie to see how she felt about it, but it just might be a great way to direct Charlie's thoughts away from his angry resentment of his father. And they could hope, once this whole, miserable business was over, that Dan's attitude about the playhouse would take a 180-degree turn. Or at least a 90-degree turn. Knowing Dan's stubborn nature, Jo wondered if 45 would be too much to hope for.

CHAPTER 19

"I'm glad you're with me, Charlie," Jo said as they climbed out of her Toyota. The disturbing transmission noise had reappeared on the drive over, but that wasn't what concerned her at the moment. They had detoured to Highpoint Road on their way to the country club to see if they could look over the scene of Genna's death. Charlie, once more, hadn't taken much persuasion.

"You don't like heights?"

Jo looked over and saw he meant that as a joke, trying to lighten up a grim moment. She appreciated the effort and smiled. "No, I mostly don't want the police — if they see me — to think I've returned to the scene of my crime. Criminals, I've read, tend to do that when they're alone."

"Do the police think it was a crime, then? Not an accident?"

"I don't really know what they think at

this point — they haven't seen fit to send me hourly updates. But for that matter I don't know what I think either. That's why I want to check out the scene. I was afraid it might still be secured, but I don't see that. Looks like we can walk right over."

Jo approached an area that had been trampled and rutted. A large section of the guardrail had been broken off, temporarily patched, and blocked with safety cones.

"This must be where the rescue crew worked. I presume it's also where she fell over."

Together they gazed down the steep incline leading to the creek. Large, uniform rocks covered the earth, obviously placed there as a hedge against erosion. Jo imagined Genna tumbling down their smooth surface, helpless to check her fall, picking up speed until she crashed on the rocks at the bottom. Jo shuddered and turned away, looking instead up the walk leading here. In the distance, less than two blocks away, she saw the top floors of the Wildwood apartments, which she and Charlie had circled in the Toyota before coming to the cliff.

"I can understand why she would walk the dog here. There's plenty of grass and trees, and the view is lovely. Even at night, seeing the lights across the way there must be beautiful."

Jo looked at the street. "It's not a heavily traveled road, but not isolated either, though late in the evening it might be fairly quiet. The dog was a small poodle I heard, not the kind to offer protection, to make Genna feel safe, I mean. But then, I'm thinking like a New Yorker. Here in Abbotsville safety might not have been as much of a concern."

"How could she accidentally fall?" Charlie asked, still looking over the rail.

Jo turned back. There was a narrow, grassy strip just on the other side of the rail. "Perhaps she dropped something, maybe her keys, or saw something she tried to reach for? That could be the reason, I suppose, that she tied up the dog first."

Charlie looked at her. He didn't believe it any more than she did.

"On the other hand, the rail isn't all that high. A person could be pushed over it fairly easily." Jo tried to picture Pete struggling with Genna. It wouldn't have been much of a struggle, slight as she was compared to his brawn. It didn't feel right to Jo, though. She just couldn't see Pete actually doing that.

Who else, though, had connections to both Genna and Kyle? Jo realized she had shifted beyond trying to prove herself innocent to wanting to prove Pete innocent as well. He had a step up on her, though, with his coworker alibi. But would it ultimately hold up? And was she trying to protect someone who was actually guilty and might go on to murder again?

"Let's go," she said to Charlie. "I've seen all I need to here."

"You'll probably find Mr. Schroder at the storage shed," the woman at the country club desk informed them, "with his crew. They'll be getting ready to smooth out those tracks someone made with their SUV the other night — kids, probably." Her eyes narrowed as she looked over her half-glasses at Charlie. "It's just extremely lucky the ground is dry, or they would have made an even worse mess."

"I don't even have my driver's license yet," Charlie complained as he and Jo walked across the grass. "Why do all teenagers, especially guys, get lumped together?"

"Now you know how I feel when I have to talk to Lieutenant Morgan." Jo wiped away a bead of sweat forming on her temple. The late-afternoon sun beat down warmly. If anything was predictable about September weather in southern Maryland, it was that it was unpredictable.

"Don't worry, Aunt Jo. You'll be able to

set him right before long."

Ah, the optimism of youth, Jo thought. Since she wasn't exactly ancient, having only recently crossed into the latter half of her thirties, Jo wondered where her own optimism had gone. Up in smoke with the explosion in New York? Or was it simply the nature of the beast to fade away over the years? Whichever it was, she rather missed the feeling, along with the comfort it provided.

"There's Garth, over there." Charlie pointed ahead to a group of teens loading rakes and shovels into the back of a pickup. "He's the one in the red shirt."

Jo saw a muscular teen with the sleeves of his shirt ripped off, presumably to better display his well-defined biceps. His dark hair had been trimmed short, and he sported a bit of chin hair just under his lower lip. He looked up as they approached, greeting Charlie with an unsmiling, but not unfriendly, "Hey!"

Jo spotted an older man who fit the description of Hank Schroder, looking every bit the aging but fit ex-Marine, and sounding like one too as he barked orders to his crew.

"Jason! Get the lead out and load these

tampers. Brett, bring that roller over, like I told you!"

"Mr. Schroder?" Jo called out as she and Charlie drew closer.

"Yeah?" Schroder squinted in Jo's direction, his leathery face wrinkling so much that she wondered if he could see out at all.

"They told me I could come talk to you about a part-time job for my nephew here. I'm Jo McAllister, and this is Charlie Brenner."

Hank Schroder, hands on his hips, looked Charlie up and down as though he were some kind of mutant weed that had just sprouted on Schroder's pristine golf course. "You want to work for me?"

"Yes, sir."

"This is hard work. You look kinda puny to me. Ever do much landscaping?"

"I cut the grass at our house, front and back. And I helped my dad put in some rose bushes for my mom."

Schroder spit, thankfully in the other direction but clearly making the point he was less than impressed. "I need guys who can lift fifty-pound bags of mulch. And work in the hot sun til the job's done. Your mama ain't gonna be bringing no lemonade and telling you to take it easy. Can you handle that?"

"I guess so."

"One way to find out. Go on with this crew to work on some repair. We'll see how you do. If I think you're up to it, I'll put you on the list for a job, soon as there's an opening."

Charlie glanced at Jo. Neither of them had expected this, and she didn't know what to tell him. Before she could say a word, though, he gamely said, "Yes, sir," and jumped forward to help with the last of the loading. Within seconds, Charlie was riding on the back of the truck over to the fourth green.

"They'll be back in an hour or so, if you want to come pick him up," Schroder said to her.

"Uh, thanks for giving him this chance."

Schroder nodded, and turned toward his own truck to follow the group. Jo thought rapidly. "Mind if I ride along with you?" At Schroder's look of surprise, she explained, "I promised his mother I'd make sure he'd be working in a safe environment. One of her brothers lost two fingers in a construction accident, and she worries."

"The kids don't handle any of the power tools here. They do all the grunt work — lifting, shoveling, raking. But come on along if you want to." He gestured toward the pas-

225

senger door of his truck.

"Thanks," Jo said, climbing in. "His mother's home with the baby, or she would have come herself," she said, feeling like she needed to further explain her presence, and hearing herself, with some alarm, start to babble. "She might have managed if she just had the twins to bring along, but she'd have trouble keeping them from running off with having to carry little Alphonse."

Schroder's only comment, thankfully, was a grunt as he put his truck into drive and took off.

Thinking it best to drop the subject of Carrie's nonexistent brood, and wondering where in the world the name "Alphonse" had popped up from, she gazed around at the landscape as Schroder drove on the paved cart lane.

"You really keep things beautiful here," she said.

"Ain't easy."

"I'm sure it isn't. Especially when there's dry periods like we've had. How do you manage to keep it all so green?"

"Sprinkling system. Pipes are underground; grass gets watered overnight."

"Really? So, what, does someone have to be here to turn it on and off?"

"Nah! It's all automatic. When it works,

that is." Jo saw the muscles in Schroder's cheek quiver, and wondered just how hard he was clenching his jaw.

"You've had problems with it?" she asked, knowing the answer but hoping she could get him to elaborate.

He shot her a dark look. "Thought I did. Wasted a lot of time working at it. Darn near tore the whole thing apart before I figured out what was happening."

"Yes?"

"Where're those fools going to? I told them the *fourth* green!" Schroder began beeping his horn and waving furiously to get the attention of the truck ahead. It pulled over, and he stuck his head out the window, spewing words Jo hadn't heard for a long time, dealing mostly as she did with the genteel ladies of her craft shop.

"Sorry," he apologized as he pulled his head back in.

"That's all right. I understand. It's not always easy dealing with people who don't have their mind on the job, is it?"

"You got that right, lady. And I don't always have final say about who gets hired around here either. Gordon's picked a few prizes."

"Yes, I heard that Kyle Sandborn might

have been one of those prizes."

Jo watched carefully, but Schroder suddenly had a need to spit, turning his head away and out the window once more. Jo was finding Schroder to be a tough nut, but she pressed harder.

"Kyle was the fellow who was killed at the craft shop. He worked here at the tennis desk."

"Yeah." Schroder stared ahead.

"He seemed to be quite a goof-off around here. From what I heard."

"Lady, I've had my fill of goof-offs. If they work for me, they don't work for me long. If they get in my way, they just better watch out. That's all I can say. I hope that nephew of yours knows how to follow orders or he won't like it here."

"Oh, Charlie can —" Jo started, but Schroder wasn't listening anymore, having pulled over and braked behind the first truck. He swung out of the cab in an instant, barking out directions in the process. Jo climbed down and watched as Charlie pitched in with the crew, hauling out tools and equipment, and then got to work. It wasn't exactly what he'd bargained for when he joined this detecting expedition, she knew, but he dug in gamely.

Jo saw she wasn't going to get anything

out of Schroder while he bustled about, clearly furious over the damage done to his course by the renegade SUV and intent on erasing all signs of it as quickly as possible. She watched him handling the crew. He'd never earn their affection with his drill-sergeant manner, and the ones who didn't work as hard or as fast as he wanted got the full blast of his wrath. Thankfully, Charlie wasn't one of them. Or perhaps Schroder held back with her there.

Eventually, the ruts got smoothed and reseeded, and the crew packed up to go. Charlie, red-faced from the heat but with all ten fingers safely intact, took his place once again in the back of the pickup. Jo climbed back into Schroder's truck as she saw him heading over. He barked a few more orders, then jumped behind the wheel and headed back toward the shed.

"The kid's not too bad. If he wants the job, I'll put him on the list. Might be someone leaving before too long."

"That's great," Jo said, feeling a twinge of guilt at the deceptions involved, but she was reasonably sure that Charlie wouldn't leave a hard-to-fill gap by not following through on a callback. "You run a very tight ship, Mr. Schroder."

"Learned a long time ago you gotta show

'em who's boss."

Jo could see that was very important to Hank Schroder. Which is why it must have really rankled to be played for a fool by Kyle Sandborn. Had he known it was Kyle, though? Schroder was being very closed-mouthed on the subject. Jo decided to try him on another one.

"On the way here we looked at the place that young woman fell to her death. Genna Hunt."

Schroder grunted.

"I had met her recently, so what happened seemed especially tragic. Did you know her, Mr. Schroder?"

Schroder shot Jo a quick look. "Yeah." Jo waited. "She's related to my ex-wife," he said, then fell silent once more. Jo was about to ask in what way, when Schroder spoke again.

"Never did like those people."

"Oh?"

"Bunch of busybodies, always poking their noses in where they shouldn't."

Schroder stared straight ahead as he said it, but Jo wondered if there was a veiled warning for her in his comment.

"I'm new to Abbotsville," she said, "so I still have a lot to learn about the town. I've noticed one big difference, though, from

New York City, where I lived. There, people barely knew their neighbors. In this town I've found quite a tangled network of relationships among the townspeople. Everyone seems to be connected to everyone else in one way or another."

"You got that right. Tangled network." Schroder seemed to mull over the words. "A net. Things get caught in nets, don't they?"

"Sometimes they do," Jo agreed.

Schroder spit out his window.

"The dumb ones, that is."

CHAPTER 20

"How're you feeling?" Jo asked as she and Charlie made their way back to the clubhouse.

"Okay. Just pretty hot. And dry. Schroder didn't even give me a soda or anything. The other guys had there own stuff to drink, but I wasn't going to ask anyone for theirs."

"Sorry you got sucked into that job, Charlie. Hank Schroder just got an hour's free labor out of you, didn't he?"

"I didn't mind. But I didn't get to talk to anyone much. It's hard when you're scraping away at dirt. And riding on the back of that truck I was too busy trying not to get mashed by that sliding roller thing."

"You deserve a big, icy drink." Jo held open the door leading to the restaurant/bar. "As do I. Schroder's truck wasn't air-conditioned. Or maybe he kept the windows open to accommodate his delightful little habit of watering the landscape with his, uh, saliva. Let's get our drinks to take out. I want to stop in at the tennis shop."

They each ordered a large Coke and gulped down a large portion thirstily; then Jo led the way to Kyle Sandborn's old job area. Tracy, the blond desk attendant, was sorting through a shipment of tennis T-shirts and looked up with a bright smile at their entrance. To her credit, it faded only slightly as she recognized them.

"Hi! How's the craft show coming together?"

"Little by little." Jo thought Tracy looked a bit stressed, despite the cheery "greeting" smile she had flashed. "How've you been?" she asked.

"Hanging in there, I guess. It's been kind of a rough week."

"Sorry if I'll be adding to it, but do you mind if I ask a bit more about Kyle?"

Tracy shook her head. "No, go ahead. Might as well."

"I wondered, since I only saw Kyle's less attractive side that day at my shop, did he have a charming side? Were girls attracted to him?"

Tracy thought for a moment. "I wasn't. But maybe that's because I saw too much of him around here. He wasn't bad looking, but that's not the only thing that matters to me." Tracy shook out a brightly striped T-shirt and slipped it onto a hanger. "I guess, now that I think about it, some of the women players used to flirt with him a bit. He was on his most charming behavior, of course, dealing with the members here at the desk. They never saw the other side of him, the side that dreamed up scandals about them when they were off on the courts."

"What I need to know is would he be likely to stir up jealousy from someone's boyfriend, if Kyle seemed to be getting too much attention from the girlfriend?"

"Maybe," Tracy said, hesitantly. "If the boyfriend didn't really know him, that is. Kyle wasn't really a studly type. He didn't go *after* girls. Not that he was gay or anything. I don't mean that. He just seemed too involved in himself, in his 'big acting career' that was coming, to care much about anything else."

"Told you," Charlie said smugly to Jo. "Pete Tober would never have been jealous of Kyle."

"But perhaps," Jo argued, "he didn't really know Kyle, as Tracy says. Perhaps he just saw the 'actor' Kyle, with Genna gazing lovingly at him on stage."

"Genna Hunt?" Tracy asked. "That girl who was killed?"

"Yes. Did you know her?"

"Kinda." Jo waited for another Abbotsville "tangled network" explanation, something along the lines of "my mother's-cousin's-dry-cleaner's-neighbor." What actually came surprised her.

"She roomed with Bethanne Fowler, our tennis pro."

"Oh!"

"Bethanne's a wreck. She canceled all her lessons this week. I was on the phone for hours, getting in touch with everyone. It's been a madhouse around here, with Mr. Gordon running in every other minute, insisting we find another pro to step in before all the tennis programs fall apart. Like we have pros sitting out there just waiting to be called!" Tracy sighed. "This was the first chance I've had to do anything with the clothing. The new shipments have been piling up. These shirts have been sitting here for days."

"Genna roomed with your tennis pro," Jo said, still holding tightly to that nugget amidst Tracy's flowing vent. She glanced at Charlie, whose eyebrows were wiggling.

"Yes. They've been friends, I heard, for years. Practically sisters."

Was this significant, or merely a coincidence? Whichever, it was the first real connection between Kyle and Genna that Jo had found so far, tenuous though it may be. It definitely warranted looking into.

"I see how hard this must be on Bethanne," Jo said, "especially coming, as it does, on the heels of Kyle's death. I image Bethanne and Kyle were rather close too?"

Tracy looked puzzled. "Close? No, I wouldn't say that at all. They really didn't like each other very much. Kyle mixed up Bethanne's lesson appointments a couple of times, and I remember that made her pretty mad. I wondered, actually, if Kyle did it on purpose, 'cause he sometimes referred to Bethanne as the 'Prima Donna,' behind her back, of course. He did have a point, though. Bethanne sometimes acted like we were all working here specially for her convenience. It got on my nerves too, but if I was too busy to do what she wanted, I told her so, and she usually backed off. Kyle, I think, needed to do more, just to prove to himself he was superior or something."

The phone rang, and Tracy excused herself.

"Well," Jo said quietly to Charlie, "that's interesting, isn't it? I wonder what else we can find out."

She glanced around, noticing for the first time several photos on the wall, and went to examine them. Several were of tennis teams: groups of men or women arranged smilingly around a trophy, with the date superimposed on the photos. The more recent photos contained a recurring figure, a young woman who was dark haired and a bit shorter than the others.

Jo gawked, and, hearing Tracy finish on the phone, called out, "Is this Bethanne, here?"

Tracy came over and peered at the photo Jo indicated.

"Uh-huh. That's her. Her teams did really well this year."

"She has quite a resemblance to Genna."

"Yes, she does, doesn't she? Bethanne used to joke that with a little makeup she could stand in for Genna in one of her shows at the playhouse and no one would notice until she opened her mouth and tried to sing."

"She's right. They could practically pass for sisters. Did Genna play tennis?"

"A little, but just for fun, not anything like Bethanne. I think she preferred the fitness classes here for her exercise. Bethanne got her a good discount on them."

Jo moved over to other framed photos. These were groups of people in evening clothes, posed in the country club's dining room.

"Those were for the Muscular Dystrophy Ball," Tracy explained. "All the big-wigs were there. It's a huge fund-raiser."

"Yes, I recognize Mayor Kunkle from pictures in the paper, and Bob Gordon. Oh, and there's a couple of my workshop ladies, Loralee Phillips — doesn't she look nice — and Deirdre Patterson and her husband, the state senator."

"Uh-huh. They always show up for those things. And there's Bethanne, over here. I'd hardly recognize her out of her tennis togs, but she looks great, doesn't she?"

"Yes, she does. She supports the muscular dystrophy cause?"

"Oh, she didn't have to pay for those dinners. Those tickets cost something like two hundred a plate. Mr. Gordon wanted her to be there so he could introduce her around as the club's pro."

"I see. A little business promotion."

"Yeah."

"Did she go as Bob Gordon's date?"

"Oh, no! Mr. Gordon always took his wife." Tracy pointed to a well-dressed, round-figured woman on one of the photos.

"That's her there."

Jo looked more closely and saw a smiling woman holding firmly to her husband's arm as they posed for the camera. Jo imagined that grip never loosening as Bob Gordon introduced his tennis pro around the room.

"So Bethanne attended on her own? No boyfriend?"

"None that I knew of. There was some talk, well, never mind."

"What?"

Tracy flushed. "It's not important. Just more of Kyle's crazy imaginings. I shouldn't have brought it up. Especially with Bethanne so miserable now, with what happened to her best friend."

Jo longed to hear more, but Tracy's face had closed down. Her sympathy for her coworker's pain was not going to allow her any leeway toward negative gossip. All Jo could do for now was file away the comment for reexamination in the future.

"Yes, I'm sure she must feel terrible over Genna," Jo said.

"Oh, definitely, especially since she blames herself!"

"She does? How?"

"Oh, you didn't know? It was Bethanne's dog that Genna was walking! Genna wouldn't have been out at all if Bethanne had come home early enough to take Mojo out herself."

"Mojo?" Charlie, who had been silent until now, yelped. "Her dog's name is Mojo? I thought it was one of those little yappy types, you know, a Toto. The kind people call Muffin, or Pookie, or something. Why'd she call it Mojo?"

Tracy looked confused for a moment, then laughed. "Oh, you're thinking of that guy that looks like a Sumo wrestler or something, on, on, what's that show?"

She and Charlie batted around the names of a few television shows, arguing in a friendly fashion over which one was the right one, but Jo didn't care much what the little dog was called. What had struck her, and she was sure would strike Charlie as well very soon, was that Genna strongly resembled Bethanne and was out at night walking Bethanne's dog. Had Bethanne, in fact, been the intended target, not Genna?

It seemed very possible, and if so, that would change everything.

Chapter 21

Jo had more on her mind than wreath making as her workshop group gathered once again for their next project. She wondered what might be in their thoughts as well, since they had become nearly as involved as she with this entire mess. You'd never guess to look at their faces, however, as one by one they filed through her door, smiling ingenuously and chattering on things as innocuous as the recent spurt of warm weather and how it might affect their gardens' mums. It began to lull Jo, at least for the moment, into the pleasant feeling that life in Abbotsville was simple and serene, and the most difficult problem facing her was how to present tonight's project.

Aware the feeling wouldn't last long, though, Jo gathered her supplies and called the group to order, after first popping open a soda from the cooler kept well stocked with a variety of drinks for the sessions.

Some of the others had already helped themselves to their favorites.

"Tonight, ladies, we're going to make this spring wreath," she paused as they ah-ed delightedly, "and I have a variety of materials lined up here for you."

"I want to hang my wreath on my front door," Javonne said. "But Harry just painted our door red — which I love — but those pink flowers you have on yours won't work for me. Can I change them?"

"Absolutely. What I have here is just the prototype. It can be adjusted any way you like. Color is the easiest."

"Your wreath turned out great!" Deirdre said, reminding Jo that she had seen it at Jo's house before it was finished, when Jo had fixed her bracelet. "I don't want to change a thing, except maybe I'll hang a tag on mine saying, 'Handmade by Deirdre Patterson.' It'll impress everyone to pieces."

Ina Mae and Loralee agreed they liked Jo's prototype, and Jo launched into the step-by-step instructions, which included wrapping ribbon about the grapevine base, making a multilooped bow, and more. The women happily got to work. As Jo expected, Ina Mae was the one to bring up the subject of murder.

"Well, Jo," she asked, "what's new on the

investigation?"

Jo noticed that the group had become so comfortable with the topic that they barely glanced up from their projects. The interest, though, was clearly there, as the chatter quieted down for her answer. Jo told them about her meeting with Hank Schroder.

"Oooh, he sounds verrrry interesting," Loralee said, her eyes flashing.

"Agreed," Ina Mae put in.

"I'd want to kill Kyle myself if he played tricks like that on me," Javonne said, and the others nodded.

"Plus, Hank Schroder has a connection to poor Genna through his ex-wife," said Loralee. "And he pretty much admitted he hated the entire family!"

"Well," Jo said, "he didn't put it quite that strongly, more dislike than actual hatred."

"People always try to soften it when they can't help but blurt out their feelings. He may have said 'dislike,' but I'll guarantee he meant 'hate.'"

The door bell jingled as a customer came in, and the group clammed up. Since Carrie was off tonight, Jo left to take care of the woman, who, it turned out, simply needed additional yarn to finish a knitting project. Jo found her the matching lot color, rang it up, and was soon back with the workshop.

"I also spoke with Tracy," she said, reaching for her soda and taking a sip. "She's the girl who worked with Kyle at the tennis desk."

"Oh, yes, I remember," Ina Mae said. "What did you learn from her this time?"

"Something quite interesting. Genna, it turns out, shared an apartment with Bethanne Fowler, the tennis pro at the country club."

"Oh?" Ina Mae looked less than impressed.

"I guess you've never seen Bethanne Fowler, but there was a picture of her at the club. She and Genna look enough alike to be sisters — same height and coloring, similar hairstyle."

"Oh!"

"And," Jo continued, "it turns out that the dog Genna was walking that night was actually Bethanne's."

"Oh." Ina Mae's face turned very solemn.

"I don't get it. What does that mean?" Javonne asked.

"It means, dear," Ina Mae explained, "that if Genna was pushed down that cliff the poor girl might have been mistaken in the dark for her roommate Bethanne."

"But I thought we were focused on Pete, Genna's boyfriend," Deirdre protested.

"You told us how angry he could get, and how jealous — over Genna, not Bethanne."

"Pete has an alibi for the night Genna was killed," Ina Mae said.

"Except," Loralee jumped in, "I don't consider it an ironclad alibi. He's still a suspect in my book."

"An alibi?" Deirdre asked.

"Pete was working late, with another mechanic, that night," Jo said.

"Oh! But you don't believe it, Loralee?"

"No, I don't. Not for a minute. I think he may have slipped out. Or maybe this other mechanic is covering for him." Loralee jabbed the stems of the spring flowers into her wreath fiercely, making Jo wonder whose face she might be seeing in its center.

The ladies hashed over the points Jo had brought up — Hank Schroder's motive, Bethanne Fowler's dog, Pete Tober's alibi — while trimming their wreaths at the same time. Clear evidence of the separation of right-brain, left-brain activities, Jo thought, as their creativity carried on in the midst of all those gritty thoughts.

Her wreath finished, Ina Mae began to tidy up her area. "I have to leave early tonight," she explained. "I'm expecting a call from one of my daughters who's traveling in Japan, and I don't want to miss it."

245

There was a flurry of interest and questions about the trip, and Loralee, who had ridden with Ina Mae, gathered up her things as well. Javonne and Deirdre were still putting the final touches on their wreaths as the other two bid them all a good night and took off. Javonne, wiring her bow in place, got back to the murders.

"I find that very disturbing, what Ina Mae said about Genna being mistaken for Bethanne."

"Yes," Jo agreed. "I plan to talk to Bethanne about it as soon as I can. She hasn't been answering her phone, so I'll just drive over to her place."

"That poor girl," Deirdre said, shaking her head. "She's probably not answering her phone because she's devastated. Do you think you should bother her with this right now?"

"That's right," Javonne agreed. "After all, it's just a guess. Maybe she doesn't need to hear this on top of all she's dealing with right now."

Jo shook her head. "I hate to add to her distress, but I think it's important enough for her to be aware of as soon as possible."

Javonne nodded, then adjusted her final flower sprig and held up her wreath. "There! What do you think?"

Jo looked at the color scheme Javonne had chosen — white flowers and green ivy, topped with a green and white plaid ribbon that had a touch of red. "I think that will look spectacular on your red door. Did you remember to tuck in all the wire ends, so they won't scratch the paint?"

"Absolutely," Javonne said, grinning. "It took Harry long enough to finally paint the door, and I'm not about to mess it up in any way. But this," she held up her wreath proudly, "will be a crowning touch, after the Christmas wreath we made last time comes down, that is. Well," she said, glancing at the clock, "time to get on home."

"Yes, I'm done here too," Deirdre said.

Jo was commenting on Deirdre's creation when the door jingled for a late-arriving customer.

"Bye, ladies," Javonne called as she sailed past them.

Jo looked over and was startled to see Hank Schroder standing there, looking as uncomfortable as he glanced around at the flowers and yarns as if he had accidentally stepped into a ladies' lingerie shop. He wore the same green overalls she had seen him in before, with a few new additions of grass stains and streaks of dried mud.

"Mr. Schroder," she greeted him. "What a surprise."

Deirdre's head popped up at hearing the name.

"Uh, yeah. I came about that nephew of yours. The phone number he gave me was kinda scribbled, and I couldn't make it out right. Got a pizza place, instead. One of my crew dropped out today — he probably knew I was going to fire him soon, so he quit. Anyway, there's an opening for after school and Saturdays, so if the kid wants the job, tell him to get in touch with me. He struck me as pretty reliable."

"Yes, I think he is." Jo wasn't sure what to say next since Charlie didn't really want the job, so she simply said, "I'll pass the word on to him."

"Okay, good." Schroder caught sight of the soda cans still scattered on the workshop table. "Say, I just came from work, and I'm wrung out. Can I buy one of those from you while I'm here?" He reached into his pocket for change.

"Oh, please," Jo said, waving away his offer to pay, "help yourself to whatever you'd like in the cooler. They're complimentary."

"You're sure?"

"Absolutely."

Schroder pulled his hand from his pocket

248

and stomped over.

Deirdre whispered to Jo, "I'll hang around until he's gone," then, in a stage voice announced, "Well, I don't know what's taking my husband so long. He said he'd be here at 8:45 to pick me up. He should be here any minute, though. With his big brother, Jeb."

Jo winced, thinking Schroder, who was not a stupid man, would surely pick up on the purpose of that announcement. Why not add that the "brothers" would arrive packing hunting rifles, with spares in the trunk? Still, she couldn't complain. There was something about the man showing up out of the blue that made Jo uneasy.

Schroder, though, after shuffling around the cooler a bit, pulled out an icy Coke can, popped it open, and poured half of it down his throat. He wiped his mouth, muffled a burp, and looked around.

"Nice place you got here."

"Thank you."

The phone rang, and Jo reached for it. The caller, however, needed to speak with Carrie about a knitting problem, and Jo suggested she check back the next day.

"Well, you tell the kid to give me a call," Schroder said, moving toward the door. "Or to just come on over."

"I will." Then, feeling the need to give Charlie an out, added, "I'll tell him to get in touch with you either way." Schroder shot her a look, and she explained. "The twins came down with the chicken pox. I'm not exactly sure if Charlie's had it yet or not, so he might not be ready to work for a while."

"Well, I hope so for his sake. I need someone now. If he can't, I'll have to call someone else." He held up the near-empty soda can. "Thanks for the drink."

Jo nodded, and watched him leave the shop, feeling a mixture of guilt and relief as she did.

As the door closed behind him, Deirdre asked, puzzled, "Charlie? Is that Carrie's son?"

"Yes, but forget the part about the chicken pox and the twins. All figments of my imagination."

"Oh, I wondered. You certainly think fast on you feet, don't you? Here, let me help you clean up; then we can walk each other to our cars." Deirdre picked up her soda can and shook it lightly, and, finding it empty, tossed it in the trash. "You done with yours?"

Jo, her throat having gone dry after the last few minutes, was pleased to find hers still about a third full. She drank thirstily, then added it to the bag Deirdre was filling with other cans and trimming debris.

"Actually," Jo said, gathering up the protective paper from the table, "I have a little more to do before I close up here. But thanks. I don't think we have to worry about Mr. Schroder. I saw his pickup drive safely away."

"Scruffy-looking man," Deirdre said with a grimace. "Well, if you're sure you're all right, I'll get going then."

Jo walked Deirdre to the door and waited until she saw her wave from inside her car. Then she locked the door and cleared the cash register. She checked a few odds and ends in the stockroom, then turned out all the lights and headed to her car, carrying along the trash bag she and Deirdre had filled to toss in the Dumpster.

The streets of Abbotsville were at their usual quiet, post–9 P.M. state, which Jo often savored on the drive home, usually opting to listen to a little soft jazz on the radio. Tonight she felt keyed up, though, as she started her ignition. Was it from going over all those points of the murder with the group? Or from the unexpected appearance of Hank Schroder at the end of the night? In any event, she didn't feel like going straight home yet, and so she turned right instead of left at the corner.

Jo headed to Highpoint Road, thinking she would drive past the place Genna had fallen to her death. She wanted to see just how dark it was at this time of night. She and Charlie had been there during daylight, and she hadn't noticed how many streetlights there were or how close they were to the spot.

Jo stopped at a red light on the way, the lone car except for one other passing in the opposite direction. As she waited, her stomach gave a surprising painful twist, enough to make her wince. It eased, and when the light turned green, she pulled ahead.

She thought of Hank Schroder and his appearance at the shop, and it suddenly occurred to her to wonder how he had known where to find her. Jo didn't remember mentioning anything to him about her shop. She turned onto Highpoint, and, as she did, came up with a possible answer. He could have asked Bob Gordon, of course, or anyone of half a dozen people at the country club who knew she was setting up the craft show. It seemed, though, a lot of trouble to go to just to locate and hire another crew member. Had Charlie impressed him that much?

Jo's stomach suddenly became a caldron of pain. She groaned, and grabbed at it with one hand, while steering with the other. Her eyes blurred for a moment. A honk from behind startled her, and a glance into her rearview mirror showed a small refrigerated truck close behind her. She must have slowed down a lot, and here, near the Wildwood apartments, traffic had increased. The driver was obviously annoyed at being unable to pass her. She picked up speed, but at the first opportunity the truck pulled around her, zooming by. She was barely aware of it, though, since by this time she was struggling to keep from doubling over from extreme nausea.

A searing stab of pain suddenly shot through her abdomen, making her cry out, and her foot reflexively pressed down on the accelerator. At the same time, she was seeing double, and one of the lampposts she had gone to check on became two and then four as it or they loomed before her. Jo battled with the pain as well as the confusion, trying, in a few quick moments, to steer, but unsure where to point the car. Her brain told her to pull over and brake, but which way was "over," and where was the brake?

Her stomach interrupted her brain, signaling extreme distress. Then there was noise, shock, and pain as her rusty Toyota came to a sudden, crashing stop.

CHAPTER 22

There was a party going on somewhere, because Jo could hear it. People talking, glasses clinking. The squeaky wheels of a portable bar. Laughing. Crying? She really wished her neighborhood would quiet down. These houses were too close together. In the morning she'd look for a place off by itself. And those bright lights. Had she forgotten to close her draperies? She needed sleep. She felt so tired.

"Jo, Jo, are you awake?"

Someone was rubbing her hand. Jo opened one eye a bit and saw Carrie. Why was Carrie in her bedroom?

"What are you doing here?" she rasped. Her tongue felt swollen and her consonants came out mushy.

"One of the nurses — Bobbie Fraehling — lives down the street from me," Carrie explained. "They wanted to call your mom, but Bobbie had them call me."

"My mom? Why would they call my mom? And who's 'they'?"

"Hospitals always call the nearest relative. Except your mom's way down in Florida. They found her name in your wallet."

Jo was totally confused. Of course Mom was in Florida. She'd been there since Dad died nine years ago. Both eyes open now, Jo glanced around. All she saw were white walls. No, they were white curtains. This wasn't her bedroom, was it?

"Where am I? What happened?"

"Don't you know?"

Carrie's eyes looked worried. Jo shook her head, then winced at the sudden pain.

"You drove your car into a tree over on Highpoint. Don't you remember? What were you doing on Highpoint?"

Jo thought hard. "I felt sick."

"Yes, they said you had thrown up. Were you trying to get yourself to the hospital?"

"No, I don't think so." It was such an effort to remember. "I think I went there to see where Genna had fallen."

Carrie nodded. "But what made you crash?"

"I remember a truck." Things were starting to come back. "He wanted to pass me. But I felt so sick." She glanced at Carrie. "I threw up?"

"Uh-huh. They found you hanging half out of the car. You must have got the door open, but your seat belt held you in."

Jo winced. "How bad is my car?"

"Why don't you ask how bad you are?" Carrie asked, with exasperation, as though Jo were a child who had just done a very foolish and frightening thing. *Don't ever do that to me again,* she seemed ready to scold.

"Okay," Jo said contritely, "how bad am I?"

"Nothing's broken, thank God. They had to put a few stitches in your scalp."

Jo touched her head. So that was why it hurt so.

"And your hair might look a little odd for a while til it grows out. Some bumps and bruises, but nothing too terrible. You were lucky."

"Yes. Apparently. Now, my car?"

"It's . . . fixable."

Jo groaned.

"Don't worry. Nothing too major. They have to straighten something around the wheel that hit the tree, pound out some dents. You should have it back in a couple days at most."

"How much will that cost?"

"I don't know, Jo. But don't worry about that. You need to rest up right now."

257

"Right. Where are my clothes? Can you take me home?"

"No, you have to rest *here*," Carrie said, spelling it out, "in the hospital. Jo, you blacked out, remember? That's serious. They want to keep you for observation."

"And how much will their observations cost me? Carrie, I don't have health insurance, remember? I couldn't afford it. So I can't afford *this* either."

"Jo, be sensible. If you go home too soon and have complications, you could run up an even higher bill. Not to mention what it might do to your health."

As if to block any thoughts of flight, a white-coated technician snapped open the curtain and stood there, holding a tray of sinister-looking needles and tubes.

"Ms. McAllister? I need some of your blood."

Jo grimaced. "It'll be on sale tomorrow if you can wait. Twenty percent off."

The woman gave a polite laugh, probably having heard similar jokes hundreds of times, as well as such accusations as "vampire" and "leech," which occurred to Jo but never reached her lips. Carrie stepped out as Jo presented her arm to be bound, swabbed, and pierced. By the time the

Band-Aid was applied, Jo realized that she really *wasn't* feeling well enough to go home and would appreciate a few hours of recovery time there under professional eyes. So when an orderly came to wheel her from the emergency area to a room, she offered no protest, only waving wanly to Carrie as well as ordering her as firmly as she could manage to return home to her family.

"I'll be back in the morning," Carrie promised, leaving Jo to watch a succession of acoustical ceiling tiles roll by on her way to her destination. By the time she reached her room, her eyes had grown too heavy to check it out, so she simply stated that it would do. She sank into oblivion on the cheerful parting words of the nurse: "Press this call button when you need the bedpan."

Carrie arrived early, shortly after Jo's food tray had been delivered.

"Well, aren't we royalty now," she declared. "Breakfast in bed!"

"And a princely one it is too," Jo said after swallowing a spoonful of her watery Cream of Wheat. "The coffee is almost warm. At least I think it's coffee."

"You're looking better — a little more color. How do you feel?"

"Good. Well, reasonably good, considering. I understand the reason for the stitches and bruises, but I've been trying to figure out what was going on with my stomach last night."

"You mean why you threw up?"

"Yes. I really felt awful, Carrie. I realize now that was the whole reason I crashed into the pole. But what brought it on? I mean, it felt like the worst flu I've ever had, or the worst food poisoning."

"Have you seen the doctor this morning? Did he say anything about it?"

"The doc who treated me last night stopped by earlier and checked my eyes and ears for possible concussion. I guess I'm okay on that point since he said I'm free to go. He couldn't say what brought on my stomach attack. Apparently, whatever was in my stomach didn't make it with me to the hospital. He seemed to shrug it off, since I don't have any symptoms left."

"There's such a thing as a twenty-four-hour flu. Maybe that's what you had, though I haven't heard of it going around lately. What did you have for dinner last night?"

"Nothing special. I brought in leftovers from a chicken stir-fry I made the other night. It didn't make me sick the first time I ate it."

"Was it in the fridge at the store until you ate it?"

"Yes, right up until the time I heated it up in the microwave, which was shortly before the workshop ladies arrived."

"Hmmm."

"There's one thing, though." Jo told Carrie about Hank Schroder stopping in just before closing time.

"That's weird. Couldn't he have just called and asked for Charlie's number?"

"You'd think so. Maybe he got tired of getting wrong numbers. I gave Charlie an out, by the way, for not taking the job. He's coming down with the chicken pox — caught from your twins."

"My what?"

"It's a long story. Anyway, Schroder went over to the cooler to get himself a soda — at my invitation. But my open can was still sitting there, and I got distracted by the phone."

"You think he might have dropped something into it? An insecticide, perhaps, from his landscaping work?"

Jo shrugged. "All I know is he was in the shop. If there's a connection, it's flimsy, but it's the only possibility I can come up with so far."

"But what would Hank gain from that?"

"That's what I can't figure out. Maybe he caught on that I was trying to connect him to Kyle's murder, and Genna's too."

"Maybe he thinks you know more than you do. Jo, I think you should go to the police with this."

"With what, Carrie? I don't have anything concrete. No way am I going to face Lieutenant Morgan with a story like this."

"Jo!"

"No, absolutely not. He'll only twist it around somehow to make me look like the guilty one." Jo pushed away the tray with her half-finished breakfast. "How about helping me check out of here so I can get back to work? The store opens up in less than two hours."

"You're not working today. I'm taking you to our place. You can have Amanda's room for a couple days, to rest up. I'll handle the store."

Jo laughed, having half-expected such a plan from her friend.

"Will you bring me breakfast in bed?" she asked, easing herself to a standing position. "And lunch and dinner too? I like a fresh rose on my tray, if you please, oh, and a linen napkin."

"I'm serious, Jo. You can't stay home alone. You've been in a car accident."

Jo located the bag containing her clothes and headed to the bathroom, clutching at the back of her gown. "I won't be at my place alone. I'll be at the store. I just need a shower and change of clothes."

"Jo!"

Jo pulled the door closed behind her to end the discussion, then winced as she caught sight of her reflection in the bathroom mirror: dark circles under her eyes, puffy eyelids, and a large chunk of hair cut away around a bandaged area where her stitches had been put in. Not exactly the look needed to greet those few customers still brave enough to set foot in her shop. Maybe Carrie was right — maybe she shouldn't go straight home.

"Carrie," she called, "let's stop at the drugstore on the way, okay? I'm going to need a few things."

CHAPTER 23

Jo dabbed her new cover-stick makeup around her eyes. It wasn't helping much to conceal the deep blue. For that matter, household putty might have trouble. The ice pack before her shower, though, had taken the swelling down some. Her hair was something else. She had been warned against a full shampoo because of the stitches, but even a shampoo and blow-dry wouldn't do much to disguise the lopsidedness of the cut. Emergency room doctors were no hair stylists.

She rifled through her scarf drawer and pulled out a brightly colored silk square salvaged from her New York days. A few folds and a couple of experimental drapes and ties about her head later, and she nodded. That would do for now. Too bad she couldn't run the shop wearing dark glasses, or a Halloween mask, though some might say that's what she was starting with.

"I made coffee," Carrie called from the kitchen. "Ready for it yet?"

"Let's take it along," Jo answered, leaning out the bedroom door. "There are two thermal mugs with lids in the left-side cabinet." She threw her makeup into her purse, along with the prescription pain pills they had given her at the hospital, and took a final check in the mirror before stepping out.

"How do I look? Scary?"

"You look fine. Good, actually. That scarf is beautiful. How about something to eat, though, to supplement the hospital gruel?"

"No time. I want to stop at the garage on the way, if you don't mind, and check on my car."

"I don't mind, if you really want to see it, but you could also just call from the store and get an update. Which reminds me, have you called your mom?"

"Mom?" Jo stared blankly. "Why?"

"To tell her about your accident, of course." Carrie set down the coffee carafe she had been emptying into the large mugs. "Jo, does she even know about all you've been going through lately? When's the last time you talked to her?"

"We've talked," Jo said defensively. "Carrie, Mom doesn't like hearing bad news, you know that. She likes to pretend every-thing is fine and wonderful, with herself and with everyone she knows. When she asks me, 'How are you?' it really is just a pleas-antry with her, like she's passing you on the street and is just saying 'hello.' She doesn't want to hear anything other than, 'Fine, and how are you?' "

"But she did hear about Mike's accident, didn't she? And she didn't dissolve into a puddle over it."

"No, I had to tell her that, of course, but I hated it. I could hear in her voice, even though she said all the right things, that she really thought it was most inconsiderate of Mike to go and get himself blown up and therefore cause her upset. She did invite me down to Florida, you remember, when I didn't know what to do next. But I knew if I went that I would never be able to say Mike's name aloud again for fear of getting that *look* that said, 'We don't talk about such things, dear.' "

"I think you're being too hard on her, Jo. Did you ever think maybe it's you that's trying to protect her?"

Jo shook her head. "Even growing up, it was always Dad I went to when I had a problem to work out. Mom was the one who wanted me always to smile, and look pretty, and be perfect."

"Well, she *was* in a dreamworld, then, wasn't she?" Carrie said, grinning.

"You got that right." Jo laughed. Her smile faded though, as she thought of her father. Had he died so early because of having to bear the stresses for two? Well, she shrugged, enough of that. She grabbed her mug and waved Carrie toward the door. "Time to work on the problems in the real world."

They stopped at Hanson's Garage. Pete Tober, not surprisingly, was not around, and Jo got the rundown on her car's needed repairs from Earl Hanson himself. It was pretty much as Carrie had said — damage around the right front wheel, along with plenty of scrapes and scratches.

"You were lucky that tree was rotted inside," Hanson said. "It gave way when you hit it. A healthy tree would have stopped you like a brick wall."

Jo thought of her stitches and aching bruises. At least she could feel them. What kind of shape would she be in if she'd hit a solid tree?

They discussed how soon Jo could get her car back — Hanson said at least another day of work was needed — and the cost. Jo did have insurance, but, of course, with a high deductible. Getting her aging, but only means of transportation in shape would set her back five hundred, and this on top of her hospital bills.

She rolled her eyes and joked to Carrie, "Maybe I should call Mom after all," then dismissed the idea as quickly as she'd said it. She'd come up with the money — somehow.

Jo gave Hanson the go-ahead on the necessary repairs, then got back into Carrie's car. As they drove to the shop, she asked Carrie about Charlie. "How are things between him and Dan?"

"Cool," Carrie said. "And I don't mean cool as Charlie would use the word. I mean chilly."

"Ouch."

"At least Charlie's keeping busy enough helping you out to not dwell on it too much. But I know he thinks Dan used Genna's death as an excuse to pull him away from the playhouse. And I don't say so, but I think Charlie's right."

"Has Charlie ever talked to Dan about what interests him so about the playhouse? How he was fascinated by the soundboard and such?"

"I don't think so. When he was still going there, I'm sure he sensed Dan's feelings about it and avoided bringing up the subject around him. Now he seems convinced anything he says to Dan will be treated as idiocy. Meanwhile, Dan sees Charlie's silence as rebellion. And I'm walking on eggs playing mediator, and not having much success."

"Give it a little time."

"Yes, maybe they'll both cool down. Or warm up. I don't know which is needed, really."

Carrie pulled into the Craft Corner's parking lot with five minutes to spare before opening time. Jo took a bracing gulp of coffee from her mug and climbed out, holding on to and adjusting her headscarf as she did. She didn't fool herself. No one was going to figure she was setting a new style trend for Abbotsville. But until her scalp could handle things like shampoo and trimming scissors, she was stuck. At least the blue in the scarf's print coordinated with the dark blue under her eyes.

Carrie handled the first few customers of the morning, while Jo stayed at the back, grateful to sit down and concentrate on paperwork. But when Ina Mae and Loralee walked in, she came forward to greet them.

"Ooh, you poor, dear thing," Loralee cried, reaching out to give her a gentle hug.

"We heard about the accident," Ina Mae said. "Tried to call you at home, and when you didn't answer, figured you must be back at work. Is that wise?"

"I'm fine, despite appearances to the contrary," Jo assured them. "Just moving a little more slowly for the time being."

"What happened, exactly?" Ina Mae asked. "You doze off? Or did a deer dart in front of you? The deer are all over the place this time of year."

"I'm not too clear on what really happened. Shortly after I closed up here, I started feeling very sick, and the next thing I knew a tree had jumped in front of me."

"Oh, my!" Loralee exclaimed, her hands to her face.

"Tell them about Hank Schroder," Carrie said.

Jo did, and Loralee's eyes grew bigger as Ina Mae's expression turned grimmer. "I'm not accusing Schroder of anything," Jo hastened to explain. "It's just that two very odd things occurred last night, one right before the other. Whether his appearance at the store has a connection to my sickness, I really can't say."

"Do you still have your soda can?" Ina Mae asked.

Jo gave her a grim smile. "I thought of

that too. Unfortunately, no. It was tossed in the trash, and the Dumpster was emptied early this morning."

"Too bad. I don't suppose they checked for anything poisonous in you at the hospital?"

Jo shook her head. "I was treated for my cuts and bruises. By the time I was conscious enough to have suspicions it was much too late. Anything that might have been affecting me was long gone."

"But you did have suspicions," Ina Mae said, giving her an eagle-eyed look.

Jo nodded. As careful as she'd been to say there was little to connect Hank Schroder with what had happened to her last night, she couldn't get past the fact that there he had been, in her store on a fairly flimsy excuse, the man who had plenty of reason to hate Kyle Sandborn, who had at least some connection to Genna, and now to her. Had Hank Schroder, in fact, tried to kill her?

The phone rang. Carrie answered it, and held it out to Jo. "It's Deirdre Patterson."

"Jo-oooh!" Jo heard Deirdre's wail as she took the phone. "I just heard!" Deirdre exclaimed, causing Jo to wonder how the *Abbotsville Gazette* managed to survive. By the time that local newspaper hit the stands, its stories were ancient history. Abbotsville's word-of-mouth was speedier than any printing press.

"I'm so sorry I didn't stay longer," Deirdre said.

"It wouldn't have made any difference, Deirdre, believe me." As Jo continued to try to placate Deirdre, she saw Javonne walk in the door, her eyes wide with concern, carrying a casserole dish. She set it on the counter and, seeing Jo on the phone, began jabbering excitedly with Ina Mae, Loralee, and Carrie. Jo covered one ear so she could hear Deirdre.

A moment later Mindy burst in, towing her twins behind her. The noise level escalated, all five ladies seeming to talk at once, when one of the twins began to wail, which immediately set off the other. Jo hastily ended her conversation with Deirdre and hung up the phone, leaving both ears open to take in the bedlam. Her head pounded, and it was too soon for another pain pill. Jo looked beseechingly at Carrie.

"Hold it, everyone!" Carrie called, grabbing a pair of scissors and rapping the handle sharply on a metal paint can. Everyone looked up with surprise, even the wailing toddlers, and Loralee quickly pulled two lollipops from her tote and put them into their little hands. This made Jo laugh as she wondered if she would see Loralee one day pull out a defibrillator from that ever-present tote of hers for a sudden cardiac emergency.

"I know Jo appreciates everyone's concern," Carrie said, "but we need to remember she's still recuperating. I happen to think," she added, throwing Jo a scolding look, "that she shouldn't be here at all, but back in bed. However, since she's chosen to ignore my advice, let's try to make it as calm and comfortable for her as we can."

"Absolutely," Javonne agreed. "Jo, honey, I brought you a ham and noodle casserole, so you won't have to cook for a couple of nights. It's Harry's favorite. You can give me the dish back whenever." She gave Jo a hug and dashed off.

Mindy apologized for her toddlers' part in the chaos. "I didn't expect everyone else to be here. The twins get upset around too many strangers." She thanked Loralee for the treats, which kept their little mouths busy — the term "plugged" occurred to Jo. Mindy chatted a bit longer, then, when she saw the lollipops dwindling down to the stick, said a hasty good-bye and took off.

"Jo, we'll be going too," Ina Mae said. "But before we do, is there some way we can help with this murder business? I don't want to see you get hurt anymore, whatever the cause. Plus, as Carrie says, you should be resting."

"I really don't know what you could do, Ina Mae, other than to keep your eyes and ears open for me. Information seems to float through the air in this town. Perhaps you can catch something helpful in the breeze."

"What about this landscape person, Schroder?" Loralee asked. "We could keep an eye on him for you."

"Do you two play golf?" Carrie asked hopefully.

"Well, no."

"I doubt he'd let your power walkers tramp around the course, Ina Mae," Jo said, "so let's just let him be for the time being. But thank you, both of you, for your offer, and for coming by." A few more careful hugs, and they were off. Once the door closed behind them, Jo turned to Carrie.

"My plan is to try to connect with Bethanne Fowler, as soon as I get my car back. But I don't want company for that. I think that particular conversation will work best one-on-one."

"Jo, I'm worried for you. I think you should leave this to the police."

"Carrie, you know I can't. I realize you're

concerned because of what happened last night. But the remedy is not to do nothing. Battered though I may be, I'm sure I must be getting closer to the truth. The best way to end all this is to push forward. The police aren't going forward, in my opinion; they're going in circles — or, rather, one great big circle with me in the center. If I don't want to get stuck there, I have to keep moving, not simply wait for the noose to tighten around me."

Jo straightened a display of wreaths that had been knocked off kilter. "And don't worry. I'm on my guard now, much more than I was before."

Carrie looked at her, worry written all over her face. "But remember, Jo, so is the murderer. He doesn't want to be caught, and he has that great big advantage."

Jo waited, knowing pretty much what was coming since she'd thought it herself, several times.

"The murderer, Jo, knows who *you* are."

That evening, Jo had just put Javonne's ham and noodle casserole in the oven to warm when the phone rang. It was Deirdre.

"Jo, I didn't want to go into this when I called you at the store because I could hear all the pandemonium going on. There's something I need to tell you."

Jo heard the seriousness in Deirdre's voice.

"Alden got this from someone he knows in the police department. He didn't say who, and I didn't ask, and I'd rather you didn't mention where you heard this either. Jo, Morgan recently got an anonymous letter."

"Oh?" Jo didn't like the sound of this.

"It accused you of having arranged the explosion that killed your husband up in New York."

Jo sank down into a nearby chair.

"Anonymous?"

"Yes."

"Well, then he certainly can't put any credibility into it, can he?"

"I don't know about that. You said he already had been looking into the accident enough to question it, so there's obviously interest in that direction already. I just thought you should know that things may heat up for you. Maybe you need to prepare yourself — gather whatever reports you have on the explosion and soon. Perhaps talk to your lawyer."

Jo laughed. Right, bring Earnest C. Ainsworthy in on this. That would help.

"This is ridiculous," she said aloud. "Who could have sent such a thing?"

"I don't know, and I agree, it is ridiculous. But there it is. I thought it was better for you to be forewarned."

"Yes. Thank you, Deirdre."

"I'd better go. Alden doesn't know I'm calling, and he's probably regretting he let it slip out. I half-promised him I wouldn't say anything, but sometimes loyalty to one's friends has to take precedence over other concerns."

Jo hung up, her thoughts spinning, wondering who hated her enough to have written that letter. Niles Sandborn? Would his grudge against her push him to such lengths? Jo couldn't see him exerting himself to that extent, but it was possible.

Deirdre never said where the letter had come from, and Jo hadn't asked. She wished she had. Surely it had to have come from New York, though, didn't it?

Or was it from someone here in Abbotsville?

Jo stared into space until the aroma of Javonne's casserole heating in the oven reminded her it was suppertime.

Too bad she didn't feel hungry.

CHAPTER 24

Jo had her car back, having picked it up from Hanson's, and was pleased with this return to some normalcy and independence. However, the price of that return — her check covering the large deductible — put her in a deep financial hole, which would deepen even further when the hospital bill arrived. She knew it would take a frightening amount of time to climb out of debt.

Much of the pleasure she expected to feel at being back behind the wheel was tempered by Deirdre's call the night before. She'd tried to put it aside for the time being, but this morning it continued to weigh heavily on her mind. In addition, she was surprised to discover that driving was making her feel shaky; a post-traumatic reaction, she figured. It would be awhile, she feared, before she would again travel on autopilot, her fingers relaxed on the wheel as she listened to her radio, rather than in her present state: steering with a white-knuckle grip and hearing every knock and chug of this rolling metal box.

But at least she could now travel solo, which was a bonus, and the first place she was going was to Bethanne Fowler's apartment for a one-on-one talk. Jo had reached Bethanne by phone and arranged the meeting, explaining that it was to talk about Genna. Bethanne had agreed, probably assuming it to be a condolence call for the loss of her good friend.

Jo approached the Wildwood apartments by the same route she had driven the night of her accident. She saw the remains of the tree she had hit, broken and partially cleared away; the sight produced a shiver and a flash of nausea as the memories flooded back. Jo blinked hard and took a deep breath before driving on and turning into the Wildwood's parking lot.

She followed the numbers to the correct building, parked, and climbed out. She took a few more deep breaths to gain full composure, then adjusted the red baseball cap that had replaced her scarf and headed for the door. She was conscious of the bruises that were still highly visible through her makeup. It wasn't her favorite look for making new acquaintances, but it would have to do.

Jo checked the row of apartment buzzers and pressed the one for 304. It buzzed back in a moment, and she pulled open the outer door and began her two-flight climb. About halfway up the first flight she heard the sound of a door closing up above. Footsteps tramped downward toward her. On the first landing a well-dressed, fortysomething-year-old man swept by her without comment. He seemed familiar, but Jo couldn't think why. Was he someone she had encountered around town? Possibly.

She continued her climb and soon found apartment 304. A couple of taps with the metal knocker brought a "just a minute" response, and Jo waited, hearing noises inside and picturing Bethanne doing some last minute cleaning.

The door opened, and the woman whose photo Jo had seen on the tennis shop wall stood before her, wearing a white V-neck sweater and dark pants. Her coloring and features resembled Genna's. But, whereas Genna had projected an air of sensitivity and naiveté, Bethanne's expression was harder and more assertive, though the touch of redness about the eyes hinted at the struggle of the last few days.

"Jo McAllister?" she asked.

"Yes. Thank you, Bethanne, for giving me

some of your time."

"No problem." Bethanne stepped back to let Jo in. "I haven't been going to work for the last few days. It's been, well, it's been tough."

"I'm sure it has, and I'm so sorry. From what I understand, you and Genna were friends since childhood."

"Kindergarten." Bethanne led the way to the living room. "Nearly eighteen years. We were like sisters. Each of us was an only child, so we latched on to each other right away."

"You could almost *be* sisters. I saw the resemblance immediately."

Bethanne laughed slightly. "Everyone said that." She fingered the turquoise pendant that hung from a silver chain around her neck. "But that was the only similarity. Inside we were like night and day. But maybe that's why we got along so well. We never competed for the same things."

"No, I guess not, since you're into tennis and she loved the theater. That's how I got to know Genna, by the way, through the Abbotsville Playhouse."

"Oh, I see. Would you like some coffee? I have a pot made."

"That would be great. Black is fine."

Bethanne left to get the coffee, and Jo sank

down on the beige tweed sofa. As she listened to the soft clatter coming from the kitchen, she looked around the pleasant but impersonal room. It held a new-looking sofa and chairs, end tables, and lamps, all coordinated and looking as though they had been scooped up in one swoop from a furniture-store display — and not a very high-end one at that. She figured this would be the usual process for two young, single women who likely considered their life here a stopgap of sorts and who had probably chipped in together on the purchase.

Where were all their personal items, though, such as photos or mementos? In their own bedrooms? Jo hoped so, since this room offered little to identify its occupants. There were no bookcases or scattered magazines. Even the pictures on the wall seemed to have been selected for their colors and size rather than the art. Then Jo spotted a sole book on the end table, lying slightly beyond the lamp, and reached over to pick it up. A book of poetry, titled *100 Love Sonnets* by the Chilean poet Pablo Neruda, translated from Spanish. She flipped it open and read a few of the lyrical, sensual lines. Was this Genna's? Perhaps a gift from Pete? If so, there was a whole other side of Pete she hadn't seen.

Jo heard a soft yip come from another part of the apartment and remembered Bethanne's dog. She returned the book to where she'd found it as Bethanne came out of the kitchen carrying a small tray, which she then set down on the uncluttered coffee table.

"So," Bethanne said, holding out a mug, "you acted at the playhouse too?"

"No, I was doing jewelry and set design for the production." Jo took a sip of the coffee. It was strong — just as she liked it. "I own the new craft shop on Main Street. The place where Kyle Sandborn died."

Bethanne froze in the middle of stirring sugar into her coffee, but only briefly, and a split second later she tapped her spoon on the edge of the mug and carefully set it down.

"I heard about your shop. Wasn't Kyle, uh, that is, didn't it happen during your grand opening?"

Jo nodded.

"Well," Bethanne took a sip from her mug, "you seem to have become closely associated with Abbotsville's two recent deaths. How very unfortunate."

"I agree. However, it's beginning to seem like nearly everyone in this town is connected to those two people, in one way or another."

Bethanne nodded. "Quite possibly. And they were connected to each other, obviously, through the playhouse. Although Kyle's death, of course, was murder."

"Yes, it was. But I'm not so sure Genna's wasn't."

"What are you saying?"

"I'm saying that I don't see any good reason why Genna would have fallen accidentally. And knowing her, although briefly, I can't believe she jumped to her own death, after first carefully tying the dog — your dog — to a tree."

At the mention of her dog, Bethanne's lip began to tremble.

"If I hadn't called and asked her to walk him . . ." Bethanne stood up and walked to the balcony window, her back to Jo. "I stayed late at the club. Jane Watson was asking my advice about a new tennis racquet. Then she wanted to try the demo. I agreed to hit a few balls with her. If I had just come home . . ."

"If you had taken your dog out yourself, *you* might be dead."

Bethanne spun around. "What do you mean? That someone killed Genna thinking it was me?"

"I think that's very possible, possible enough for me to warn you."

"But why? Why would anyone want to kill me?"

"That's what I hoped you could tell me."

Jo watched Bethanne's face as a series of emotions flew across it — disbelief, anger, then fear. "I don't know! I can't imagine."

"Bethanne, so far the only person I can connect with both you and Kyle is Hank Schroder. Hank had good reason to have murderous feelings toward Kyle. Did he have any problems with you?"

"Hank? No, nothing. He was responsible for keeping the tennis courts clean, and once in a while his crew did a lousy job and I had to get after him about it. But I don't see that he'd want to kill me for that. That's crazy."

"Nothing else? Anything more personal?"

"Personal? With Hank?" Bethanne's lip curled at the thought. "We had very little to do with each other. Unless he had some kind of perverted fantasies about me, there was nothing between us other than what I've told you."

"Fantasies? Did you ever get any uneasy feelings in that direction?"

"No," Bethanne waved a hand dismissively. "Just making a sick joke. Women in short tennis skirts sometimes draw unwanted attention." She sat down across from Jo. "Hank Schroder never struck me as a person who spared a thought for anything beyond his work."

"Could he have felt you jeopardized his job by making complaints?"

"I doubt that. Everyone knew running that crew of high school kids was a major hassle. I never went to Bob Gordon about it, always directly to Hank. I doubt he took it personally. Look," she said, "I really don't think someone was after me. Or poor Genna either. It had to be an accident. Maybe she was reaching for something on the edge. She could have tied up Mojo before doing that, to keep him back."

"Maybe. What about Genna's boyfriend, Pete? Could he have been with her? I know there were some problems between them, and he has an explosive temper. Perhaps an argument between them turned violent?"

"Pete?" Bethanne frowned. "I know what you're saying. Pete really has anger issues. But I've seen him lately, and he's devastated over this. There's no way he could have caused Genna's death. Really. No way."

Jo nodded. "I tend to agree with you on that. But I still think there's a strong possibility Genna may have been mistaken for you. Even if I can't figure out yet by whom, I think you should be very careful."

The yip Jo had heard earlier from the back of the apartment escalated to frantic barking. Bethanne got up. "Mojo doesn't like to be closed up too long." She walked down the hall and opened a bedroom door, releasing a small dog that reminded Jo of the toy poodle her Great-aunt Martha had owned, years ago. The dog scampered excitedly to the living room, sniffing first at Jo's feet, then bouncing on and off the sofa, trying to get on her lap or lick her face. Jo fended him off, laughing.

"Mojo!" Bethanne scolded, scooping him up into her arms and holding him tightly. "Sorry, he gets excited with visitors. That's why I try to keep him away."

"That's quite all right. Oh, your necklace!" The little dog had wiggled about and nipped at Bethanne's turquoise pendant.

"Stop that, Mojo." Bethanne pushed the dog's muzzle away and set him on the floor.

"That's a lovely piece," Jo said. "I noticed it right away. Isn't it a Roberta Sawyer? The New Mexican designer?"

Bethanne looked down at her pendant, rubbing it clean, and smiled. "I'm not sure. It was a gift. All I know is it's very beautiful. And unique."

And expensive, Jo added, mentally. She knew the jewelry designer by reputation and had long admired her work for its simplicity and subtle Southwestern touches.

"Well," Bethanne said, "I'm afraid Mojo is telling me he needs to go out." The dog had started running back and forth to the door, barking excitedly. Jo got up as Bethanne reached for the leash hanging near by.

"I don't know what I'll do about him once I go back to work," Bethanne said. "When it was Genna and me here, he was never alone for very long because of our alternate schedules." At mentioning her lost friend, Bethanne's eyes glistened, and she crouched down to the little dog and clicked on his leash.

"Poor thing," she said, hugging him. "He misses her, I know, almost as much as I do. I've found him wandering around her room as though he's still expecting to find her there." She looked up at Jo. "Genna was the one who came up with his name. Mojo. Funny thing, though. Part of the reason we both liked it was because it means 'good luck charm.' "

She looked somberly at Mojo, and ruffled his fur.

"Isn't that a crock?"

CHAPTER 25

Jo followed as Mojo led Bethanne out of the building. They parted ways in the parking lot with Bethanne promising to heed Jo's warning and be cautious. Jo hoped she meant it, though she wasn't sure she had convinced Bethanne that she might be in danger.

As she climbed in her car to head back to the shop, Jo remembered that Carrie planned to take off at one o'clock to run errands. If she wanted lunch, she'd better pick it up before going back. She drove to the Abbott's Kitchen, a couple of blocks down Main from the shop, where she often got carryout. Carrie had often joked that Bert and Ruthie Conway had been running the lunch shop since colonial days, and the aged and dusty brick building made the joke seem likely. Inside, though, all was spic-and-span, and Bert's sandwiches, in Jo's opinion, were to die for. Her mouth watered at the thought of her favorite turkey-bacon roll-up, dripping with Bert's special sauce.

As she walked through the door, Rafe Rulenski was just settling down at a small table, having picked up his lunch order at Ruthie's counter. He looked up and immediately pulled out the chair next to his.

"What a pleasant surprise. Won't you join me, Mrs. McAllister?"

Jo hesitated. She had planned on carry-out. But spending a few moments getting to know Rafe Rulenski a bit better was tempting. "That would be nice," she said, smiling. "But I'll have to be quick." She gave her order to Ruthie, who nodded and winked one aged eye, obviously recognizing what had become a regular choice for Jo, then called it back to her husband.

"Want coffee with that?" Ruthie asked.

Jo decided she'd had her fill of caffeine for a while, and chose bottled water instead. She paid, then carried her water to Rafe's table.

"If we're going to dine together, you'll really have to start calling me Jo," she said.

"Deal."

Rafe still had his day's growth of beard, and he wore a denim jacket over his usual dark T-shirt. Something seemed different about him, though, and it took Jo a moment to realize it was his manner, which was missing the fire she had seen at the theater.

"What's happening with the show?" she asked.

Rafe groaned. "Nothing. Nothing at all, that's what's happening. The death of two of your stars tends to do that to a production."

"I can imagine the troupe is pretty upset."

Rafe nodded. "Of course. It's all quite tragic, but we can't let this mean the death of the Abbotsville Playhouse as well."

"It could be that serious?"

"We were living on borrowed time as it was. If we can't pull things back together . . ." Rafe took an enormous bite of his sandwich and chewed glumly.

Ruthie called out that Jo's turkey-and-bacon was ready, and Jo hopped up to get it. As she settled back at the table, Rafe asked, "What's with the new look?" indicating Jo's baseball cap and bruises.

"My car and I had a little battle with a tree the other night. The tree won."

Rafe grunted. "Bummer."

"I've been having a few other problems of my own since Kyle's murder. The police have been squinting at me with suspicious eyes because he was killed in the back room of my shop."

"Oh yeah! I'd forgotten about that. So that was *your* shop?"

"Uh-huh. Plus I was the one who found him, and the knitting needle that killed him very likely came from my stock."

Rafe stared at her intently, but Jo wasn't sure if it was from concern for her or if he might in fact be planning his next play: *The Little Craft Shop of Horrors.* Would he have her character sing a little ditty? she wondered. Perhaps tap dance her way into the storeroom? What would she be declared at the end — guilty or innocent?

"Surely," he said, "that's not enough to incriminate you, is it? I mean, *somebody* has to find the body. And if he was killed in your shop, who more likely than you? Nor should it come as a huge surprise that he was killed with something from your store, especially if it wasn't premeditated."

"That was my point, exactly. Unfortunately, my strongest defense was that I'd never seen Kyle before he showed up for the clown gig. That was recently blown away by his Uncle Niles, who claims I met Kyle several times up in New York when I placed my jewelry at Niles's shop. However, I have no memory, whatsoever, of those meetings." Jo took a bite of her roll-up.

"Ah, Uncle Niles," Rafe said. "I remember him from the memorial service. He struck me as an oily character."

Jo dabbed a paper napkin at her mouth as Bert's special sauce threatened to dribble down her chin. "That's how I'd describe him too. We had some problems, business-wise, in the past. He may be deliberately trying to hurt me because of that."

Rafe took a few swallows from his Coke can. "I'll be going up to New York tomorrow. I've got an opportunity to pick up a few bucks doing a commercial voice-over. How about I check on Uncle Niles with a few people I know in that area? Maybe I could even stop in and talk to him myself. He wasn't grieving too much to give me his business card during the service."

"You'd go to that trouble?"

"Sure, why not?"

"It's just, well, I mean, that would be great if you could. I'd really appreciate it."

Rafe smiled. "Don't expect too much. But I'll see what I can dig up."

Jo smiled back. "I'm really sorry about the playhouse. I hope you can pull it back together."

"We'll see. Maybe I can put the squeeze on a few major contributors."

"Yes, I've heard there have been things in

the past like the Thespian Ball to raise money."

"Right. All the crème de la crème of Abbotsville show up to eat caviar and show off their new gowns for the cause."

"But it *does* raise money, doesn't it?"

"Oh, yes."

"Why do I get the feeling you'd rather have a root canal than suffer through those balls?"

Rafe rubbed at his face. "I'd skip the *anesthesia* to not have to go to one of them. They're excruciating."

"They can't be that bad, can they? After all, everyone there is interested, to some extent, in the theater, so you get to talk about your favorite subject, don't you?"

"They're interested, all right. And each one wants to tell you how you should do it. Or has a relative who's written an "absolutely wonderful" play about Millard Fillmore's early life they want you to look at. Our beloved state senator tried to impress upon me the importance of our plays having a message — like, say, battling roadside litter or wearing bike helmets."

Jo grinned. "Surely not that bad."

"Nearly."

"What is Alden Patterson like?" Jo asked. "I've only met his wife."

Rafe shrugged. "Typical politician, I guess. Bright enough, ambitious, hopeful of living off the taxpayers as our governor, someday. Has all the necessary requirements, including the beautiful, adoring wife."

Jo thought about the scrapbook Deirdre had chosen to make highlighting Alden's career. That certainly fit in with Rafe's impression.

Jo heard a tapping noise and looked to the front window. There stood Loralee waving happily, her ever-present outsized tote on her arm. "Hi, Jo," she called, her voice muffled by the glass. "See you tonight?"

Jo waved back, nodding.

"There's another one of my Thespian Ball terrors," Rafe said, watching Loralee move on.

"That sweet lady? Why?"

"Exactly because of that sweetness. She oozes it. Puts me in danger of Type 2 diabetes every time she comes near."

"Oh, come now," Jo laughed.

"And she always shows up with the other one, the tall woman with gray hair."

"Ina Mae?" Jo guessed the name right away, since she rarely saw one without the other.

He nodded. "Two odd ducks, but between them I don't think they miss a thing going on. Let slip a four-letter word in private across the room and there one of them is, looking at you like she's just added that to her book of "Everything that's wrong with Rafe Rulenski."

"Like that would really worry you?"

"Well, not normally, of course. But I can see Ms. Sweetness there, gently swaying the vote of Betty Big-bucks who can't decide between writing a check for the playhouse or a check to the Orphans' Fund."

"Those wretched orphans, grabbing all that money that should properly go to the arts."

"Then the tall one," Rafe went on, ignoring her as he worked up steam, "she comes to the balls supposedly to support the playhouse, but she has her own agendas, like, having kids in our plays? Forget about it. Child exploitation! Plus, they might miss out on five minutes of homework time. And animals? I know she was the one who sent the animal rights people to stop us from having a live parrot on stage once. Claimed the lights were too hot for the bird. We had to get a stuffed one, and have someone wiggle it and make cawing noises every once in a while so it would look alive." Rafe crumpled his sandwich wrappings into a tight ball.

Jo had to press her water bottle to her lips to keep from laughing over the image of the parrot-wiggler. Was he credited in the playbook as such, she wondered? *Jason Krabable — Parrot Shaker.* As for Ina Mae, Jo knew she volunteered at the local SPCA. And she *did* have strong opinions — about animals, children, and just about everything else.

"I can see that life as director of the Abbotsville Playhouse is not an easy one, Rafe. Here you are, trying to entertain people, and you're expected to actually *deal* with them too."

Rafe looked at her, still scowling from his rant, but then relaxed into a sly grin. "And I usually *can* deal with them, ultimately. That's one of the advantages of theatrical training. When faced with imbeciles, one can look enthralled. It's just that it's exhausting." Rafe rubbed his eyes and then looked back at Jo. "But I'll twist those arms. The Abbotsville Playhouse isn't down yet, don't you worry."

"Good. My friend Carrie's son, Charlie Brenner, will be one of the many who are glad to hear that. Charlie was really intrigued by the lights and sound workings before things came to a stop.

Rafe almost looked like he knew who Jo

was talking about, and nodded. Obviously he wasn't one to keep track of the "little people." It was another example of the invisibility Charlie had remarked on. Would Charlie be back, though, if the playhouse did get up and running? From what Carrie had said, Dan had not given an inch along that line, which did not bode well for the father-and-son relationship.

Jo glanced at her watch. "Speaking of my friend, it's time for me to relieve her at the shop." She gathered up her sandwich wrappings and dropped them in a nearby trash container. Rafe did the same and walked out with her. They parted on the sidewalk, Jo wishing him good luck in New York, and he accepting it.

As she walked to her car, Jo mulled over Rafe's unique impressions of people. His statement about actors and their ability to pretend stuck with her, making her wonder. If someone had an honest face, did she easily accept everything they said as fact? Did she believe someone was innocent simply because they acted sincere?

She gave herself a shake. After all, she wasn't born yesterday. She'd dealt with many a crafty businessman, and she was confident in her abilities to read people. There was, however, the little matter of that anonymous letter sent to Morgan.

Reaching her car, Jo noticed that the scratches in its paint seemed to glow in the bright, midday sun. As if on cue, the stitches in her scalp began to throb and a wave of nausea fluttered through her stomach. Were they reminders of the need for caution in this murderer's pursuit?

More likely, Jo thought, they were reminders of the need to drive carefully, though she'd definitely aim for both. She put the Toyota in gear and headed for the shop, wondering when all her questions would finally have answers.

CHAPTER 26

"I'm here," Jo called out as she walked through the door into an empty Jo's Craft Corner.

"I'm here too," Carrie's voice sailed back from the bathroom. "Be right out."

"Take your time." Jo stashed her pocketbook on the shelf beneath the cash register and glanced at the receipts. Carrie had made a few sales that morning, mainly from the knitting supplies. The knitters of Abbotsville seemed to have zeroed in on the times she would be available at the shop with her expert advice. Jo also saw a message from Betsy Davis, the basket weaver scheduled for a table at the country club craft show. It gave only the woman's phone number, with no indication of the reason for the call. Jo hoped she wasn't backing out. At this late date it would be impossible to find a replacement.

She heard the bathroom door open and

called out to Carrie, "Did Betsy say what she needed to talk with me about?"

"No, only that you could reach her until two."

Something in Carrie's voice didn't sound right, and Jo looked up. Her friend's eyes were red-rimmed.

"Carrie, what's wrong?"

Carrie shook her head. "I'm sorry. I didn't mean to bring it all with me to work. But when things slowed down, I couldn't help thinking about it. Charlie and Dan had a big fight last night."

"Uh-oh. About the playhouse?"

"It was, but I doubt either of them would admit it. They'd claim it was all about the lawn, which Charlie didn't mow like he was supposed to. He claimed that was because it was still too wet from the rain we had a couple nights ago. Dan thought that was just a crappy excuse and told him so. Then Charlie retaliated by saying Dan thought everything Charlie decided was crappy, and Dan told him not to speak to him in that tone, and, and, it just got worse after that." Carrie teared up, and Jo reached out to give her a hug.

"They'll both feel bad about it once they simmer down, Carrie."

"I didn't see any signs of that this morning. Charlie stomped off to school early, without breakfast. And Dan wouldn't talk about it at all with me; he just glared at his fried eggs as he shoveled them into his mouth and then washed them down with hot coffee. He'll probably have indigestion all day and blame it on Charlie."

"Men can be so stubborn. I'm sorry you got caught in the middle."

Carrie sighed. "That's it. I'm in the middle, but I can't help if neither of them will talk to me. Ah, well." Carrie took a final bracing sniff. "I better get going. I've got a bunch of errands to run. If I keep busy maybe a solution to all this will pop into my head."

"I'm sure it will all work out." Jo watched as Carrie gathered her things and left with a wan smile. Though she'd tried to be upbeat for Carrie's sake, Jo had a sinking feeling about this. The breach between father and son had been developing for quite a while as each pulled in their separate directions, and Jo hadn't a clue how to help repair it.

With a sigh, she reached for the slip with Betsy Davis's phone number and punched it in. Betsy's answering machine picked up, belying the basket weaver's supposed availability until two. Frustrated, Jo left her message and hung up, feeling highly annoyed.

It wasn't the uncompleted call that really bothered her, though, just as Charlie and Dan's fight wasn't about unmown grass. In addition to concern for the family that meant so much to her, Jo had the ongoing escalation of Russ Morgan's insinuations weighing on her, plus the recently added suspicions of just about everyone she knew in Abbotsville.

That last part was something she was going to have to work through. It made no sense to mistrust everyone, when in actuality only one person must be lying to her. The trouble was, at this point she couldn't say who that was. Jo began to wish that she'd never stayed to share lunch with Rafe. His negativity had managed to rub off on her, disrupting what she had hoped would be a clear-cut track to the truth. That track now appeared more like a maze through tall grass, where every new turn seemed to erase the path behind and present instead a fresh set of hidden problems up ahead.

The door jingled, and Jo pushed aside her depressing thoughts to greet her customer. No matter what her troubles, she still needed to earn a living, or she'd end up being the hungriest murder suspect in Abbotsville.

■ ■ ■ ■

Mindy Blevins was the first to arrive for the scrapbooking workshop. "Cute," she said, indicating Jo's camouflaging baseball cap.

"Glad you like it. You'll be seeing a lot of it until my hair evens out."

Mindy looked closely at Jo's bruises. "They're starting to fade. How do they feel?"

"Not bad. I've stopped the prescription pain pills altogether."

Mindy took her place at the worktable as Deirdre walked in. When Deirdre did a double take, Jo realized they hadn't seen one another since the accident. Deirdre peppered Jo with concerned questions on her condition but made no reference, of course, to their phone discussion of the previous night. Ina Mae and Loralee were the last to arrive, with Loralee carrying a plate of homemade pineapple squares.

"They're mostly for you, Jo, a little treat for your convalescence, but I made extra for everyone to share tonight." Jo thanked her gratefully, remembering that she hadn't eaten since her lunch with Rafe. The others moaned with delight over the frosted pastries and debated their possible caloric content.

"Are you sure you're up to running this workshop tonight?" Ina Mae asked quietly, her eyes scrutinizing Jo's face. Jo assured her she was, though in truth she could feel fatigue starting to set in. And though she'd stopped taking the strong prescription pain pills, she thought a Tylenol or Advil wouldn't be a bad idea.

However, she managed to put on a positive smile. "How's everyone's project coming along?" she asked as they spread out their photos and tools. She got four varieties of responses, ranging from "wonderful" to "I need a bit of help."

Loralee's was the last, and Jo went over to look at her pages. Loralee was putting together a scrapbook for a five-year-old granddaughter who lived in Seattle and had spent a week visiting during the summer. Loralee wanted the scrapbook to be a source of special memories of the visit, and planned to send it to the granddaughter at Christmas.

A quick glance at what Loralee had done so far brought to mind Rafe Rulenski's complaint of Loralee as a diabetes inducer: the pages nearly dripped with cotton-candy pinks and gossamer fluff. Jo knew Loralee's granddaughter was named Caitlin, but if her name were Tinkerbell, or maybe Barbie, the pages would fit her just as well.

"I want to create a page for our day at the beach in Ocean City, but I can't think where to start," Loralee said.

Jo quickly pulled out some sheets of blue paper, with the idea of toning down some of the intense pinkness of the scrapbook. "How about one of these for background?" she suggested, and when Loralee pursed her lips, Jo pointed out, "It will coordinate with the blue in your ocean shots. Then," Jo grabbed some red paper, "you could frame your shots with this to pick up the red in your beach umbrella."

Loralee played with it for a bit, placing a few photos over Jo's papers. "It's very nice," she said, "but I wonder if it might also be good to pick up the pink from Caitlin's swimsuit."

"That would work," Jo agreed. After all, it *was* Loralee's scrapbook. She offered a few starfish and sand bucket prints to further decorate the page, and moved on, leaving Loralee to create to her own taste.

"How is your book doing, Deirdre?" she asked.

"Oh, it's coming along great. This is so

much fun." Deirdre flipped to her previous page to show Jo, and Jo leaned over to see photos of two Afghan hounds in various poses.

"Well, aren't those beautiful dogs," Jo said, somewhat surprised.

Mindy leaned over to see. "They're gorgeous. But I thought your scrapbook was supposed to be about your husband."

"It *is!* And Caesar and Max are part of Alden's family." Deirdre beamed at the dogs' pictures, obviously as proud of them as Mindy was of her twins. Mindy shot a look to Jo, and Jo remembered how Mindy once told them about Alden Patterson's minimal tolerance of his wife's dogs. Jo made a tiny shrug, and Mindy smiled and turned away.

"Jo, did you ever get to see that tennis person?" Ina Mae asked. "Genna's room-mate?"

All the faces at the table turned once again in Jo's direction.

"Yes, I talked with Bethanne. She seems quite broken up over what happened to Genna."

"Did she have any theory on what happened?"

"She couldn't believe it was anything but

307

an accident. Nor could she accept the possibility that someone may have killed Genna while under the impression it was her."

Ina Mae nodded. "A difficult concept for anyone."

"I don't know," Loralee said, her scissors poised halfway through a shimmery sheet of pink. "I mean, about Genna not being the intended victim. I'm still very suspicious of Pete, Genna's boyfriend."

"I am too, absolutely," Deirdre agreed. "That violent temper of his, and all."

"Bethanne told me Pete is devastated. She's convinced his grief is genuine and that he could never have done anything to harm Genna."

"Well, I still say," Deirdre insisted, jabbing her calligraphy pen about for emphasis, "that Pete — oh!" Deirdre's pen caught an open bottle of green ink next to her, knocking it over. She quickly righted it, then grabbed for the paper towels Jo always kept handy, and frantically blotted.

Mindy helped, after first whisking her own materials out of the way of the creeping spill. "Be careful," Mindy warned Deirdre, "don't get ink on your ring!"

Jo hadn't noticed Deirdre's ring, and, as they all pitched in to change the worktable's protective papers, she glanced at it. Worn on her right hand, it was a lovely and unusual piece.

"Is that new?" Jo asked. "It's beautiful."

Deirdre wiped at her green-smudged fingers and held her hand up, smiling as she looked at it. "Not too new. I probably haven't worn it to the workshops before. Alden picked it up on one of his trips."

"He has very good taste."

"I think so too." Deirdre looked pleased.

"My mother had a lovely collection of jewelry, some of it rings," Loralee said. "Before she died she divided it up among the daughters. I have some nice pieces with amethyst that I haven't worn for years. I should bring them out."

"Oh, I love old jewelry," Mindy cried. "If I could afford it I'd have scads of it. Billy's afraid to let me anywhere near an antique shop."

The ladies chatted on, but Jo had tuned out. She moved over to Deirdre's scrapbook, which had been pushed aside during the cleanup, and flipped back a few pages until she found what she was looking for. So absorbed was she that apparently, at first, she didn't hear Deirdre speak to her.

"Jo!"

Startled, Jo looked up. "What?"

"I said, did my book survive?"

"Yes." Jo flipped through several pages. "I don't see any ink splotches, Deirdre." She held the scrapbook out to her.

"Well, good. Wasn't that lucky?"

Jo nodded. "Yes. Very lucky."

Jo felt her head throb painfully, and, thinking about what she had just seen, wished she hadn't left her prescription pills at home.

CHAPTER 27

Jo drove up the country club's drive, past maple trees whose red fall leaves shone like glowing embers in the sunlight. It was Wednesday, Jo's day off, and the one day of the week she closed the shop. Though she was dressed in jeans and a light sweater, topped with her red cap, she wasn't coming for a round of golf. Jo had murder on her mind.

She had spent a restless night tossing and turning between her sheets as worrying images jostled about her head, all including Deirdre and Alden Patterson. Jo had hidden her observations last night at the workshop, hoping somehow she was wrong. It could all simply be coincidence, and Jo could be jumping to the worst possible conclusions. On that slim chance, she was coming to the club with questions for Tracy. The answers she found could settle her mind, one way or the other.

Jo thought about the ring Deirdre was wearing, which she said had come from Alden. It had a beautiful design that was simple as well as elegant, and Jo had recognized it immediately as a Roberta Sawyer — the same woman who had designed Bethanne's pendant. Coincidence? Certainly possible. Except for the man Jo had passed in the hallway of Bethanne's apartment. He had seemed so familiar, but she couldn't think why until Deirdre's ring stirred up the memory.

Jo had never seen Alden in the flesh, but she had seen photos of him. A check through Deirdre's scrapbook had confirmed his identity. There he had been, posing side by side in several shots with Deirdre, often with an arm around her, smiling. Alden Patterson was definitely the man in Bethanne's apartment building. Was it too much of a stretch to assume he had been at Bethanne's *apartment* and that Bethanne's pendant had come from him? Though not long stretches, they were painful ones, and if correct, the worst was yet to come.

Jo parked and headed up the walk to the tennis shop. Several courts were occupied on this perfect tennis day, and the *thunk* of racquet against ball reverberated soundly.

One yellow missile flew over the green fencing, landing near Jo, and she picked it up to toss it back to the player, who waved gratefully. As Jo approached the shop's door, two people pushed their way out, a woman in a blue warm-up suit and a man carrying racquets and a basket of balls. Was this Bethanne's temporary replacement pro, Jo wondered? They smiled at Jo, the man holding the door open for her before moving on.

Walking in, Jo found Tracy occupied with a customer at the front counter, and Jo caught her eye as she moved toward the clothing racks. She thought she caught a glimpse of Ryan in the back employee area, and was glad. Of the two, Ryan was definitely the more forthcoming, and Jo needed straightforward answers today. She waited, biding her time among the T-shirts and hats, and then came over to Tracy's counter as soon as her customer left.

"I have some important things to ask you," Jo said, getting straight to the point.

"Okay," Tracy said, her eyes blinking somewhat nervously.

"Is that Ryan back there?" Jo asked. "I'd like him to be in on this too."

Tracy, obviously sensing Jo's gravity,

turned and called, "Ryan, can you come out here?"

Jo heard the sound of boxes being set down, and then Ryan, dressed in shorts and the country club's signature green polo, came through the doorway.

"Yeah?"

"Mrs. McAllister wants to talk to the two of us. About Kyle, I think."

Jo nodded. "That's right. And about Bethanne."

"Bethanne?" Ryan asked, his eyebrows going up. "She hasn't been in for a while."

"I know. I've been to talk to her."

"You have?" Tracy said. "How is she?"

"Hanging in there. But this is what I need to know. I have reason to think Bethanne has been involved with Alden Patterson. Can you confirm that for me?"

Tracy's face flushed pink, and she and Ryan exchanged looks.

"I'm not asking for frivolous reasons, believe me. This could be very important. You told me before that Kyle had been watching people here at the club, and speculating on affairs between them. Were Bethanne and Alden two of those people?"

Tracy looked unhappy, but Ryan smirked. Tracy spoke first.

"Kyle never actually said that to me."

"Yeah, me neither. But I wouldn't have been surprised if he did."

"Ryan!"

"Oh, come on. You don't think there was something going on? You knew about all those extra lessons. You've seen the way they always look at each other."

"It didn't necessarily mean anything. Mr. Patterson was always nice to me. He wasn't a flirt or anything."

"He's smart enough to pick the ones he knows will flirt back."

Tracy frowned but didn't argue.

"Those extra lessons," Jo asked, "did they happen to be late at night?"

"Uh-huh," Tracy admitted. "The courts are lighted. Bethanne explained to me that Mr. Patterson had a very busy schedule, but that she didn't mind staying late. She said he took his game very seriously." She grimaced, as though realizing how lame that was.

"Who was on duty here at the shop when the lessons were going on?"

"Probably Kyle, right?" Ryan said. "He liked being the only one around here."

Tracy agreed. "I think it was usually Kyle."

Jo nodded. "Thanks. I guess that's all I need to know. I appreciate your help, but keep this to yourselves for now, okay?"

As Tracy was nodding, the shop door opened and two players walked in, mopping at their sweaty faces. Jo turned to leave, and Tracy asked, "Did Bethanne say when she might be back?"

"No, she didn't." She paused. "But I have a feeling it won't be soon."

Jo headed back toward her car, so deep in thought over what Tracy and Ryan had said that she nearly missed hearing her name called. It was the woman with the half glasses from the front desk. She had run outside, eager to catch Jo before she left.

"Mr. Gordon saw your car here. He wonders if you could stop in and discuss a few things about the craft show."

Jo winced. Right now she felt she had far heavier things to deal with than the craft show. However, she doubted she should say, "Don't bother me now; I have a murder to deal with," so she followed the woman back toward the main entrance of the club. On the way, Jo caught sight of Hank Schroder's white pickup coming in their direction. She wasn't sure if he saw her, but his truck made what looked like a sudden right turn onto one of the drive's offshoots.

Bob Gordon popped up from his desk as Jo entered his office.

"Mrs. McAllister," he cried, jovially, "great to see you." He then peppered her with a variety of questions on the status of the craft show, which Jo answered as best she could without her notes at hand. All the while she tried not to stare at the framed photo hanging on the wall beyond his head — a photo of Gordon and his wife, Alden and Deirdre, and Bethanne.

"So we're unsure of Betsy Davis at this point?" Gordon asked, referring to the basket maker who had called Jo yesterday. Jo had been able to reach her only this morning.

"I'm afraid so. She's had some problems with her supplier, plus a recent flare-up of arthritis in her hands. She's not a hundred-percent sure she'll have enough baskets to set up a good table."

"That's unfortunate." Gordon frowned. "Her baskets have come to be a big draw over the years."

"She sounded like a person who would not consider showing up with less than her best presentation."

Gordon nodded. "That's her, though most of her customers, I'd say, would be thrilled with her rejects." Gordon brightened. "Well, if she doesn't pan out, I'm sure you could fill the gap with your own craft items."

Jo gulped, though she hoped not visibly. In the past days she'd barely spared a thought for what she would bring to the show. "Certainly!" she said, in as sincere a tone as she could manage. Did Carrie have some needlework projects to contribute, she wondered? Preferably an eight-by-ten-foot afghan, or a quilt or two? She could only hope.

Gordon escorted her through the halls of the club, chatting on about finer details of the show and stopping to introduce her to various people, until Jo managed to tear herself away. She left Gordon at the door and trotted back to her car, eager to head for home. It was time to put her thoughts together.

As she drove, Jo wished she could talk to Carrie. But Carrie had told her she would be busy at Amanda's soccer game that evening, because she was in charge of refreshments for the team. Jo was on her own.

She pulled into her garage and went through the side door into her kitchen, tossed her keys on the counter, and plopped on the sofa, carefully avoiding the broken-spring cushion. It was dinnertime, by the clock, but Jo had no desire for food. She *should* be celebrating, she reflected grimly.

She may have finally discovered who murdered Kyle. Once she laid all the facts before Lieutenant Morgan, she would likely be off his hook. Unfortunately, it wasn't turning out to be that simple.

But life never was simple, was it? Jo sighed. Long-term plans went awry; people you thought you could trust let you down. Deirdre's husband, the man who had appeared so lovingly thoughtful by gifting his wife with a beautiful ring, had in fact been cheating on her. Bad enough, certainly, but as things often do, one wrongdoing led to another to cover up the first, and a young man ended up dead, and then an innocent young woman.

Now more lives were poised to be destroyed, this time through Jo. Could she, *should* she do it? Was she certain enough of her conclusions to set in motion things that could send someone to prison?

CHAPTER 28

Jo didn't know how long she had been sitting on her couch, staring sightlessly at the drab wallpaper across the room, but she realized the once bright daylight beyond her windows had faded to dusk. She had been going over and over all that she knew about the murders. Was there something she had missed?

Alden Patterson had a strong motive for murder — to protect his career. But would he actually kill Kyle and Genna? It seemed unlikely. For one thing he probably wouldn't mistake Genna for Bethanne, dog or no dog. Then, his visit to Bethanne that day Jo encountered him suggested he had no murderous intentions toward her and that he wasn't terribly concerned about hiding their relationship.

On the other hand, Deirdre's stake in covering up Alden's affair was in holding on to her own way of life, which she liked quite well. Jo had seen that in her scrapbook. Instead of the record of Alden's successes that Deirdre had claimed it to be, it had become in fact a testament to the distinctions of her own life. Every photo included herself. Every record of Alden's step up the political ladder featured Deirdre front and center. Even her prized dogs had taken precedence over Alden, dogs that — according to Mindy Blevins — she had admitted he didn't much like but that symbolized, with their uniqueness and expense, Deirdre's own status.

Did that prove her to be a murderer, though? After all, Deirdre had been so helpful with Jo's investigation. On closer examination, though, Deirdre's "help" had always directed Jo away from the truth. She continually pointed Jo away from the clubhouse and toward the playhouse and Pete Tober.

Jo could imagine Deirdre, who knew neither of the women well, mistaking Genna for Bethanne. But could she see her committing such violence? Pushing a young woman to her death? Stabbing a young man dressed as a clown? Jo didn't know.

Jo sighed, and pulled herself off the sofa, heading toward her bedroom. The phone rang as she walked in, and she reached for the extension on her night table. Her voice came out in a hoarse, "Hello?"

"Jo, sweetie, it's me."

"Mom? Hi, how are you?" Jo sank down onto her bed.

"I'm fine, dear. It's been too long, hasn't it? I've meant to call at least a dozen times. How are you doing there, in that little town you've settled in? What is it called? I keep forgetting."

"Abbotsville."

"Yes, that's right. Is your shop all set up now?"

Jo thought back. It seemed like a million years since her grand opening. How excited she had been that day. How quickly it had all fallen apart. But her mother, she knew, hadn't called to hear about problems. She didn't want any specks whatsoever on her rose-colored glasses.

"Yes, the shop's up and running, Mom."

"Wonderful! I'm going to tell all my friends here to stop in when they're in the area."

Jo couldn't picture anyone wanting to detour to Abbotsville on a trip to Washington, D.C., or Baltimore, just for Jo's particular craft supplies, but the thought was there. Carol Wagner did what she could for her daughter, and her daughter accepted it, knowing her mother's limits.

Jo heard the clink of glassware on the line and pictured her mother standing in the kitchen of her little house, designed for senior citizens who might have mobility problems, although Carol Wagner had no concerns in that department. Possibly the youngest member of her small, central Florida community, Jo sensed that her mother enjoyed her position of relative youth, as well as the ease of the maintenance-free situation and effortless sociability. She had moved down there shortly after Jo's father died of heart trouble, and seemed to have never looked back, except for the occasional contact with her daughter.

"So, when will you be able to come down here for a nice vacation? We have a lovely pool you can swim in as my guest."

"It might be awhile, Mom."

"Oh, I do hope not too long." Jo's mother began telling Jo about the almost daily swims she had been taking since she moved into her home, and which neighbors she usually encountered, tales Jo had heard a few times before. She began to tune out, and when the story expanded to descriptions of recent ailments of said neighbors, Jo barely listened, simply filling in any pause with automatic "uh-huhs." At one point Jo thought she heard a noise from the area of her backdoor and she cocked one ear to listen. Some little night creature, perhaps, looking for crumbs? The noise didn't continue, and she tuned back in to her mother's chatter, just in time to hear the finale on Harriet Kreitner's knee replacement.

"Uh, Mom?" she broke in, when Mrs. Wagner took a breath.

"Yes, dear?"

"Remember when we lived in Larksdale? On Rosewood Lane?"

"Of course. You were in elementary school then, weren't you?"

"Uh-huh. Remember the Milburn brothers? They went around one summer bashing mailboxes."

"Oh, yes. Why do you mention it?"

Jo heard the tinge of annoyance creep into her mother's voice. *Why do you mention things I'd rather not think about?* she might as well have asked.

"I was just wondering. Nobody knew for a long time who was doing the bashing. But then you happened to see them one night, right?"

"Yes."

"Was it hard turning them in? I mean, you and Dad were friends with the family and all. But somebody had to stop them. Was it

324

very difficult?"

"Oh, I sent your father to talk to that policeman we knew. I told him to make sure we were kept out of it. I think they kept an eye on the boys and caught them in the act a couple nights later."

Jo should have known. Dad was sent to take care of it, and Mom, as usual, side-stepped the issue. Jo wouldn't have that luxury, however. No sidestepping possible here, only a straightforward march to Russ Morgan's gray steel desk.

"Why do you ask, dear? Has someone been damaging mailboxes there?"

"No, Mom." *A murder or two, but our mailboxes are just fine.*

"Well good. I want everything to be well for you, Jo. Especially after, you know."

Yes, Jo knew. That little unmentionable incident up in New York. "Everything's okay here," she assured her mother. Jo had long stopped crossing her fingers when she said such things to her mother. They didn't qualify as lies, she reasoned, when they were exactly what Carol Wagner wanted to hear. They always made her mother a little happier, and Jo was just as glad to cooperate. Unfortunately, they always left Jo feeling a little lonelier.

"I guess I'd better let you go, Jo. You probably have a lot of things to do."

Jo didn't argue. She promised to pass on her mother's best to Carrie, and to think seriously about driving down to Florida. They finished with a breezy "love you" on each side, and ended the call, Jo's hand lingering on the phone as it rested in its cradle. What if, she wondered, she had taken up her mother's invitation after Mike's accident to move somewhere near her? Would she have been better off? Would it have been worth it to live a life of pretend happiness in year-round sunshine in order to avoid the troubles that had rained down on her where she was?

Jo sighed, and dragged herself off the bed. Perhaps a little food and drink would help with the gloom, although the only kind of drink that would really help was not what she would allow herself tonight. A clear head and alcohol-free breath were what she needed for her meeting with Russ Morgan tomorrow, if she finally decided she should go.

She went to her kitchen and pulled open her refrigerator to stare inside: a few aging eggs, wilted lettuce, and a covered dish of leftover macaroni and cheese. She pulled out the dish and was heading for the microwave when the phone rang. Who would that be? she wondered. Her mother, with one more neighbor's story she had forgotten to share?

Jo headed toward the phone, macaroni in hand. A figure suddenly stepped out of the shadows, and Jo screamed, dropping her dish, which clattered to the floor.

"Let it ring," Deirdre said, her suggestion reinforced by the gun in her hand. "We have more important things to take care of."

CHAPTER 29

Jo stared at the gun in Deirdre's hand. A small, silver piece that fit easily into her palm, it looked almost like a toy. But Jo didn't doubt the deadliness of it, nor, from the look on Deirdre's face, her intentions. All doubts about the woman's capacity to commit murder had definitely been erased.

"How did you get in here?"

"You're careless with your keys, Jo. I borrowed the one to your back door one day during a workshop and copied it. How helpful of you to label each key. You thought it had slipped off your ring onto the shop floor. That was my way of returning it."

Jo remembered the incident. She hadn't even missed that particular key until one of the workshop ladies — Mindy? — spotted it lying near her desk. Jo had indeed assumed it had simply fallen off somehow, and tightened up her key ring with one of her jewelry pliers, apparently locking the barn door, in effect, after the fact.

"Why don't you clean up the mess on your floor, Jo? I wouldn't want you to accidentally slip and fall."

Jo stared at Deirdre, wondering if she could be serious. A menacing wave of the pistol convinced her, and Jo grabbed a fistful of paper towels and mopped at the macaroni, all the time aware of Deirdre hovering closely. Jo's mind raced, trying to think what she could do to get away from this woman who clearly planned to shoot her, but nothing foolproof came to mind. Karate kicks were not in Jo's repertoire, unfortunately, and the only weapon she had at hand — her kitchen knives — were not faster than speeding bullets. Maybe she could distract Deirdre, somehow.

"How did you know I was starting to figure it out?" Jo asked, reaching for a final curled noodle with her towels.

Deirdre smiled an eerie smile. "You seemed so interested in my ring last night, Jo. And then my photos. It made me worry. The photo I put in my scrapbook of Alden and me at the Muscular Dystrophy Ball didn't include Bethanne — I had trimmed her off, as she needed to be. But I looked up my original copy. Bethanne is wearing a pendant that Alden must have given her. I could see how similar it was to my ring, though I hadn't noticed it at the time, since I didn't have my ring yet. You saw that pendant, didn't you Jo? When you visited Bethanne."

Jo nodded.

"I thought so. I realized, then, you were starting to put it all together. Obviously, I had to stop you before you got too far."

Obviously.

"I guess I can understand you wanting to kill Bethanne," Jo said. "She must have made you furious, luring your husband into an affair. I presume you mistook Genna for her when she was walking the dog?"

Deirdre frowned. "Yes, that was a mistake. Unfortunate, since Bethanne quickly became less accessible."

Jo caught the coldness of Deirdre's attitude toward Genna's death. "Unfortunate" and "mistake" instead of what it truly was: a terrible crime. It gave Jo chills.

"And Kyle was a threat for what he knew?"

"Of course. Would we want to be blackmailed the rest of our lives? And risk having Alden's career destroyed? You know how the media is. Always looking for the least bit of dirt on candidates. Alden is heading for the governorship. Everyone says so. And after that — who knows? The Senate, or even the White House!"

Deirdre had grown agitated, moving about as she talked, waving her pistol for emphasis. Jo backed slowly toward her trash can with her handful of noodle-filled towels, watching Deirdre and trying to remember which knives had been left in the knife block that sat on the counter, and which lay buried in her dishwasher.

"Perhaps Alden should have considered that before he got involved with Bethanne."

Deirdre's anger melted into rueful pity. "Men can be so weak, can't they? For all his brilliance, Alden managed to let himself be drawn in by that tennis slut. If it weren't for me watching out for him, who knows where he'd be? When I pointed out the risks he was taking, Alden agreed it had to end."

Deirdre said it as calmly as if she and Alden had discussed the downside of wearing polka-dotted bow ties to public appearances. Jo wondered how calmly these "risks" had in fact been pointed out. She reached the trash can and turned to deposit the towels. The knife block sat a few inches to the right, and Jo saw two handles poking out of it: the boning knife and the small paring knife. Which one should she try to grab?

"When did you become aware that Kyle knew what was going on?"

"The night that Alden met with Bethanne at the club to break it off with her. I had slipped over to monitor the situation, determined to step in if she gave him a difficult time. But then I saw that ridiculous person from the tennis shop, creeping around, spying on them."

Deirdre looked at Jo, incensed. "Bethanne was being perfectly reasonable at the time, but Kyle, I knew, had no sense of what was important. He would think his pitiful acting career, getting money to bankroll it or publicity to fuel it, was more critical than who eventually guides our state, or our country, toward peace and prosperity."

"And of course, who stands beside that governor or president," Jo added.

"Alden wouldn't be where he is except for me," Deirdre declared. "I deserve the rewards of being First Lady."

That's what it was all about, of course. Deirdre didn't really care about the country's need for Alden. Deirdre cared most about her place in the spotlight, once the elevated positions were reached. Something else now occurred to Jo.

"My car accident. Did you have something to do with that?"

"Of course. You were getting too close, determined to talk to Bethanne. It was a spur-of-the-moment decision, though, so I had to use what I had at hand." Deirdre gave a small laugh. "Alden always claims I carry a small pharmacy around with me. I have to admit I've gathered up quite a variety of pills. It's not always easy being the wife of a politician, you know. There's enormous stress involved, which brings on sleep problems and such.

"The doctor I went to see in Baltimore prescribed the Restoril I used on Kyle. I wouldn't dare go to Doctor Davidson here in Abbotsville. The people in his office know me, and you know how easily things get out. Besides, the office staff of my Baltimore doctor is extremely overworked, and they don't always guard their cache of drug samples as they should. They make it so easy to reach for a few packets on your way out from the examining room." She smiled, amused. "I'm not even sure what I dropped into your soda that night."

"You intended to kill me?"

"As I said, I didn't have time to plan. I wanted to at least slow you down. You were starting to move much too quickly in dangerous directions. I *tried* to convince you it was the jealous boyfriend who killed Kyle. There I was, showing up for all those wretched workshops of yours, just to guide you onto safer paths. This could have all been avoided if you'd only cooperated."

As Deirdre paced, ranting on about her supposed hardships and pressures, then crowing over her clever handling of them, Jo reached back for the paring knife, hoping Deirdre's agitation covered the movement. She slid the knife into the back pocket of her jeans, grateful for the recent weight loss that made them loose enough to do so easily.

"What about that anonymous letter you called me about?" she asked, anxious to keep Deirdre talking.

"Again, something intended merely to slow you down."

Something intended to get me arrested for murder. "So you wrote it?"

"Certainly. Taking all the proper precautions, of course. How helpful all those television crime shows can be. I used the library's computer to print it out, wore gloves to prevent fingerprints, and swabbed the envelope's flap with a wet cotton ball to avoid leaving DNA. Not that I thought they'd ever go to that much trouble on a simple letter, but one never knows."

"I assume, then, you plan to eventually eliminate Bethanne, as a proper precaution, of course," Jo said.

Deirdre sighed. "It's so true that a woman's work is never done. At first she was being sensible, and willing to step quietly out of the picture, for her own sake as well as ours. But she seems to be an ongoing temptation for Alden. If she had only gone away and caused problems for someone at a tennis club in Arizona, for instance, she would have saved a lot of trouble for us all.

"But enough of this. It's time to get moving." Deirdre picked up Jo's keys from the counter. Jo took a step toward Deirdre, but Deirdre stopped her with a firm thrust of her pistol. "First, though, remove that knife from your pocket."

Jo's heart sank.

"Slowly," Deirdre added, watching intently as Jo silently followed the order.

"Drop it on the floor and kick it to that far corner."

Jo did so, watching her only hope spin out of reach.

"Now walk ahead of me into the garage."

Deirdre pulled open the connecting door and waved Jo out. She held Jo's keys in her left hand. Where did she plan to take her? Surely Deirdre couldn't drive and hold the gun on her at the same time? Jo's hopes began to revive. If Deirdre ordered her to drive, perhaps she could manage an escape after all.

Jo stepped down the single step into the garage and moved past her workshop room toward her car.

"Stop," Deirdre said, and Jo heard her keys jangle. She looked around and saw Deirdre locate the key to Jo's jewelry workroom and fit it into the lock. She waved Jo in.

"What — ?

"Just get in!"

With Deirdre's pistol nearly in her face, Jo got in. But what was going on? Did Deirdre plan to let her live after all? Did she intend to simply confine Jo there while she escaped? That didn't make any sense. Deirdre didn't want a life on the run; she wanted a life of prestige and power.

Jo heard the lock turn, then footsteps walk to her car. The car door opened, and in a moment Jo heard her ignition turn over. She expected to hear the garage door open next, but instead she heard her car door slam shut and Deirdre's footsteps return.

No, oh no!

"Don't do this, Deirdre!"

"Don't worry, Jo, it will be quite painless." Deirdre's voice came from near the door.

"You won't get away with it! Alden's

career will be over!"

"Ah, but I will, Jo. I've had time to plan this. You see, when they find you, they will think you committed suicide. I will come back in the morning for our appointment to discuss a jewelry commission. Remember that brooch design we were going to discuss? No? No matter, it will be scribbled on your calendar. What a horrible discovery I will make then. Perhaps I'll even get one of your neighbors to help me find you. Of course I will have unlocked this door, first.

"And the police will eventually find a letter — hidden somewhat sloppily in your bedroom — that will obviously be from Kyle — threatening to blackmail you about your husband's murder. It will become so clear that your conscience overcame you and you chose suicide, surrounded by your beloved jewelry implements. Lieutenant Morgan will have no trouble whatsoever believing it."

Jo saw immediately how right Deirdre was. Morgan would take it as confirmation of what he'd suspected all along. His case would be tidily and efficiently closed as Jo was proclaimed responsible for the recent Abbotsville murders.

"Good-bye, Jo. I'm sorry. I truly am. But you wouldn't listen."

Jo heard the door to her kitchen close, and Deirdre's footsteps faded away as she headed toward Jo's bedroom to plant her false evidence. Within moments Jo faintly heard her back door close and pictured Deirdre slipping easily to wherever she had left her car, unseen by neighbors who were likely staring at televisions rather than out their windows.

All the while, Jo heard her car engine chugging away, pumping carbon monoxide into the closed garage. Jo rattled the knob on her workshop door and then threw her weight against it. Again. It barely moved.

It had never occurred to her that she might be locked in this room, accidentally or not. The door locked and unlocked by key, which she carried on her key ring. She only locked it when she was out of it, never while she was inside, working. And if she had her key ring with her, there was no need to keep a spare inside the room. It wasn't a freezer, after all, simply her workroom. She never, never anticipated something like this.

"Help!" she cried. "Help! Help!"

Even as she did so, she realized the futility of it. There was no way her voice would carry through this door and the length of the garage, especially over the sound of the engine. She began to panic.

Mike, Mike, what can I do? I can't think. Help me.

Jo drew a deep calming breath, trying not to imagine what might be going into her lungs. She had to keep her wits about her. There must be something she could do to save herself. She couldn't let Deirdre get away with everything. She couldn't let her go on to kill Bethanne and who knew what other unfortunate person who happened to be in the way of Alden's career climb. But what could Jo do to get out of here?

Jo realized she had remained standing in the dark all this time, listening for Deirdre's movements. She flipped on the light switch and looked around at her jewelry bench. Was there something there she could use to break out?

Her jewelry tools, unfortunately, were meant for delicate work, not for demolition. She picked up a ball-peen hammer. Was it weighty enough to break the door's lock? Jo hefted it, deciding at best it could put artistic-looking dents in the metal, if placed correctly. Was there anything there to pick the lock with? Jo remembered joking with Carrie about sending off for a lock-picking set. How she wished she had one now, along with the skill to actually use it.

Except that Jo didn't have time to diddle

with the lock, even if she had half a chance of being successful. Her garage was small, the room she was in was not airtight, and she would be running out of oxygen before long. She wasn't sure how long she had, but she knew she wasn't in a position to dally.

Jo's searching gaze, which had been roaming across the door, suddenly stopped. The hinges! Maybe she could take off the door hinges. Jo scrambled through her tool bench for something to use. She grabbed a steel punch that looked about the right size and knelt down to look at the bottom hinge, and then groaned when she saw the rust. Was that likely to make things harder? Probably, but she got to work, placing the steel punch against the lower end of the pin and tapping firmly with her hammer. The pin didn't budge.

Jo felt a wave of dizziness and fought it off. Kneeling near the floor probably placed her closest to where the bad air flowed into her room. She looked around for rags, grabbed a couple from beside her bench, and stuffed them into the space between door and floor. The garage air would still enter her room, but hopefully, now, more slowly. She resumed tapping at the pin, frustrated with the limits on the swing of her hammer. The hinge was less than a foot from the floor, and she wasn't feeling any give whatsoever. Until at last she felt the pin move, just a bit.

Encouraged, she adjusted the punch and tapped again. Another shift. *Tap, shift. Tap, shift.* The pin moved excruciatingly slowly, but it was moving. Jo tried not to think about her car's exhaust as she worked. She tried to ignore the nausea that had crept into her stomach. Was that due to the air? She couldn't think about it now. *Tap, shift. Tap, shift.* Finally the pin poked enough above the hinge for her to grasp it, and she pulled and wiggled the rusty metal, feeling skin scrape off as she did so, until the pin came out.

One done, one to go. Jo stood to work on the upper hinge, feeling the room sway as she rose, but shaking the feeling away. She reached up to the top hinge, images of Deirdre's deadly work running through her mind as she tapped. She pictured Deirdre at the grand opening, which, in retrospect, was not so grand. Still she remembered the busyness of the day: the milling crowds, the crying children, the circus music. As Jo had been rushing about, attending to customers, Deirdre had blended in as one more stranger, slipping through the crowd, casually helping herself to punch, carrying a drugged paper cupful to the overheated clown outside, then watching and waiting until the drug took effect and he staggered to the back room.

Had she planned the use of the knitting needle to throw more suspicion on Jo? Probably. Deirdre, Jo was convinced, despite all her pretense at concern and offers of help, would have been delighted to see Jo charged with Kyle's murder. She would have happily continued to play along as one of the sympathetic workshop ladies, commiserating over Jo's plight, wringing hands that in private would be clapping with joy. Jo, however, remembered Loralee's jaundiced look while discussing Deirdre and her dogs that one night. Had Loralee noticed a few cracks in Deirdre's façade and seen through the deception? Jo wished she had coaxed out Loralee's thoughts right away, instead of brushing it all off as a trivial personality clash.

Tap, shift. Tap, shift.

Jo thought of that night she had invited Deirdre into her home after fixing her bracelet in this workroom. She had been tired after a long day, she remembered, but sensing Deirdre's interest and suspecting loneliness, Jo had chided herself that it wouldn't kill her to be hospitable. She laughed grimly at the memory. What irony. It didn't kill her then, but what would it do to her now? No, she wouldn't think in that direction. Keep working on the hinge.

Tap, shift. Tap, shift.

Jo pictured poor Genna, out walking her roommate's dog, possibly even wearing one of Bethanne's own warm-up jackets. Had she been caught totally by surprise? Jo guessed so. Deirdre would know she needed to catch her victim off guard to avoid any struggle or screams. Jo imagined Deirdre rushing out from a hiding place, or perhaps strolling several steps behind in the shadows, then, as Genna paused near the edge of the cliff, pushing her over the rail before she could react. Jo pictured Deirdre coolly fastening the dog's leash to a nearby tree, caring more for the well-being of that little creature than she had for the young woman she'd just killed.

Tap, shift.

Jo's head had begun to throb badly. The pounding at her temples seemed to match the rhythm of her car's chugging. Her body was telling her in several ways that it badly needed cleaner air. She realized her tapping had slowed down and she forced herself to pick up the pace. Her arms, reaching above her head to the hinge, ached, and she lowered them to rest a moment, inadvertently dropping her steel punch and small hammer in the process.

Jo stared down at the tools as they lay on the floor, her mind suddenly blank. There was something she needed to do, she knew that, but she couldn't think what that was. Her hammer and — her tools. Oh, yes. She needed to pick them up. She needed to work at the hinge. She bent to pick them up and had to steady herself by grabbing at her bench as dizziness overwhelmed her. She waited a moment for it to pass, then retrieved her tools. What did she want them for? Yes, that's right. The hinge.

Tap, shift, tap, shift.

The pin in the top hinge poked up, and Jo pulled at it with her cramped fingers, wiggling and working until it came free. She knelt down and grasped the door by the knob and lower edge, pushing away the rags, and pulled. The door didn't budge. It felt so heavy, heavier than she could manage. She felt so tired, so sleepy. Should she just lie down? Just a minute? No! She had to get the door off. She tugged. The hinges separated.

Jo struggled with the door to shift it sideways and pull it from its lock, as the weight threatened to push her backward. She managed to push it aside enough to step through, then staggered out into the garage. She stood, looking at her car in the small amount of light spilling from her workroom. It sat there, perfectly still, as she heard the engine under its hood run rapidly. That suddenly seemed very funny to her. That the engine was running but the car wasn't. Jo giggled, then stopped herself. She should probably turn the car off. That seemed like a good idea, but Jo couldn't remember how one did that. Was there a switch somewhere on the car? Something to flick up or down?

Mike, do you remember? How did we turn our car off?

Maybe she should forget the car and just go. She took a step toward the kitchen door and staggered, grabbing on to the door-frame of her workroom. The connecting door seemed a long, long way away. She was so tired. Perhaps she should just sit down and rest awhile. But something seemed to shake her; someone seemed to say to her: *Move! Keep moving! Get to the door.*

"I can't," she protested. "My legs won't move."

Move!

"I can't," Jo insisted, tears filling her eyes. But she did. One foot swung forward, and she shifted her weight onto it. "It's so hard," she cried, but she managed to slide her other foot forward, then lean onto it.

Keep going!

"I'm trying!" One more step.

Another one!

Jo's legs were like cement blocks that she had to push through four feet of water in a slippery-bottomed pool. But she moved, one inch at a time, as the Toyota spewed out its poisonous fumes.

Again.

Again.

Jo could barely see at this point, but she stretched out one leaden arm, flailing from side to side until, leaning forward, she touched wood. She gasped, then fumbled over it until she touched the metal of the door knob, turned it, and pulled. The door opened toward her, and she held on desperately, aware, somewhere in the fog of her brain, that losing her balance and falling backward to the floor meant losing her life. But a single, rising step still stood between her and escape.

Jo tried to lift one foot up onto the step, but her brain's signals seemed to be scattering like buckshot. Her toes wiggled and her knee flexed, but her foot remained flat. She tried with the other foot. Wiggle, flex, tremble. Nothing worked as she wanted it to. She knew, somehow, she couldn't stay there, so Jo threw herself forward, landing halfway into her kitchen, and gasped from the floor at the fresher air. It helped, for a moment, and she lifted herself onto her elbows and pulled, determined now to drag herself all the way out.

You can do it.

But then the fog swirled thickly again, engulfing her, and she couldn't see, couldn't move, couldn't think. Her head dropped to the floor and she felt the smoothness of the linoleum on her cheek, so cool, so nice. She could just . . .

Jo suddenly felt strong hands grasping her shoulders, pulling her forward.

"No, no, I want to stay . . ." she protested.

But the hands gripped harder, pulling, pulling, and the last thing Jo remembered was a macaroni noodle sliding past her cheek and onto her neck.

Missed that one, she thought, then closed her eyes.

CHAPTER 30

"You've been blessed with a perfect day for this craft show, Mr. Gordon." Ina Mae stood in front of the St. Adelbert's Ladies' Sodality table, facing the country club manager.

His head bobbed in agreement. "We couldn't have ordered it any better. And what a turnout! I'd have to say this is the best crowd we've had in years. Perhaps ever. The weather is a factor, of course," his voice growing serious, "but I think many people are here because of Mrs. McAllister."

"Oh, certainly. You might say this entire show is a tribute to her." Ina Mae leaned closer to Bob Gordon. "And I wouldn't be surprised if she put in a good word with *someone*," she raised her eyes heavenward, "for this beautiful, sunny day."

"Absolutely," Loralee chimed in. She set down the pink quilted picture frame she had been examining. "It would be just like Jo to continue thinking of others, no matter what."

Bob Gordon opened his mouth to speak when the voice from the next table caused him to turn.

"Oh, please!" Jo cried out, laughing. "Like I have a hotline to heaven, and special ordering privileges?"

Ina Mae smiled at her. "Well, don't you think you have a *few* perks owed you, after all you've been put through recently."

"My perk is being here at all, for which I'm very grateful. If anyone is owed a debt, it would be Charlie Brenner for following his gut feelings and showing up right when I needed him most."

"Yes, that was extremely clever of him, I have to say. Carrie and Dan have raised a fine boy."

Jo looked over at Carrie, who was busy at the other end of the table helping a woman decide among several of Jo's seasonal wreaths, and saw from the pleased smile and pink cheeks that she had heard. Jo knew if Dan were nearby that he too would be grinning with pride. Charlie's actions that night were truly heroic, and he had definitely grown several inches in the eyes of his parents.

A club employee called Bob Gordon away,

and Ina Mae and Loralee were distracted by one of the Sodality ladies. Jo, left to herself for the moment, gazed over the lush green of the club's golf course, her thoughts going back to that night.

She hadn't been aware of much once she lost consciousness on the kitchen floor, but she had revived sporadically as the paramedics treated her on her front lawn. She remembered urgent voices shouting and red lights flashing. Charlie had called 9-1-1 and pulled her from the house, frantic, he'd said, until the ambulance finally arrived.

"I was following Mrs. Patterson," he'd explained to Jo later. "I got bored hanging around Amanda's soccer game, and rode my bike to the Forest Home Drugstore to check out the magazines. I heard someone mention the playhouse while I was looking through *Cycle Week,* and I looked up. Mrs. Patterson was talking with some other women, and they were saying stuff like what a shame the playhouse closed down and would it ever reopen, things like that, so of course I listened in. I wanted to know what was going to happen too."

Charlie had told her this as Jo was recovering at the University of Maryland Medical Center, where she'd been taken for treatment in the hyperbaric chamber. She remembered how he had paced about her room, the adrenaline pumping through him once again as he described those moments.

"But they didn't have any real information. They were just yakkin' away about how much revenue was being lost by this latest cancellation, and all. So I started flipping pages of my *Cycle Week* again. Then I heard Mrs. Patterson say she would ask Mr. Rulenski about maybe setting up another fundraiser when she saw him, which would be very soon since she was meeting with him in about fifteen minutes, so she was sorry she had to take off now, yada, yada, yada."

Charlie had stopped at the foot of Jo's bed then, his lip curling at the significance. "She was lying. Mr. Rulenski was in New York. I knew because I kept checking with his assistant — what's-her-name with the glasses — in case rehearsals started up again."

Jo nodded. Rafe had told her, too, about his plans to go up to New York for a commercial job. "So you followed her?"

"Yeah! I wanted to know what was going on. I mean, I didn't know too much about her, but in this town everyone's connected to everyone. Maybe I thought she was going to meet up with Mr. Schroder and I'd hear him telling her how he'd killed off Kyle Sandborn."

Jo laughed. "Poor maligned Mr. Schroder."

"Well, maybe not anything that exciting, but I was curious. So I hopped on my bike and tailed her. She's got a cool car. Did you ever see it?"

Jo nodded, grinning at the teen-interest sidebar to his story.

"But I'm on my bike so I'm invisible. Like, who thinks twice about some kid on his bike, right? And instead of following her to the country club or some place like that, I see her pull onto your street. And she slows down in front of your house but doesn't stop. It's like she's checking it out. So I slow down too, and keep in the shadows. And I see her go around the corner and park, then get out and walk down that street that runs in back of your house. I saw her go into your backyard. But it was dark, and I couldn't get that close, so I didn't know she didn't knock or anything, but snuck in. I just figured you knew she was coming and said to come in that way for some reason."

Charlie scowled. "If I'd known what she was really doing, I would have charged right in."

"I'm glad you didn't, Charlie. She had a

gun. It could have been very bad."

"Yeah, well maybe," he said, somewhat skeptically.

Jo saw he believed he could have somehow overpowered Deirdre before she pulled her trigger, just as every actor on TV so easily did seven nights a week. "The best thing," she insisted, "would have been to call the police."

"Yeah, now I wish I had. But I just hung around thinking if she didn't stay long I'd follow her some more, see where she went next, and talk to you about it the next day. I was getting worried, 'cause it was getting late and I knew my folks'd be mad if I stayed out too long. Anyway, I saw her come out, but something seemed funny 'cause she seemed real tense, looking around and all. She got in her car, and I kept behind her. She drove faster this time, and I had a little trouble keeping up, but I finally saw her pull into her driveway and her garage. I knew it was hers 'cause the mailbox outside said 'Patterson' on it."

"You could have just gone home then, Charlie. What made you come back to my place?"

"I don't know." Charlie looked truly puzzled. "I started to. But something just didn't seem right. Here she had told the others she was going to meet with Mr. Rulenski and instead she goes to your house. Then, using the back door and all, it just seemed funny. I decided to go back and just see, even though I was cutting it real close with the time by now."

"You ended up breaking in."

Charlie nodded. "I was real scared to do that. I just wasn't sure, you know? But you weren't answering your door, and when I walked around I could see your kitchen light was on. Then I heard your car running, but the garage door was locked. That really worried me, so I decided to break the window in your bedroom and climb in."

Thank God he had, Jo thought as the sound of a golf cart winding its way down the path brought her back to the present.

"Jo." Loralee broke into her thoughts. "Can I get you something to eat from the refreshments table? They have lovely frosted brownies. Maybe coffee?"

"Thanks, Loralee, but I have a drink here I'm working on. And Javonne brought me a fully loaded sub earlier, so I'm bursting at the seams."

Her workshop ladies — minus Deirdre, of course — had been fussing over her since her return from the hospital, refusing to allow her to cook for herself or even wash a dish. Jo felt she could get used to this very easily. Dan and Charlie had repaired her broken window before she even had time to think of it, and Carrie, Jo was sure, though she hadn't admitted it, had mopped and cleaned inside.

Jo glimpsed Hank Schroder's truck in the distance, and remembered how he had shown up at her door a few days ago, typically not asking but *informing* her that he had extra grass seed that would go to waste and since her front lawn was pretty torn up from the emergency workers, he would rake it smooth and reseed it for her. He had brusquely waved off her offer of payment, saying, with the beginnings of a grin that threatened to crack his leathery face, that he owed her one for that free soda he got from her the other night.

Hank Schroder, Jo learned with a shock, had a sense of humor.

"I know you're just renting," he'd gone on to say as he got to work, "but I also know your landlord, Max McGee, spends half his time in Florida and doesn't worry about maintenance."

"I think he might be sweet on you, Jo," Carrie had later teased. Jo had waved the thought away with a laugh until she recalled that the entire time Hank toiled away at her lawn, he hadn't spit once. That, plus the fact that he had taken extra time to spread fertilizer on the straggly rose bush — his version of bringing flowers to a lady? — had made her wonder.

"Can I hang this wreath outside?"

Jo refocused to see Dawn Buchmann standing before her, holding up one of Jo's hand-trimmed Christmas wreaths. Her wreaths had been selling well today, which pleased Jo. She liked the thought of her creations decorating doors throughout Abbotsville — a much happier result of her opening up the Craft Corner, than the other, terrible things that had followed it.

"Yes," she said, answering Dawn, "but the wreath will last longer if it has protection from wind and rain, like a front porch or at least an overhang." Jo smiled down at Dawn's toddler dozing angelically in the stroller beside her. "Cory's quiet today," she said. "In the park he ran about like the Energizer Bunny."

Dawn grinned. "This won't last. I'm shopping fast while I have a chance." The young mother picked out a few other items to add to her selected wreath, until, hearing Cory begin to stir, she declared what she had gathered would do, and dug into her purse for cash to pay. As Jo bagged Dawn's purchases, she asked softly how Pete was doing.

Dawn grimaced. "He's still taking it hard. Pete really, really loved Genna."

"Has he gone back to work yet?"

"Yes, but they say he's like a walking zombie there. Everyone's trying hard to get him through this."

"It's good he has so many friends." Jo handed Dawn her bags and watched as she pushed the stroller off through the crowd.

She thought of the conversations she had eavesdropped on between Pete and Genna, both after the theater rehearsal and at the garage. Jo had mistakenly assumed that Pete was pressuring Genna to move in with him, when in fact he was pushing her to move away from Bethanne. Pete, it turned out, didn't like Genna having a roommate who thought it was perfectly fine to sneak around with a married man. He felt Genna deserved a more trustworthy friend. In fact, rooming with Bethanne had ended up being the worst decision of Genna's life, but even Pete couldn't have anticipated why that would be.

Jo remembered the book of poems she had originally thought was a gift from Pete to Genna. How she wished it had been, instead of in fact being from Alden to Bethanne. Jo wished she could look down this beautiful lawn and see Pete and Genna strolling hand in hand, heads together as they read from the book's pages. Instead . . . Jo sighed.

"Tired?" Carrie asked.

Jo looked over and smiled, shaking her head.

"You haven't had a break for a while. Why don't you stretch your legs? I can handle the table."

"Maybe for a couple minutes," Jo agreed. "Can I bring you anything?"

Carrie shook her head, holding up her half-filled soda cup, and Jo adjusted her baseball cap — a new blue one in honor of the show — and wandered off. She walked near Betsy Davis's table, pleased that the basket maker had managed to participate after all. Clearly, from the crowd of customers gathered around her table, many others were just as pleased. The waterfowl carver's table had drawn several of the men in the crowd, and Jo saw the table manned by the Methodist group doing a brisk business.

Jo heard a wail and turned, realizing her ear had grown attuned enough to identify its source: one of Mindy Blevins's twins. Jo told herself she should learn their names because the poor things shouldn't perpetually be known as "the twins." Perhaps, she thought, once they passed their wailing stage and she could actually converse with them, she would get the names down. She spotted Mindy, and when Mindy in turn caught sight of her, she sent her husband off in the direction of the ice-cream table with the toddlers and came over to Jo.

"How're you doing?" she cried. "I don't know how you managed to put all this together in your state."

"With lots of help," Jo insisted. "By the way, thanks for the dish of lasagna. It was great."

Mindy flapped a hand. "It was nothing. Have you heard the latest about what's going on with Deirdre?"

"Only that she's still being held in custody, despite her husband and lawyer trying their best to get her out on bail until the trial."

"Can you believe it? And they're actually claiming insanity and insisting she needs treatment."

"She was sane enough to try to fly out of the country the minute she learned I'd survived. Thank heavens I came to enough to tell somebody what she had done, before she got away."

Jo remembered the struggle with the paramedic over her oxygen mask. He thought she was delirious, but she was thinking clearly enough by then to want to clear her own name from the false evidence Deirdre had left behind.

"I *knew* there was something about her I didn't trust," Mindy said.

"You did?"

"Absolutely! I mean, this was a woman who didn't know beans about doing crafts. Plus, anytime I happened to show her a really cute picture of the babies, she'd pull out a photo of her dogs. I mean, I ask you!"

Jo grinned. Deirdre should have known better, if she were trying to ingratiate herself to the group, than to offend a doting mother that way.

"Loralee didn't like her much either," Mindy said.

"I picked up on that, and I've been meaning to ask her why."

"Ask me why what?" Loralee slipped next to Jo from behind, with Ina Mae closing the final gap in the small circle.

"Why you didn't like Deirdre, even before all this happened," Jo explained.

Loralee made a face. "I've watched her at the charity balls. She was all charm, but I could see it was only to the people that could be useful to her. Deirdre had lofty goals, that was clear, but the better I got to know her, the more it seemed those goals were set only to prove that she was better than everyone else." Loralee shifted the bag in her arm, tucking the pink frame deeper inside. "It was sad, really," she said. "Even those dogs of hers, whom she obviously cared about. They couldn't be just any dogs. They had to be expensive, high-maintenance pets to impress everyone."

Loralee squeezed Jo's arm. "I'm just so sorry I never shared any of this with you before. You might have been more wary of her."

"There's a big leap from seeing a person as self-centered," Ina Mae said, "to seeing them as a potential murderer."

"Yes, there is," Jo agreed. "I had trouble with that myself, until she actually showed up in my kitchen with a gun. If you had said anything much earlier, I probably wouldn't have taken it very seriously."

"Terrible woman," Loralee said, her lower lip beginning to tremble.

"Why don't we check out those baskets now, Loralee?" Ina Mae said, obviously deciding it was time to change the subject. "It looks like the crowd has thinned a bit around the Davis table."

"I'd better get back to the kids," Mindy said, taking off in her own direction, leaving

Jo on her own. She glanced over at the Craft Corner's table to see if Carrie needed help yet. Things looked quiet, so she decided to pop into the clubhouse for a quick visit to the restroom before setting her friend free for her own break.

The light indoors was much dimmer than the bright sunshine outside, and Jo's eyes worked at adjusting to the changed light. As she headed down the hall, she saw only a shadowy form standing at the doorway of the restaurant, but as things grew clearer, she realized it was Lieutenant Morgan. She instinctively stopped.

This was silly, Jo told herself, even as she edged closer to the wall. Morgan was no longer the enemy. His simmering suspicions had been extinguished as soon as he learned about Deirdre's attempt on Jo's life. He had told Jo so, at the hospital, when he came for the details of her story, and related the events of Deirdre's arrest at Baltimore–Washington International Airport. He had even apologized, much to Jo's amazement, for any "inconvenience" his investigation may have caused her.

She had brought up the anonymous letter Deirdre had sent, and he had waved it off, saying — though Jo only half-believed it — that they seldom paid any attention to such things. She and Morgan had parted on good terms, so Jo should be able to walk up to him casually and wish him a good afternoon. What was holding her back?

She heard the clicking of high heels, and her gaze shifted farther down the hall, beyond Morgan. A woman wearing a light, fluttery dress came toward them. Morgan reached out for her hand, and he leaned forward to place a kiss on her cheek. She slipped her arm through his, and they disappeared together into the restaurant, Jo pressing deeply into her shadowy niche as she watched.

So there was a woman in his life.

So what? That certainly didn't matter to her.

Did it?

Jo decided it was past time to get back to Carrie. She quickly went to the restroom and then hurried back out to the craft show.

"Have a good break?" Carrie asked, as Jo slipped back into her chair.

"Uh-huh."

"Anything wrong?"

"Not a thing."

Carrie's gaze remained fixed on her, so Jo added, "Except the refreshment stand ran out of mocha chocolate chip ice cream."

"Mmmm."

"Hi, Mrs. McAllister." Jo, glad for the distraction, looked up to see a pretty girl in a flowery sundress, her blond hair curling around her face.

"Tracy! I almost didn't recognize you with your hair down. And not standing behind the tennis desk in a green polo. This must be your day off."

"Yeah." Tracy grinned. "Busman's holiday, huh? But I wanted to see how the craft show was going. And I, uh, kinda wanted to talk to you, to tell you I was sorry for not helping you more."

"Tracy, you helped me a lot!"

"Really? I just felt like I should have done more. It was just hard, you know, talking about the people I worked with behind their backs and all."

"I understood that, Tracy, really I did. And I admired your loyalty. There was no way you could have known what all was going on."

"I wish I did. I felt so bad when I heard what happened to you."

"Thank you, Tracy. The good thing is that it's all over."

Tracy nodded, her face serious. "Did you know Bethanne quit?"

"She did?"

"Uh-huh. She found a job at a tennis

place in Texas. She said she wants to put this all behind her."

"Oh, well, I wish her good luck." Jo knew Bethanne would have to testify in Deirdre's trial eventually, but didn't mention that to Tracy. It would be quite a while before interest in Bethanne's part of the whole mess waned and she could live more or less anonymously again. There had been a high cost for Bethanne's brief fling, and the payments, Jo feared, would last a long time.

Tracy said her good-byes and Jo thanked her for stopping by. Carrie, who had been sitting nearby, said, "She seems like a nice girl."

"Yes, she is." Carrie had a speculative look in her eye, and Jo asked, "What?"

"Oh, nothing, I was just wondering. Do you think she and Pete Tober might make a good pair, someday?"

Jo laughed. "Ask me in a year or two, when they might be more ready."

"Okay. I'll make a note of it. Oh, there's Dan and Charlie. Yoo-hoo! Over here!" Carrie waved them over.

Jo watched the two head over, delighted to see the easygoing compatibility evident in their body language and facial expressions. It had been missing for too long.

"How's the work going?" Carrie asked

once they reached the table. She leaned over for a quick kiss from Dan.

"Pretty well. We moved most of the furniture out of the living room. I forget what we decided about the bookcase. Did you want it left downstairs, or what?"

Dan had a short lull in his remodeling business and to Carrie's delight was getting a start on putting down hardwood floors in the downstairs areas.

"The bookcase can go upstairs in our room. Remember, we measured the corner by the front window to see if we could squeeze it in there? It should fit."

"Okay. You and I can handle that, right Charlie?"

"No problem." Charlie nodded. Jo remembered that Carrie said Charlie had recently started weight lifting. He was interested in building up his fifteen-year-old muscles, perhaps stinging a bit from Hank Schroder's remark, that day, on his puny build.

"I don't know about moving that highboy we got from your Aunt Aggie," Dan said. "I'm thinking maybe we should ask Phil from next door to give us a hand on it."

"Dad! The highboy's nothing!"

Dan grinned at Charlie. "That old monstrosity's no featherweight, son."

"Monstrosity!" Carrie protested.

"If Charlie could drag my dead weight," Jo put in, "all the way from the garage entryway to the front lawn, he's got some good muscles on him."

"I didn't drag you that far, Aunt Jo," Charlie said, looking perplexed. "You were only a couple feet from the front door."

"What?" Jo *knew* she hadn't made it that far. She *remembered* being pulled across the kitchen floor. Or did she?

"Yeah, I almost stumbled on you when I came from the bedroom. It was dark right there."

"That's right, son. I remember you telling us about that." Dan clapped Charlie's shoulder, his chest swelling just a bit. "Well, we'll give the highboy a try, just the two of us. But right now we've got to run down to Home Depot for . . ."

Jo saw Dan's lips moving but she had tuned out. *Was* she mistaken? The memory had seemed so clear. But her brain *was* fuzzy at the time, starved for oxygen amidst all the carbon monoxide coming from her lungs.

Jo looked off, over the green lawn, then up to the bright blue sky.

Mike? Do I remember right or not?

"See you later," Dan said as he and Charlie turned to go.

"Good luck," Carrie called, then, as they disappeared into the crowd, said to Jo, "I never thought I'd be so glad for Dan not to have a job, at least temporarily. Just think, before long I might be able to pack those silly dust sheets away for good." She reached for the sweater draped over the back of her chair and pulled it over her shoulders. "Brrr, I think the temperature's dropped lately. You feeling cold?"

Jo shook her head.

"No," she said, hugging herself. "As a matter of fact, I just had quite a warm feeling come over me, something I haven't felt in a very long time."

She smiled.

MAKE JO'S WOODLAND WREATH YOURSELF — IT'S EASY!

(See the actual wreath at http://
www.maryellenhughes.com)

Materials:
1 24-inch Canadian blue spruce artificial wreath
2 Curly willow branches
1 4-inch bird's nest
4 1/2 yards of #9 plaid wire-edged ribbon
Raffia
1 bunch mini mountain-holly sprigs
1 bunch red berry sprigs
7 Mixed sugared fruit (60mm.)
6 Pinecones
1 21/2-inch sitting red cardinal
1 21/2-inch flying red cardinal
Wire, pipe cleaners, glue gun

Fluff your wreath. Cross the curly willow branches at the base and wire together, and then wire them to the wreath on a diagonal. Clip wire ends. Pull top end of one branch around top of wreath and wire to end of second branch.

Make a looped bow with 4 yards of ribbon. Secure in center with a pipe cleaner. Make a flat bow with several strands of raffia and place behind ribbon bow. Attach both to wreath at base of willow branches with pipe cleaner. Repeat for a smaller bow with remaining 1/2 yard of ribbon and raffia, and attach to wreath diagonally across from first bow.

Tuck bird's nest horizontally into wreath to left of large bow, and glue in place. Glue sitting cardinal in nest. Glue flying cardinal diagonally across from nest.

Tuck holly and red berry sprigs about the wreath, and glue in place.

Tuck sugared fruit and pinecones around the bows and about the wreath, and glue in place.

Design by Julie Black
(http://www.blackeyedsusanflorist.com)

CARRIE'S CHILI

Carrie makes a chili much like the recipe my mother sent me years ago, which my family always loved. It's tasty, easy, and great for cool nights.

1 lb. lean ground beef
1 medium onion, chopped
2 to 3 ribs of celery, diced
1 16 oz. can of tomatoes
Small can of tomato sauce, if desired
1 10 3/4 oz. can of condensed tomato soup
1 teaspoon of salt
1/8 teaspoon of pepper
1 teaspoon of chili powder, or more to taste
1 16 oz. can of kidney beans, or pork and
  beans (we like pork and beans)

Cook ground beef until it loses its red color, then add onions and celery and cook 5 to 10 minutes more. Add tomatoes, tomato soup (undiluted), and the seasonings, and simmer 1 1/2 hours. Add tomato sauce or water if it is too thick. Add the beans 10 minutes before serving, just enough to heat through.

ABOUT THE AUTHOR

A Milwaukee native, **Mary Ellen Hughes** received a degree in medical technology from Alverno College before moving to Maryland to work at the National Institutes of Health. The author of two previous novels, she is a member of Mystery Writers of America and the Chesapeake Chapter of Sisters in Crime. When not on the tennis court or visiting craft shows, she is likely to be working on her next Craft Corner Mystery. You can visit her website at www.maryellenhughes.com.